A PLAIN VILLAGE

Stories of Country Life

GEOFFREY EYRE

Mardle Publications

Also written by Geoffrey Eyre

Nutwhistle Farm
ISBN 978-0-9554608-2-1

The Poaching Gang
ISBN 978-0-9554608-3-8

The Case for Edward de Vere as Shakespeare
ISBN 978-0-9554608-4-5

Curlywigs
ISBN 978-0-9554608-5-2

A Plain Village

Published by Mardle Publications

www.mardlepublications.com

mardlebooks@gmail.com

© 2015 Geoffrey Eyre

Typeset by John Owen Smith, Headley Down

ISBN 978-0-9554608-1-4

Printed by CreateSpace

A Plain Village

Contents

1

Molly and Polly

The village I am writing about is named Mardle. It is not picturesque but it is still lived in mostly by country people, and you cannot say that about many villages these days. It has remained a working village where agriculture continues to be a main provider of employment for the people who live here. My name is Alan Ablewhite, I was born in Mardle, as was my wife Ruth. At the time of writing I am forty-eight years old, and by profession a teacher.

A narrow country lane passes the side of our house, which is close to the village church. Known as Beckles Lane it is gravelled for about a hundred yards and then continues for about half a mile as a stony track. After this it narrows into a bridle-path and finally winds its way over Beckles Hill, our local high point.

There are only two dwellings in Beckles Lane, two cottages owned by the Beckles Estate, our local big land owner. The first cottage is large, originally built for one of the estate gamekeepers with a big family. The second is much smaller and farther on down the lane, and it is occupied by a mother and her daughter.

The names of the mother and daughter are Molly and Polly respectively. Of all the people who live in Mardle these are the two my wife and I see most often. This is because Molly and Polly spend their days out of doors wandering the countryside. We are so used to seeing them it is almost as if they are a permanent feature of the landscape.

Our front windows look out over the village, from the back our view is of Beckles Hill. This used to be bare when grazed by sheep but the lower slopes are now covered by small yew trees and juniper bushes. There is a network of ancient tracks all round us. Some are little more than footpaths, others are bridleways for horses and their riders, or green lanes very muddy in the winter months.

We see quite a few walkers in the course of a year. Mostly they are single hikers, map in hand, wondering which of the many tracks to take, and few of them are signposted. Occasionally a pony club will make its way past, and every winter at least once we see a straggle of hardy Ramblers with their woolly hats and backpacks defying the weather. But of all the people who walk these ancient track-ways Molly and Polly must be the two who know them best.

Mother and daughter are almost identical in size and shape, and wear the same old-fashioned clothes. This gives them a distinctive silhouette I recognise at once, whether seeing them at a distance on the hill, or in the lane as they return home on a dark evening. In the winter they wear bonnets, and layers of old coats one on top of another, as though they were cloaks. They walk slowly but there is no mistaking their bulky figures as they loom out of the December rain and mist. If I catch a glimpse of them in the headlamp beam of my car they seem like two cloaked and hooded apparitions from a previous century.

Winters soon pass. Molly and Polly love the spring and summer months when they can spend all day every day roaming the fields and footpaths. We have grown used to seeing mother and daughter make their slow descent of Beckles Hill. There is a long field-edge path down which they amble without haste. It is one of their favourite routes and leads into the lane just below our house.

Apart from their distinctive way of dressing the two women are so alike that it is obvious they are mother and daughter. They have nut-brown complexions with wind-reddened cheeks, hardly surprising since they spend almost all their waking hours out of doors wandering the countryside. They also have eyes that light up with happy laughter when someone speaks to them.

Molly is seventy years of age, her daughter much younger, only thirty, with a mental age that is younger still. Poor Polly is sorely handicapped with unintelligible speech, but she can walk and she can smile. She is the most gentle and sweet-natured creature imaginable, a description that could apply equally well to her mother.

Polly loves the summer flowers, the more colourful the better. In the cornfield at the bottom of the hill she can always put together a large bunch of white marguerite daisies and dark red poppies which she will hold up to show us if we are in the garden when she passes by with her mother. After which my wife Ruth always makes the same heartfelt comment.

'What will become of poor Polly when her mother dies?'

2

The Grave Digger

The larger of the two cottages in Beckles Lane is occupied by my friend Tom Mundy and his wife Joan. Tom is well known in the village, and for many miles around. As a gardener and handyman he runs an efficient one-man business. If he says he can spare you an hour the week after next that is exactly what he means.

Tom can subdue acres of grass, trim the highest hedges or cut down trees, being prodigiously strong as well as possessing all the right tools and the know-how. To many people he is indispensable, particularly when they are in trouble. He has a set of rods for unblocking drains, a tall ladder and a head for heights. After every gale he has tiles to replace and fences to mend. Mardle would not function without him.

Tom and I were born in the same year and grew up as boys together, although elsewhere in the village. I was an only child, Tom had three sisters but no brother, so we made common cause and our boyhood friendship has endured into middle age. Our lives began to diverge at the age of eleven. My parents were tenant farmers on the Beckles Estate but had become increasingly disenchanted with farming and decided that I should receive sufficient education to make an alternative career possible. I was allowed no distractions from my studies and that meant saying 'no' to Tom Mundy when he called with his fishing rod or rabbit gun and wanted me to join him for an expedition to the river or the steep slopes of Beckles Hill.

Tom and his wife Joan are the nearest neighbours to Molly and Polly, the mother and daughter who roam the hillside tracks. Their much smaller cottage is farther down the narrow lane and I know that Tom and Joan keep a protective eye on it and on the two women who live there. Both cottages belong to the Beckles Estate and Tom is an ideal tenant, trusted by the estate to watch out for poachers and to use his gun on predatory birds and animals. It is a spacious cottage with as much garden as he wants, since he has only to shift his fence to take in more. In the winter months Tom acts as head beater for the twice weekly pheasant shoots, a main source of income for the estate.

As there is less outside work in the winter Tom fills in his time by rearing poultry for Christmas. This is a considerable enterprise which takes up half his garden. It also involves a lot of work and a large outlay of money. Turkeys have big appetites for expensive food and need to be securely housed at night safe from foxes. His wife Joan helps him, as does their daughter Valerie who works in London but always takes a week off at Christmas when they are flat out with the plucking and table preparation. This needs to be done as quickly as possible so the extra help is much appreciated.

Tom's wife Joan leads an equally busy life. For many miles around she is known as Nurse Mundy, or Sister Mundy, and is treated with great respect. She left the state service long ago to become a freelance nurse in the private sector and gets plenty of well-paid work looking after the many wealthy invalids who inhabit the big houses in the area. She is recommended from one to another and is treasured as a discreet and experienced nurse whose advice is sought on a wide range of sensitive medical problems. At the end of September she is always particularly busy. 'My Christmas party babies,' she says proudly. 'They never fail me.'

Neither Tom nor Joan has ever had a holiday to my knowledge, and are unlikely to have one in the near future, because they cannot leave their animals or abandon their seasonal back door trade in bedding plants, cut flowers and vegetables. Nor would they know what to do with themselves if they did. This is because they are not aware of spending their lives in paid labour and would find it hard to distinguish between what is work and what isn't. They get up early and toil cheerfully all day, during which time I am sure that it never once crosses their minds to wonder whether they are happy or not.

Tom also digs the graves in Mardle churchyard, as well as being paid to keep it tidy. This puts a slight constraint on our friendship. I know it is irrational but the thought of him one day digging mine makes me uneasy. He has notched up several of my relations on his spade handle already, including both my parents, and he comes from a long-lived family. Unless I can somehow survive to a great age, and avoid accidents along the way, there is a chance that he will still be around to do the business for me too. So I keep on the right side of him, just in case.

3

Itchy Feet

Today there died in Mardle a quiet and inoffensive man, a farm worker whose name was Fred Harmer. He was fifty-two years old and he died from lung cancer.

This surprised no one since he was never seen without a cigarette, hand-rolling his own with a sticky black tobacco that needed lighting and relighting every few minutes. He had no special skills but had done every job on the farm and was a useful man to have around, able to turn his hand to anything. He worked at Doggrells Farm which is not far from our house across the fields, and there is a footpath past his cottage which leads into Beckles Lane. He used it regularly so we counted him as a neighbour and came to like him.

This was not difficult because Fred was a good-natured man who would slide back the window of his tractor cab and wave to anyone who seemed friendly. Neither he nor his wife Doris were local people. They came with the reputation of a couple who never stayed anywhere long and seemed to have worked on farms all over the south of England. A situation that changed after they came to live in Mardle.

'Yes, we like it here and we've made up our minds to stay,' Doris told us when we met her in the lane one day. 'There's just me and Fred, so we can please ourselves.'

My wife Ruth sensed their vulnerability and behaved protectively towards them. Few people have much interest in farm workers provided they are well-behaved and do their work. The Harmers seemed to have learned from experience how to keep their heads down and not draw attention to themselves. Ruth liked them because they took a childlike pleasure in simple things. They had an old car and every drive they took in it together was viewed as a treat to be enjoyed, even if only an excursion to the town to buy fish and chips followed by an ice cream afterwards.

There was a kind of innocence about them that was very appealing and once Ruth had pointed this out to me I took more interest in them myself. Most of us are dissatisfied in some way, even though we live in the midst of plenty, so it was humbling to meet the Harmers who had very little in terms of income or luxuries but who were pleased just to have found a nice place to work and live.

Something was bound to spoil this happy existence and in Fred Harmer's case it was the damage to his health caused by cigarette smoking. Fred was a willing victim to his addiction. 'Don't want to give it up,' he would gasp defiantly between bouts of coughing, his hands resting on his knees and shoulders heaving. 'A man's entitled to his pleasures, isn't he?'

Some pleasure, and it had been obvious for some time that his dreadful hand-rolled cigarettes were ruining his health. During his fifth year at Doggrells Farm he had a long spell off work with bronchitis. It did not respond to treatment so the doctor sent him to hospital for an X-Ray. A massive growth on his left lung was revealed so the diagnosis of lung cancer came as no great surprise when the news reached us, but it was distressing all the same.

Fred Harmer lost his job and died in hospital a few months later. Ruth helped his wife Doris to arrange the funeral and cope with all the necessary paperwork that follows a death. The poor woman had no one else to help her with the formalities. She said that Fred was the one with the schooling, not that he had very much, but enough to fill in forms and use a telephone. She did not have the faintest idea what to do when he died, and had no one to turn to in a community that was not her own.

Doris was adamant that Fred should not be cremated but should be buried in Mardle churchyard instead, saying that after a lifetime of wandering they both considered Mardle to be their home and wanted to stay here permanently after death. Although Ruth made sure this wish was granted the funeral was pathetically brief. Mardle no longer has a rector and is part of a group ministry covering several villages. The officiating priest was a part-timer and made little effort, no relatives had turned up and only a handful of villagers attended. With Ruth on one side and Tom Mundy's wife Joan, a motherly soul, on the other, poor Mrs Harmer was helped through the service and the committal and taken home afterwards. Tom dug the grave and duly filled it in again, notching up yet another inhabitant on his spade handle. Within an hour Fred Harmer disappeared without trace, it was almost as if he had never lived.

Once again Ruth used her contacts and local knowledge to good effect by securing Doris a small council flat in our nearby market town and arranging income support to secure a long-term future for her. Everyone in Mardle has a story, and this is the story of Fred and Doris Harmer.

It did not take us long to find out from their small bundle of personal documents that they were not husband and wife but mother and son. Doris told us that she had been a young, a very, very young, teenage mother. Her parents were farm workers with other children and could offer only enough support to prevent mother and baby being separated at birth. An illiterate country girl with a young child faces a difficult future and all too soon her family cast her adrift to fend for herself. She found a room and a series of jobs until eventually Fred was able to leave school a year or two early and begin full-time work.

They stuck to what they knew best, farm work, and eked out a precarious living on the fringes of the agricultural industry. They picked freezing Brussels sprouts in winter and choked on combine dust in the summer. They hoed and weeded, hauled and lifted, and somehow survived all this back-breaking work.

Although farm jobs are not so easily come by as in the past there is still a cottage or a caravan or a stable-block flat available for the man willing to accept low wages in return for no questions asked. Fred fitted the bill and spent long hours in stifling chicken sheds, or standing in cold water picking watercress. However dirty or difficult the job he took it, and the accommodation that went with it, and moved in with his mother. They never stayed anywhere for long, having itchy feet as they say in the country.

From an early age the habit of sleeping together had been formed, for the simple reason that most often they only had one bed to sleep in. Farmers prefer to employ reliable married couples and since they had the same name they took the line of least resistance and allowed people to assume that they were man and wife. Doris was a pretty woman who looked after herself while Fred was more weathered and ground down with hard work. Add in the ravages of cigarette smoking and the difference between their ages was not noticeable enough to provoke curiosity. No one has much interest in itinerant farm workers and they passed without comment as Mr and Mrs Harmer, a childless married couple with neither relatives nor friends.

I have never seen Doris Harmer again but my wife tells me that she has become a bag lady who roams the back streets and car parks all day, returning to her tiny flat only to sleep. A sad end. Tom Mundy also keeps me informed. He says that flowers appear on Fred's grave at regular intervals during the course of a year. Sometimes they are garden flowers, or in the height of summer, wild flowers. But not as a bunch. The flowers are laid out one by one along the length of the grave, and arranged with great care.

We live next door to the church and if I am passing through the churchyard I always remember to glance over to the corner where Fred is buried. There is something inspiring as well as tragic to see the flowers so carefully placed, particularly when they are wild flowers picked nearby, or sprigs from an ornamental shrub. No one has ever seen Doris putting them there. She must come all the way from the town in the early hours of the morning before even farm workers are stirring, and that is a fair old walk for a bag lady just to place flowers on a grave.

Mother and son had shared a close and loving relationship for every single day of Fred's fifty-two years on the earth. A close and loving relationship that did not end with his death.

4

The Home Farm Cuckoo

Although the Beckles Estate is much reduced from its peak extent in the last century, many of the farms having been sold off, it is still a thousand hectares in size and requires the services of a full time manager. This is Jamie Paterson, a Scot. As the estate manager he has an important job, it gives him considerable leverage and a big say in how things are run in the village. Most local people take care to keep on the right side of him, myself included.

Although he has lived and worked in England for thirty years Jamie Paterson has never been softened up by the good life. He is the proudest of Scotsmen, a small, fiery, sandy-haired man, fervently patriotic. He dreams of the fully independent Republic of Scotland to which he and his wife will one day return. Thirty years south of the border have not put the slightest dent in his ferocious accent, and he is particularly hard to understand when in a rage.

Which he is regularly. He is a man who refuses to be messed around and no one with any sense picks a fight with him. The mobile phone was invented so that he can have one glued to his ear, or so it seems when I meet him, and someone on the other end is usually getting the rough edge of his tongue. Jamie is a neurotic worrier who cannot bear the slightest delay. He begins chasing up suppliers the day after placing his order, and is generally considered to be an awkward customer hard to please.

Jamie's wife Agnes is also a Scot, and if anything she is even more staunchly patriotic than her husband, equally frustrated at the delay between devolution and full independence. Their love of country binds them together.

They never for a single hour relax their enthusiasm for Scotland and all things Scottish. It makes them feel special and different, it provides them with a ready-made topic of conversation in the family home, and it gives them a stake in their future.

The Patersons have only one child, a son named Dougal, now aged eighteen. He lives at Home Farm with his parents but from early childhood has been a regular visitor to my house next to the church. Because Ruth and I have no children of our own we made Dougal welcome whenever he wished to call, and it has been a pleasure to watch him growing up into a fine young man.

Although loyal to his parents Dougal has been increasingly unhappy at home and found in my wife Ruth a sympathetic listener for his adolescent problems. He confessed to her several times that he was baffled by his parents. Understandably so, I think I would have been baffled by them too, in his situation. This is because Jamie and his wife Agnes have made no secret of the fact that they are deeply disappointed in their son, and have been for most of his life. Dougal loves books and classical music, not something they can understand.

My wife Ruth regularly expresses surprise that our house has not collapsed under the weight of the books I have aggregated over the years. I love having books around me and cannot resist buying new ones. It is my overflowing bookshelves which have been the main attraction for Dougal, and the explanation why he has visited our house so often. I think he knows my books almost as well as I do, and has borrowed many of them over the years.

Nor is this my only association with Dougal because he attends the school where I teach. This is known locally as 'the College'. Formerly one of the old grammar schools it is situated in our nearby market town, some three miles distant from the village. Dougal is a prize-winning pupil at the College, a senior sixth former who has been accepted for Oxford. A bright future is confidently predicted by all those who have taught him as he progressed through the school years but this is little consolation to his parents who complain bitterly about the wrong path his education has taken. They blame the College for not giving their son the right sort of education, or not the education they would have preferred for him. More specifically they blame me because they think I could have done something about it and chose not to.

I can explain some of the background to this unhappy state of affairs.

When Dougal was three years old he began to speak with a rather nice English accent, much to the surprise and annoyance of his Scottish parents. They had sent him to a play group in the next village and so had only themselves to blame. Children do not learn speech just from their parents, they learn it mostly from other children, and it is fixed for life if you then send them to a good prep school. The Scots are great educators and this is exactly what the Patersons did next, having saved up the money for many years.

Dougal's education flourished, and with it his posh English accent. He could not help the way he spoke but soon came to realise that it did not meet with the approval of his parents, who disliked it intensely. And not just his beautiful English speaking voice, they were equally dismayed by his English-ness. So at an early age he was provided with an innocent means of profoundly irritating his parents with every word he spoke.

He had a good ear for language and in the uncompromising way of intelligent children he developed and strengthened both his English speaking skills and his Englishness during every waking moment. Nor could his parents reasonably complain since it was the money they had forked out on his school fees which had fixed for life the impeccable vowel sounds that would chime very sweetly in his Oxford dining hall but might grate a little if he ever visited his long-lost cousins in Dumfries.

This was bad enough but his complete lack of interest in sport was the next source of disappointment for the unhappy parents. Agnes had been an international hockey player, Jamie had played for some top rugby teams in his youth, and they both prized physical fitness and success in sport above all else.

Rugby football was Jamie Paterson's passion in life. Although he had hung up his boots this did not stop him from becoming an active member of the town's rugby club where he coaches the second fifteen. He also took up the whistle, being an expert on the complicated rules, and such spare time as he has is spent at the rugby club in one capacity or another. Dougal's distaste for the game remains a bitter and lasting disappointment.

Jamie had longed for a son and the moment Dougal was born his imagination surged on ahead. He pictured a day twenty years into the future when Dougal pulled the dark blue shirt of Scotland over his head and trotted on to the pitch at Murrayfield to win his first international cap. Against England, of course. Hoisting huge penalty kicks, then running in the winning try, modestly accepting the congratulations of his team mates while the crowd cheered. Not just a father's dream but a Scotsman's dream, and one that refused to fade.

Jamie never gave up hope that one day Dougal would suddenly express a desire to play. He kept coaxing him to join in a coaching session but Dougal had no intention of going anywhere near a rugby pitch as long as he lived. When persuaded to watch on television a few minutes of the ritual conflict between Scotland and England he made a point of applauding when the England team scored.

'England is where I live, which other team should I support?' he enquired of his parents in his perfect English accent.

'Don't say such things to your father,' Agnes scolded him.

But Dougal was not frightened of his father. He said, 'It's where you live too, Dad. I can't understand why you're so keen on Scotland seeing that you left it at the first opportunity and obviously never intend to go back.' 'Don't speak to your father like that,' his mother scolded him again, but she was on a loser, and they both knew it. Not one to give up easily she had bought him a hockey stick as a present for his seventeenth birthday but he had smilingly declined to give it a try. Dougal did not like muddy fields, no matter which game was played on them.

His Englishness called into question their Scottishness. He found their fervent patriotism faintly ridiculous, and said so. 'You keep telling me about the tartan and the haggis and the skirl of the pipes but you have both lived here longer than you ever lived in Scotland. Isn't it time for a rethink about where your home is?'

'No!' mother and father cried with one voice. 'We're Scottish and proud of it.'

'You don't even go there for holidays,' Dougal pointed out. 'Last year it was Spain, the year before it was Turkey, and the year before that it was Italy. When do the bonny banks and braes get their turn?'

His parents were not amused. They repeated these conversations to me when I called one afternoon during the Easter break. It so happened that Dougal was not in the house at the time and although the purpose of my visit had nothing to do with his education Jamie and Agnes seized it as an opportunity to air their grievances with the College. I was steered through into their sitting room to discuss Dougal's future prospects and had to nod sympathetically and grunt understandingly while Agnes provided mugs of tea and passed me the plate of bannocks.

They were appealing for my support. They seemed to think that Dougal would listen to me, that I could talk some sense into him. They had set their hearts on him becoming either an Edinburgh trained veterinary surgeon, an Edinburgh trained doctor or an Edinburgh trained engineer, whichever he preferred. Neither was possible because Dougal had no interest in either mathematics or science and had opted to study arts subjects instead. This was contrary to their wishes, expressed forcefully at every parent evening.

They were afraid that Dougal would never be able to earn a

good enough living with an arts degree and wanted me to do something about it before his time at the College ran out. This was their strongly held point of view so I had to be defensive as well as diplomatic, while doing my best to calm their fears. I tried hard to convince them that they were worrying unnecessarily, aware as I did so that they did not believe me. My words fell on stony ground.

My sympathies were entirely with Dougal. Jamie and Agnes frowned at the idea of play-acting and dressing-up so he had to keep quiet about his active membership of the Drama Club to avoid further unpleasantness at home. His involvement with the Classical Music Society was another cause of friction, as was the way he spent his pocket money on CDs and books.

'Not from me,' Agnes said emotionally, choking back a sob as she showed me his well-stocked bookcase. 'He doesn't get it from me.' She was referring to his fondness for music and literature which she found incomprehensible, and could not pretend otherwise.

'From me neither,' Jamie growled, picking up one of Dougal's CDs and examining the label. 'Beethoven', he read aloud in disgust. 'String quartets!' He shook his head in angry bewilderment. 'The lad should be out in the fresh air kicking ball with the team, not sitting around indoors listening to classical bloody music.'

'That's not all,' Agnes said tearfully, her cheeks pinking with shame. I waited apprehensively. Something told me she was about to come to the point, to confide dark parental fears that their eighteen year old son would develop homosexual tendencies from reading poetry. 'No,' she whispered. 'He's learning to play the clarinet. We don't know what to say, do we, Jamie?'

'I never thought to see a son of mine wasting his time like that,' he grieved. 'I told him 'no', and I mean 'no'. I'm not having him make that awful wailing noise in my house. If he wants to play a musical instrument when he's left home and supporting himself and spending his own money then good luck to him. But I'm not going to pay for his music lessons, and that's final!'

I have never found it easy to convey to disappointed parents the uncomfortable explanation that they themselves are usually to blame, as in this case where it was far too late for change. The excellent education they had provided for their son had made the boy cultured and intellectual, not qualities rated highly by either of his parents. The mystery of genetics is beyond the wit of man to understand. That Jamie was Dougal's father was not in dispute, he had also been present at the birth so they had not brought the wrong baby home by mistake. Yet the boy might as well have been a changeling he was so different from his parents, and likely to become even more different as the years passed.

Dougal was the cuckoo in the Home Farm nest.

A well-grown eighteen he was taller and heavier than his parents. The frugal and thrifty Patersons were lean, taut and angular. Dougal came in a more plump and rounded package, with a healthy, pink, good-natured face. Jamie and Agnes were over-anxious workaholics, with equally jagged tempers, while Dougal was calmly self- assured. Neither had the slightest sense of humour but needless to say their son was witty as well as articulate. Even my wife Ruth drew the cuckoo analogy to see Dougal's placid features towering over his harassed parents while they fussed and scolded.

Although not highly regarded at home Dougal's many fine qualities were fully appreciated at the College where he fitted in and was much happier. And would be happier still when he went up to Oxford. As a sixth former and prefect he was first choice to accompany prospective parents on a tour of the College. Dougal's smooth staff-officer good manners put even the most awkward new parent at ease in a moment. I had no doubt that he would make a great success of his life.

Dougal was a son that any right-minded parents would be proud of. That Jamie and Agnes should be disappointed in him defied belief, yet such was the unhappy state of affairs at Home Farm in Mardle. It was not much happier for me either because the time had come to tell them what Dougal would be reading at Oxford. He had led them to believe that his subject was English Literature but flinched from telling them that his real intention all along had been to read Theology instead.

He asked me if I would soften them up when a suitable occasion arose so that it did not come as a complete surprise when he told them the rest of the plan. Which was to take Holy Orders as a clergyman in the Church of England, a vocational career he had set his heart on. How his parents would react to this news neither he nor I could guess but it was unlikely to meet a favourable response, so I could well understand his wish to avoid an angry confrontation.

It was time to leave the unhappy couple alone so I extricated myself from this tense family situation without another word, recognising a lost cause when I met one. As I headed for the door I saw Agnes dab at her eyes, and Jamie lay a consoling hand on her shoulder. They should have been proud, instead they were angry and disappointed. I let myself out and trudged home, almost as upset and dejected as they were. There is another episode in Dougal's life which is worth retelling. It comes later in the book.

5

The Egg Man

Eddie Pritchard is a small-time chicken farmer, well known In Mardle and the surrounding villages because he delivers his eggs from door to door in a dilapidated old van. On the sides of the van are brightly coloured pictures of hens and a cockerel which he painted himself, using house paints. Eddie is known locally as 'the Egg Man'.

I have to say at once that he is not our most popular inhabitant. In fact he is generally considered to be a pest and a nuisance, and that is on his better days. Eddie Pritchard is a tenacious door-stepper who expects a cup of tea and a chat at every call. He will hinder anyone and everyone, and is a great time waster.

He is not so much interested in your troubles as concerned that you should listen to his, at length. Eddie unburdens himself with nothing held back. His egg round is more like a serial group therapy session. It makes him feel better but makes everyone else feel worse. I think we would all prefer that he kept the more intimate details of his domestic problems, financial difficulties, medical history and unsatisfactory sex life to himself.

He expects me to be sympathetic because we attended school together for many years, including the school where I am now a teacher. I try to avoid him but he delivers in the evenings and weekends, and of course during the school holidays, so he catches me in more often than not. Five years ago I was filling my car at the local garage when his hand-painted egg van pulled up at the opposite pump. He came over and grabbed my hand. I could see that he was upset about something and soon learned why.

'You're never going to believe this, Alan,' he said, still mangling my hand in agitation. 'My wife has left me.'

There is not much anyone can reply to such a statement except to murmur expressions of sympathy. So I said, 'Sorry to hear that, Eddie.'

'I never thought she would do it,' he continued, shaking his head in disbelief. 'Never.'

'These things happen. I'm sorry.'

'Went off to stay with her sister and wrote me a letter to say she isn't coming back and intends to divorce me. I still can't take it in.'

'Understandable,' I said. 'Must have come as a shock.'

'It certainly did. I thought I was stuck with her for life. I never dreamed she would leave of her own accord.' He punched the air with his fist and shouted, 'Free! I'm free! Dear God, I'm free at last!' Ignoring my stern frown of disapproval he said, 'I'm having a party tonight. This calls for a celebration, and you're invited.'

So much for married bliss although I guess poor Mrs Pritchard had put up with a lot before deciding she could take no more. Living with someone as hopelessly dysfunctional as Eddie would have driven any woman to despair. He confided to me on a previous occasion that his wife had treasured her virginity above all else, and consequently had not enjoyed her married life. Which meant he had not enjoyed it either so perhaps a separation was in both their interests.

Being a poultry farmer is not the easiest way of making a living, and Eddie's business suffered from the various health scares associated with salmonella and bird flu. Free-range eggs are his main source of income. He has birds in cages as well, a more reliable means of egg production, even if it is one he keeps quiet about, for obvious reasons. It ensures that his boxes are kept filled, although not exclusively with free-range eggs as he would have you believe. He delivers to pubs and restaurants and the many nursing homes in the area, as well as from door to door in the village. Between them he manages to make a living. The general feeling is that it would be a much better living if he worked harder and talked less.

Eddie thought a new age of sexual freedom had dawned when his wife left him. Eagerly he advertised for a house-keeper, rubbing his hands in anticipation. He hoped to strike it lucky with a good-looking woman who would do all the shopping, cooking, gardening, washing, cleaning and mend-ing, and then oblige him between the sheets as well. A tall order but he had several applicants to choose from and not surprisingly he chose the youngest and prettiest.

She soon proved to be a competent housekeeper but any hopes of resuming his sex life with a more responsive partner suffered an early setback. The woman informed him that she was devoutly religious and trying to make up her mind whether to enter a convent or not. From his point of view it took her an agonisingly long time to make up her mind but eventually she chose the veil, which gave him the chance to advertise again.

Having learned nothing from his previous experience Eddie chose the youngest and shapeliest of the second crop of applicants. She moved in and soon began to look extremely permanent. Her housekeeping skills could not be faulted but when bedtime came and Eddie tried his luck she told him that she was a rape victim still traumatised by her experiences and unable to bear a man near her. It would be many years if ever before she felt like sex again, too bad if that was what he was expecting.

Eventually she too moved on and Eddie tried again. Unfortunately for him the new woman also had a readymade excuse to keep him from her bedroom. She announced proudly that she was a lesbian but that she liked it at the farm and intended to stay. And stay she did for many months until she too found somewhere better and moved on.

My unfortunate friend the Egg Man was demoralised after these failures and tried to manage on his own for a few months. He was hopeless around the house and it soon got in such a pickle that he decided to advertise yet again for the housekeeper of his dreams. Once more he had to seethe with frustration. The new woman told him she was sympathetic to his requests but had lost every shred of interest in sexual activity since undergoing her hysterectomy operation. She was sorry but she was sure he knew how she felt.

He didn't, but wanted tea and sympathy every time he delivered the eggs and would sit disconsolately at my kitchen table lamenting his bad luck. 'You wouldn't think it would be so difficult, would you?' he sighed. 'Or is it just that they don't fancy me and think up all these silly excuses? I never had this trouble when I was young. Tell me, Alan. Why do you think none of them want anything to do with me?'

Although I knew the answer to his question I could not bring myself to tell him. True, Eddie had a painful hip and had lost most of his hair but he was otherwise in reasonable shape for a middle-aged man. What he didn't have was any idea how to treat women, and seemed incapable of learning. Or of changing his uncouth ways. But this is not something one man can tell another, even an old school friend, and wisely I never tried.

Instead I tried to cheer him up. 'Doesn't sound as if she intends to stay long. Perhaps you will have better luck next time.'

Next time was a real corker. She carried a lot of weight but it was nicely distributed, and she had a sinuous way of walking in high heels that drew thoughtful looks from Eddie's neighbours, who knew a bit of all right when they saw one. Eddie's hopes of exercising his seigneurial rights soared again, and everyone in the village hoped that he had drawn lucky at last. If only to stop him feeling so sorry for himself.

One look at his face next time he delivered the eggs gave me his sorrowful answer. It was yet another disappointment, and more sexless nights alone in his own bed.

'What went wrong this time?' I asked him as he sat down at the kitchen table to tell me his latest tale of woe.

He sipped the mug of coffee I made him and gave it to me straight. 'She had false teeth.'

I waited, not sure if that was sufficient by way of explanation. 'Plenty of people have false teeth, Eddie.'

'Not these days they don't, not women her age anyway. I didn't realise it when I saw her the first time. They looked like ordinary teeth but they weren't, they were falsies, two full plates, top and bottom.'

'I still don't see the problem.'

'The wretched woman doesn't get on with them. They aren't comfortable. Most of the time she doesn't have them in.' He winced and made a grimace. 'I know I'm being unreasonable but women don't look so good without their teeth. She looks quite nice when she's dressed up to go out and got them in, not bad at all actually. But the rest of the time...' He shook his head sadly. 'Not what a man wants to come across first thing in the morning. Believe me, it is not a pretty sight.'

'Sorry it didn't work out for you, Eddie.'

'I don't know why I can't take it over the false teeth but I can't. She keeps them in a glass of water and carries them about with her. Sometimes I find them looking at me in the bathroom, sometimes in the kitchen. She likes her food and puts them in to eat, then takes them out again. She rinses them under the tap and dries them on her apron. It puts me off.'

'I think it would me, too.'

He heaved a sigh of desperation. 'Anyway she's going, I've given her the push. She didn't want to stay anyway.'

'Will you try again?' I asked him.

'Not much choice, Alan. I shall take the first bloody woman who turns up. Couldn't be worse than any of the duds I've had so far.'

He shouldn't have said it because some weeks later I saw coming out of the village shop a woman wearing muddy gumboots. A woman no longer young. She wore glasses and had big red hands that looked as if they had done their fair share of hard work. She was heavily built and drably dressed, a woman who plainly had no illusions about herself and did not pretend otherwise. She drove off in the brightly painted egg van so there could be no doubt who she was, and my heart sank.

It sank not on Eddie's behalf but mine, because I would have to listen yet again to his latest lament of unrequited love. From the woman's appearance I knew she was not quite what our unlovable Egg Man had in mind. He explained that he was so demoralised by his previous experiences that when she turned up seeking the position he just hired her without asking any questions or bothering about her appearance. A woman far removed from the beddable temptress of his dreams.

To begin with he simply co-existed with the new house-keeper. She was a woman of few words who did her work and kept out of his way. She had two rooms upstairs and took herself off early in the evening and did not reappear until the morning. 'A telly addict,' Eddie informed me. 'Watches it in bed. Stays up half the night.'

He did not tell me how he knew she watched it in bed but said that her most common reply when spoken to was a grunt. 'Was this necessarily a bad thing?' I asked him. He had to admit that it wasn't. She seldom spoke and so they never quarrelled.

'Olive,' Eddie told me. 'That's her name.'

Not being beautiful Olive did not give herself airs. Not being young she did not have big ideas. She did not flounce about if anything went wrong, nor did she mind getting herself dirty. She helped him with the chickens and did odd jobs around the farm as well as cooking him some nice meals. This was when he started to take a bit more notice of her.

Olive seemed to know instinctively which foods he liked, and which he didn't. His wife and all the other women in his life had regularly served up things he could not bear such as liver, herrings, spaghetti, garlic, diced beetroot, bean sprouts, brown bread, margarine, skimmed milk and spinach. Especially spinach. If he said anything they answered back triumphantly that such things were good for him. Then punished him for complaining by dishing up more of the same.

No longer. Although an unpretentious cook Olive came up with the goods. Big Sunday roasts, followed during the week by steaks and chops and tasty mixed-grill fry-ups. With favourites such as treacle pudding or jam roly-poly with custard for his afters. Eddie soon began to look a little less lean and twitchy and a little more comfortable and contented. Olive never refused if he asked her to stop what she was doing to make him a mug of tea. She would even offer to cut him a sandwich to go with it, or to fix a quick snack, if only beans on toast.

Having an obliging woman in the house was a new experience for the Egg Man, and it made him very thoughtful. He was aware that his life had become a lot more pleasant. Olive did her work without getting in his way or making difficulties. She remembered where he liked to keep things, fitted in with his routine and never seemed to notice his many bad habits. Instead of constant irritation and conflict Eddie discovered that his domestic life was surprisingly harmonious.

So for the first time in many years he had a woman who pleased him, and who he did not want to leave. On the contrary he very much wanted her to stay and tried hard to be a little less slovenly, such as remembering to take off his filthy gumboots before he came indoors. He started to say 'please' and 'thank you' and generally behave in a more house-trained fashion.

'She's actually got quite a nice smile,' he confided in me one week when he delivered our dozen eggs. This seemed to surprise him. He became even more thoughtful, and behaved in a subdued and chastened manner.

Eddie was not a fan of television but as this seemed to be Olive's only interest in life he took the trouble to watch the soaps in order to learn the names of the characters and pick up something of the plots. One evening he invited her to watch the television with him on his front room settee instead of upstairs in her room alone.

She accepted. So, much to his astonishment and delight, Eddie found himself in a courtship situation. Which meant he could not afford a wrong move, and took care not to make one. He started doing things that would have been unthinkable before, such as to make someone else a mug of coffee and offer the biscuit tin.

Eddie had left it late to learn some manners, but fortunately not too late. He humbled himself by doing what he should have done many years before, treating a woman with respect and tenderness. Having learned some sense at last he did not rush things and eventually the right moment presented itself. One evening they found themselves laughing helplessly at a comedy programme. Eddie told me he didn't know how it happened but his arm just seemed to slip naturally round Olive's shoulders.

She cuddled up, and so the Egg Man finally found the domestic happiness he had longed for all his life.

6

Straight Between the Eyes

The sudden death of someone you know always comes as a shock.

One warm summer morning at the start of August I was reading the Sunday newspaper on our garden seat when I heard the back gate open. It was my friend and neighbour Tom Mundy. When he did not speak I looked up in alarm and was startled by the grim expression on his face.

'Bad news?' I asked, laying the newspaper aside and getting to my feet. 'Has something happened?'

'Peter Baigent,' Tom replied. 'Seven o'clock this morning. Silly bugger blew his brains out with a twelvebore shotgun.'

The death of someone of similar age is always unsettling and the bad news took a few moments to sink in. Peter Baigent was a local farmer and landowner, a man who was well liked in the village.

'Not a nice way to go,' I said, wincing.

'It certainly wasn't. Splattered far and wide from what I hear.'

The local police sergeant is Tom's brother-in-law so I had no doubt that he heard rightly. 'Who found him?' I asked.

'His wife.'

'Not very nice for her either. This is a bad business, Tom.'

'Certainly is. If I can find out any more details I'll let you know.'

He headed back to the gate and I hurried indoors to tell my wife the bad news. Ruth was just as shocked as I had been. Peter and Nicola Baigent were not close personal friends but we knew them well enough to feel the loss.

'What a terrible thing to happen,' she said in a subdued

32

voice.

'I can take over in the kitchen if you want to go and see if there is anything you can do. I think Nicola would appreciate it.'

Ruth was already taking off her apron. 'Poor Nicola. Yes, I must go. Not that anyone can help very much in a situation like this.'

The death of a neighbour by suicide is soon common knowledge. The entire village was appalled by the news, as was the wider farming community. It certainly cast a gloom over the day, not helped when Tom Mundy made his promised return visit. This particular death had made a deep impression on him too, and he told me what had happened in grisly detail.

It is not easy to kill yourself with a shotgun because of the length, the triggers being just out of reach when you stare down the barrels. Those who try often end up blowing half their faces away without killing themselves outright. To do the job properly it is best to use a short stick to push the triggers down, preferably with the gun butt standing firmly on the ground, the method chosen by Peter Baigent. According to Tom Mundy the stick had been neatly cut and trimmed, and forked at the ends.

As with most suicides involving farmers he had shot himself in the middle of the forehead, knowing this to be how animals were dispatched in the slaughterhouse. Those who use a handgun mostly opt for the temple but Peter Baigent had gone out the classic way, straight between the eyes. My father had taught me how to use guns and look after them so I was well aware of the explosive force of a double-barrelled twelve-bore shotgun at close range. I did not need to have it explained to me what it had done to Peter Baigent's head.

Tom Mundy was equally troubled by this unnecessary death and made grimaces of sorrow and disbelief. He said that Nicola Baigent the dead man's wife, now his widow, had been woken by the shot, found the bed empty beside her and feared the worst, running downstairs with a coat thrown over her nightdress. She was still dressed like this when the police arrived.

Her husband had bolted the big double doors of the barn from inside but like most wooden barn doors they were a loose fit and she had soon managed to wrench them open. On entry she would have seen a terrible sight, one that would most likely haunt her for the rest of her life. Her two young sons had followed close behind. She ran screaming to try and stop them from seeing their father's grossly injured body, but they had seen it just the same.

My wife Ruth and Nicola Baigent are on friendly terms because they are both involved with the biggest single event in our local calendar, the annual agricultural show. Our nearby market town has a flourishing Agricultural Society. Ruth is the junior partner in a firm of estate agents founded by her grandfather and she acts as secretary to the Society. She has been in charge of organising its Annual Show for the last ten years, and it is a big job. As with many country shows the emphasis has shifted from farming to leisure activities, many involving horses. The competition events go on all day in the main arena so there are many arrangements to be made beforehand. Nicola Baigent is in charge of the horse side of the show which takes place on the last Saturday in August every year. It is held in the park of Beckles Court, our local big house, both house and park lying within the Mardle parish boundary.

As a teacher I am on holiday in August which means I am available to help my wife with the show, mainly fetching and carrying, running errands and generally making myself useful. We live less than a mile from the Baigent's farm and as soon as the schools break up for the long summer holiday the show preparations begin in earnest. If the phone rings Ruth says, 'That will be Nicola,' and it usually is.

'Try not to let it upset you too much, Alan,' she said sensibly as we got ready for bed.

'I went to see Nicola last week. You asked me to collect something from her for the show.'

'I remember.'

'Peter was there. I didn't say anything to you when I came back but he was deeply distressed about something and acting strangely. I wasn't too surprised when I heard the news.'

'It was a tragedy waiting to happen. Nicola and the boys had done everything they could but if someone has made up their mind to kill themselves stopping them is never easy.'

We were referring to the fact that Peter Baigent had tried to commit suicide at least once before. The family had successfully concealed his mental condition from all but a handful of people, among whom we were included.

'The funeral won't be much fun either,' Ruth said. 'Poor Peter. What a ghastly way to die.'

Peter Baigent was well liked in the village because he was generous with both his time and his money in a good cause. He had a handsome wife who had once been a famous show jumper, two fine young sons still at school, and a manor house inherited from his father, a wealthy businessman. The last man who should have wanted to take his own life.

I think I was so deeply affected because of the exceptionally fine weather at the time. Had it been a cold wet day in dark December there would have been a glimmer of understanding that a farmer might be dejected enough to wish to end his life. Instead of which it had been a day of unbroken warm sunshine in the first week of August. I am an early riser and had enjoyed that magical hour soon after dawn when the night has ended but before the day has begun. Yet it was at this time of warm and pleasant stillness that Peter had slipped carefully out of bed so as not to wake his still sleeping wife and crept down to the barn where he had already hidden the gun, the cartridges, and the neatly trimmed stick to work the triggers.

It troubled me greatly, and I could not sleep for thinking about it. Did Peter take a last look round before going into his barn and bolting the huge wooden doors behind him? Did he spare a glance for his manor house, his avenue of trees, his cornfields sloping down to the river? Did he listen one last time to the birds greeting the dawn in song before slotting the cartridges into his gun and lowering his forehead to the barrels? I should like to think that he did because he was certainly leaving a lot of lovely things behind.

As a young man he had held a commission in the army and was referred to in the village as Captain Baigent, an indication that he was well liked and willingly given his modest rank as a mark of respect. He was a charming man, gentle of manner and unfailingly courteous, even to the most unwelcome of salesmen calling at the farm office. This was situated in the stable courtyard of his beautifully kept country house and it was his custom to come out and greet his callers if he saw them arrive.

He was proud of his trim figure and wore youthful buttery-cord trousers with gleaming brogues and expensive twill shirts. Also a cloth cap which he would remove to swipe at his two overweight Labrador dogs. They were only too pleased to flop down when he came to a stop and held out his hand to the caller. This was how he greeted me earlier in the year, although I had come to see his wife Nicola rather than him.

'Not more sponsorship needed?' Peter groaned when I arrived at the farm. 'Have mercy on us, Alan. We've all given until it hurts, and still you want more!'

    'It's in a good cause.'

He chuckled and offered me a cigar, producing it from his shirt pocket. When I refused he said, 'I'll smoke it myself then. Come round the corner where Nicola can't see me from the house. I'm supposed to be giving up.' He grinned at me cheerfully as he puffed away. He had a decency and a boyish good nature that were hard to resist.

Nicola Baigent also conducted her life with commendable style. What is the point of having money, being well educated and coming from a good family unless you put on a bit of a show? When she was not looking down on the world from eight feet in the air with her feet in the stirrups she was sitting behind a huge Chippendale style desk, surrounded by books, pictures and silver cups.

It was two years ago that I discovered the Captain's secret.

It was the first Sunday in September and I was still running errands for my wife. She was clearing up after the Show, mainly writing 'thank you' letters, but needed something to be collected from Nicola Baigent. I sat opposite Nicola at her big desk while she searched for the document Ruth wanted. She could not find it and apologised for keeping me waiting. This was no hardship at all, Nicola being an exceptionally good-looking woman in the best of health, and in the prime of life.

While we were making conversation a man's voice kept calling out from the next room, 'Who is it, Nicola?' To which she replied, 'Stay there, darling. I'll come and see to you as soon as I've finished.'

Peter Baigent chose not to take this well-meant advice and came in to find out for himself who it was. He was unshaven and wearing a dressing gown.

His movements were slow, and his voice dull. He said, 'Hello, Alan old chap. Thought it was you. Got it sorted yet?'

His wife made it plain that she did not expect me to reply and waited pointedly until he took the hint and shuffled slowly past us and out into the front hall. 'Easily the best of the one-day shows,' he said in a flat voice. 'You do a good job all of you. A damned good job. I want you to know that.' He climbed the stairs slowly and not long afterwards I could hear him moving around in one of the rooms overhead.

A husband with two taped wrists takes some explaining away but Nicola managed it. She said, 'Peter isn't awfully well at the moment.'

'I can see that he isn't.'

'He has been to a clinic. The treatment was rather severe.'

'I'm sorry.'

I was, extremely sorry, and listened in silence as Nicola admitted that he had tried to take his own life, or at least to harm himself, and had done so on a previous occasion. She has one of those exquisite patrician voices that do not need to be raised above a murmur to be clearly heard. Nothing is more disarming than courtesy. All members of the family were scrupulously polite and behaved as though nothing was wrong, a strategy that worked right up until the end.

Modern psychiatric treatment is very effective and for long periods at a time the trim little Captain was able to drive about in his Range Rover with no one the wiser. The problem for his wife and two boys was that the attacks of suicidal depression came without warning, and after long periods of rational behaviour. They had few clues that would alert them to a sudden change in his mental stability.

After his death Nicola spoke to me more freely, indeed seemed pleased to unburden herself a little. And since I was one of the few people outside the family who knew of his problem, and had kept quiet about it, she told me of the effect it had on her and her two sons.

They had gradually developed an instinct for knowing when he was most at risk, the grain harvest being a time when he was more than usually agitated. Two years ago at the Show she had been watching the dressage competition and suddenly noticed that her husband's Range Rover was no longer parked at the ringside. She sensed danger and left immediately, jumping into the saddle and galloping to the farm at top speed.

Her horse was entered in the hunter classes so she was able to clear hedges and five-barred gates in a headlong dash for home across the fields. Arriving at the front door in a flurry of gravel she dismounted in a flying leap and ran round the house in a frantic search for her husband. Finally racing upstairs where she found him lying in a bath of hot water with his wrists cut. He was slumped in the water as though dead, the blood still rising in little twists and spirals. But he had not carved deeply enough and she was able to pull the plug and rescue him. His taped-up wrists I had seen for myself.

On an earlier occasion he had climbed out of the river still alive. No one was really sure whether he had tried to drown himself or not and gave him the benefit of the doubt. After the wrist-cutting incident Nicola and her sons hoped that he would always be a failed suicider who lacked the last desperate inch of courage to extinguish his own life. He left himself an escape route which allowed for rescue in the nick of time.

The last occasion on which I saw Peter Baigent alive was a week before my neighbour Tom Mundy brought me news of his death. By this time in late July preparations for the Show were well under way and I volunteered to visit Nicola to sort out some problems which had arisen over sponsorship of the pony classes.

The elder of the two boys opened the door and Nicola called me through. I found her sitting sideways on her chair behind the ornate mahogany desk. This was because her husband was kneeling on the floor with his face hidden between her breasts. Neither of them moved. I made as if to go out again but she motioned me to stay. It was a sight I will never forget.

After a minute or two Peter got to his feet and said, 'Hello, Alan old chap,' his customary greeting. 'Which of us have you come to see? Nicola, I hope. You'll get more sense from her than you will from me.'

'Yes, Nicola,' I said, indicating the bundle of entry forms I had brought with me. 'Ruth doesn't bother with emails. She just sends me instead.'

'Like it,' he said, greeting me with a friendly squeeze on the arm. 'Much more sensible to let the womenfolk handle everything.' He spoke with an expressionless voice but his politeness did not fail him, and he even managed a smile.

'Shall I call back?' I offered. 'Now doesn't seem like a good time.'

'No, stay and talk to Nicola. I must go and see how the combines are getting on.' He managed another sickly smile. 'It's a busy time of year for us poor old hard-up farmers. Do you know how much they pay us for a ton of wheat these days?'

Although his inherited wealth had protected him from the suffering endured by many other farmers, his precarious mental state could not cope with the problems which beset the agricultural industry at the time. Nicola told me that he had nightmares about the harvest, imagining among other disasters that his huge cornfields were being devoured from end to end by greedy crackling flames.

On that last morning, when I had seen her cradling his head between her breasts, she told me that he had woken during one of those false dawns when the sky lightens prematurely, quite common during the summer months. The sky had been suffused with a pink iridescent glow and he had leaped from the bed in terror, believing that field after field of standing corn was being destroyed by lurid flame.

Because he was so distressed Nicola kept all his medication under lock and key, doling it out to him like a nurse at the prescribed times. Together with her two boys they had devised a rota so that there was always one of them close to him throughout the day. The boys had taken his shotguns to pieces and hidden them in various places around the house, including the box of cartridges. The swimming pool was drained, the car keys removed, likewise the bolt on the bathroom door. They had done all they reasonably could but it had not been enough.

Any hope that he would always be a reluctant suicider who did not really mean it was disproved once and for all in the most violent way possible, because a week later he shot himself early in the morning. Guns are always available in the country, cartridges can be bought from the local hardware shop, the stick to work the triggers he had cut from a hedge and prepared in advance.

There is no escape from shotgun barrels pressed into the forehead, no chance of a last minute rescue between pushing down the triggers and the blast of lead shot. He had meant it, and this time he had done it, and proved us all wrong. Nicola told me that the moment she heard the shot and woke up she knew that this time he would be dead when she found him.

As she ran downstairs in her nightdress, pulling on an old raincoat as she went, she knew that the marriage bond had been severed, that she was alone again and not half of a married couple. Knew that she would no longer be signing her

40

Christmas cards 'from Peter and Nicola', or make up a foursome at golf, or sit with him on an airliner, or sleep beside him in bed. Even before she reached her husband's mutilated body she knew she was a widow.

I must admit that I too miss the stylish little Captain with his harmless vanity and simple good nature and would like to remember him in happier times. I shall try not to think of him lying in a bath of hot water while other people were enjoying themselves at the Show. Watching the little wreaths and spirals of blood rising from his severed arteries, realising that he had not sliced deeply enough but lacking the courage to try again. Perhaps he should have done so because it would certainly have been a more easeful death than the violent one he suffered later from the barrels of a shotgun.

Funerals are few and far between in a small population of healthy people and generally take the form of thanksgiving for lives usefully led. Peter Baigent did not come into this category and I have to say that I found his farewell service in Mardle church a harrowing experience. Outside in the sunshine afterwards I stood for a moment with my pal Tom Mundy. We were both equally cast down.

Grim-faced he said to me, 'Death is never easy. That's true, isn't it?'

'Yes,' I said. 'Yes, Tom. That's true.'

We stayed silent but shared the same thought, namely that however it comes, or whenever it comes, no death is either easy or welcome. Least of all our own.

7

Packhorse Meadow

Ralph Chadwick is easily the wealthiest inhabitant of Mardle, and probably for many miles around. Making money from any form of agriculture is hard at the best of times but Ralph has managed it and has become something of a celebrity in the farming community. He and his wife Beth and their son Trevor live at Giants Farm here in Mardle. The farm is so called because there is a shallow depression in the hillside known locally as the Giant's Footprint, and it is marked as such on the larger scale ordnance survey maps.

I need to describe Ralph, or at least to describe the impression he makes on people. He is the third generation of Chadwicks to own Giants Farm, and like his father and grandfather before him he is a competent farmer and a successful businessman. Ralph was spoiled as a child, allowed to do more or less as he pleased. He was brought up to expect his own way and still turns nasty if he doesn't get it. Now aged fifty he is completely selfish, always absorbed in his own affairs to the exclusion of all else. He never wastes breath enquiring about other people's health or problems. He isn't interested, and doesn't pretend to be. When you meet him he launches immediately into whatever is concerning him at that particular moment.

Ralph is physically strong, with a mass of black curly hair. This is now greying at the edges, otherwise there is no obvious decline in his robust health, ambition or energy. On the day I called he was in shirtsleeves with the sleeves rolled up to expose thickly muscled forearms and massive hands. I have heard him variously described as a blacksmith, a fairground prize-fighter and a Roman emperor, which gives you the general idea.

Bullying comes naturally to him. It is his preferred way of doing business, it always works, and he sees no reason to change. Long before he succeeded his father at the farm Ralph had mastered the art of conversation control. Any interview on whatever subject is always steered in the direction he wants, with sudden changes of pace, and equally sudden changes of mood in which a smile is changed to a ferocious scowl. Any argument with Ralph is of short duration. More disconcertingly he thinks with extreme rapidity and knows what you are going to say after the first few words, which makes conversation even more uncomfortable for those on the receiving end.

My wife Ruth is a second cousin to Ralph, her mother being a Chadwick, and she has always been included as a member of the family in celebration gatherings and guest lists. In recent years Ralph and I have become friends, in fact I think I am probably his closest personal friend, and apart from his wife the only person whose opinion he seeks. Since I know nothing of agribusiness finance, which is the subject usually exercising Ralph's mind, I assume it is because neither of us have anything the other wants, and so we have no need to dissemble with one another when we meet and talk.

Ralph had sent me a message asking if I would call and see him when convenient to do so. When I was shown into his office at Giants Farm he greeted me with the words, 'I'm in trouble, Alan.'

I knew this was not literally true, the reason being that Ruth had told me in advance what was causing the concern. 'Are we talking about Packhorse Meadow?' I asked him.

'Buying it seemed like a good idea at the time. Now I'm not so sure.'

'Doesn't it depend on what you intend to do with it?'

'That's the problem. I may not be able to do anything with it. I may have to leave it exactly as it is. Which doesn't please me, having paid a lot of money for it.'

'You are under pressure not to develop it in any way? Not even a return to agricultural production?'

'Got it in one, Alan. Those bloody eco-people are coming after me. They say it is a precious wildlife habitat that must be preserved at all costs. If they have their way I won't even be allowed to run a tractor from one side to the other. Which is why I wanted to buy it in the first place.'

The troublesome piece of land in question, Packhorse Meadow, was a narrow fifty-acre strip of scrubby ground on the extreme western side of our market town, the side nearest to our village of Mardle. It was landlocked, there being no means of access from a road. It could only be reached through a long footpath leading out of one of the town car parks. This is known as Priory Car Park which gives the clue to its ownership. Only a few ruined walls now remain of the medieval priory which once occupied the site and the diocese had long ago sold off all the adjacent land. Only this piece remained and had been used for recreational purposes for so long that the local residents assumed it had become common ground.

Packhorse Meadow was popular with dog walkers because their pets could be let off the leash to exercise themselves and do what dogs have to do. In the spring children went there to scoop tadpoles from the pond, in the autumn there were family expeditions to pick blackberries, and for the rest of the year young couples went there to become better acquainted. More crucially the Meadow contained several prehistoric burial mounds which were protected as ancient monuments, although these were so buried beneath shrubs and small trees that they could hardly be seen for what they were. Combined with its lack of access there was not the slightest chance of the local authority granting planning permission for building development, or for any other change of use. As far as anyone could see Packhorse Meadow was safe and would remain unchanged for ever.

Unfortunately for all concerned they had reckoned without Ralph Chadwick. One look at the map on his office wall explained why Ralph wanted Packhorse Meadow. He owned the land on the northern boundary, and likewise the land to the south, but to get from one side to the other involved a long journey round narrow lanes. Not easy for his big tractors and the even bigger tackle hitched on behind them. Buying the plot in between would have solved the problem nicely.

Ralph's solicitors are Vokes & Vokes, their offices are in College Street close to where I teach. Their senior partner Walter Vokes had conducted the delicate opening negotiations with diocesan officials. They had long ago given up hope of making any money from this piece of derelict church land and were understandably keen to close the deal. Both sides were acutely aware that conservation issues are more sensitive now than ever before, and they knew this one would be dynamite. They kept the conveyancing as secret as possible but in spite of all their precautions news of the purchase leaked out. The local eco-warriors were on to it like a flash, and eager for a fight.

Ralph was not a man who liked to be thwarted and started to scowl with his arms tightly folded. Not a good sign, I knew. He repeated his main reason for buying Packhorse Meadow. 'A short cut for my tractors. Does that sound unreasonable to you, Alan?'

'It isn't me you have to persuade.'

'It's not as if I'm going to start a new pig unit or put up a slurry extraction plant. I'm not planning to build houses or open a landfill site. Why all the fuss?'

'Apparently a goldfinch colony has established itself there in recent years. And there are some rare meadow orchids. True or not, the opposition will use them to resist any change of use on your part.'

'Sounds like dirty tricks to me. What about all the thistles, ragwort, docks, stinging nettles and rubbish strewn about? Why don't they mention those? You could fill a lorry with the old prams and bikes people have dumped there over the years.'

'I think you should ask Walter Vokes to assess the legal

implications of a return to agricultural production. Even if it was a few centuries ago the Priory would most likely have grazed cattle and sheep there. If so there are bound to be records that would support your case.'

He cheered up a bit on hearing this. 'That's a good idea, I'll get him on to it right away.' Then he sighed. 'I need the information now, not in three months time. You know Walter, he won't be hurried.'

'I'm not sure that's entirely fair, Ralph. Caution in a lawyer is not a bad thing.'

'Lawyers get paid for slowing things down. Delay is money in their pockets.'

'A compromise, perhaps. Fence off the footpaths and put a few beef cattle in for the winter.'

'I don't like to see farming land go to waste. Not when I've just paid a lot of money for it. Those church people weren't very holy when it came to business. They screwed every last penny out of me.'

'What does Beth think about it?'

'Let's ask her.'

His wife Beth was usually near at hand when Ralph wanted her and she soon appeared to provide tea, Madeira cake and sympathy. She could see that Ralph was angry and frustrated so lost no time in calming him down. She smiled and touched him on the arm. 'It hasn't happened yet. These things have to run their course, you must be patient and not do anything to make the situation worse.'

'I'm not a patient man, Beth.'

'People don't like change. You must be tactful.' She appealed to me. 'I think he should hear it from you, Alan.'

'I'm afraid Ralph doesn't do tactful.'

She laughed at this and insisted that Ralph should eat a piece of cake and stop grumbling. Which he did, if not for long. It is always interesting to see how a husband and wife behave in their own home. Ralph's forceful character is softened in his wife's presence. She is a small quiet woman, very pretty and feminine, but with a good grasp of his business interests. They have an act they put on for visitors. She scolds him gently while he pretends to glower. It is nicely done.

Beth soon worked out what was really troubling her husband. 'Are we talking about Amelia? Is that why you're so despondent?'

'I thought we had got away with it when the sale finally went through. That wretched woman has spies everywhere. It would have been even worse if she had found out earlier.'

'But now she has?'

'Yes. Although what she intends to do about it I have yet to find out.'

I can join up the dots here. The Amelia he was so agitated about was Amelia Ashby, the local head busybody and do-gooder. She leads a shadowy organisation known as the Beckles Valley Trust which fights against any planning application they do not approve of, which means just about all of them. Amelia had taken him on before and emerged triumphantly victorious, so he had good reason to be worried.

He said, 'Amelia will never agree to a change of land use. She could give us a lot of grief if it goes to a tribunal. Not to mention the expense.'

I had to admit that Ralph was right. 'Planning committees tend to agree with her about that. It's likely to be her trump card.'

Ralph said, 'Tell me something, Alan. How does this Ashby woman come to wield so much influence? No one elected her to anything as far as I can remember.'

'It pays to keep on the right side of her, even I know that. She's no friend of ours at the College.'

'Nor of mine, either.'

Ralph scowled, and when Ralph scowled the room went dark and thunderclouds gathered. I did not encourage him to say more because I knew that much the same was said about him, although never to his face. Ralph also reacted strenuously when his interests were threatened, and a violent clash with Amelia Ashby was now a certainty. They had opposing views on almost everything and neither would ever back down. It was inevitable they would be enemies, and they were, implacably so.

Tea break over, Ralph wanted to get back to work so we moved towards the front door, conversing as we went. Giants Farmhouse is a huge rambling early Victorian mansion with as many rooms as a hotel. Ralph's mother furnished and decorated it to a high standard, expensively and expertly, with the result that he and his wife Beth have lived their married life in style. It is spacious, a luxury few of us can afford, space being the most expensive of all building materials.

Beth enquired after Ruth and asked how the work for the Show was coming along, the summer already having reached the month of July. On hearing this Ralph immediately switched his attention to the Show, something else that was often on his mind. He had been smiling but suddenly scowled. Discussion of one enemy triggered hostile thoughts about another. He turned to me and said, 'Paterson hasn't moved the cattle out of the park yet. It's time. Would you like me to remind him?'

'Ruth has it all under control. I think she has agreed a date with Jamie.'

'Paterson is an awkward cuss. Refer him to me if Ruth has any trouble.'

'It's premature at this stage. I don't foresee any problem.'

'The grass was much too long last year. People complain-ed, and I don't blame them.'

Ralph was on the boil again and once more Beth calmed him down. 'You don't need to worry, darling. The Show will run like clockwork, as always. Ruth and her helpers will see to that. Stop fussing about the grass.'

Ralph grumbled for a few more minutes and then gave up. 'I know Paterson is a difficult man but the park wasn't at its best last year. Is it something to do with being Scottish and not liking to see people enjoying themselves? The Show won't survive without trade sponsors. Between them they put up a lot of money, and they deserve a little consideration.'

'What are you entering?' I asked him.

'We've got a young Simmental bull that could do well. Too immature for this year but it will get him used to the show ring. Should do well next year, or even the year after that. I've never had the Champion. That would be nice. Father put up the Cup.'

We had reached the lofty entrance hall of Giants Farmhouse where he pointed to a large portrait of his father, Lionel Chadwick. It was painted in old age, even if a portly and pink-faced old age, and had pride of place in the hall. Ralph's father Lionel had been president of the town's Agricultural Society as well as chairman of the College governors. Ralph was not a committee man himself but he was proud of his father and had commissioned the portrait as an eightieth birthday present.

People are always interested in a dynasty because not many businesses survive into a third generation, and Ralph's son Trevor was set to be the fourth. I will write more about them later to explain how Giants Farm came into existence and was successfully managed by a succession of alpha-male Chadwicks. Ralph's parting words to me as I left were, 'What the hell am I going to do about bloody Amelia?'

I only wished I could tell him.

8

Amelia Ashby

Amelia is unmarried and lives in College Close. This is the best address our nearby town can offer. It is a horse-shoe shaped arc of small and medium sized town houses, mostly Georgian although one or two are considerably older, and some later ones are Edwardian, but they are all exquisitely proportioned and lovingly maintained. Entrance is through a carriage arch beside the alms-houses, and the houses them-selves overlook the College playing fields. Although ours is a plain country town it possesses this small architectural gem and the fortunate people who live there make sure it stays that way.

They know it will because Amelia Ashby has promised them it will, and when she promises something it is always delivered.

Amelia had wealthy parents who left her comfortably off for life. She had a good early career as a barrister and still has business interests in London. She travels up regularly, staying overnight for the theatre or a concert before returning the next day. Investment income allows her to devote her energy, talent and free time to local affairs. She has an enviable lifestyle and swishes about looking very pleased with herself.

Amelia punches above her weight and has an impressive list of victories to her credit because she heads The Beckles Valley Trust. The Trust was originally formed as an association to safeguard the interests of the people who lived on the southern side of the town but it soon developed into a watchdog body keeping an eye out for unwelcome planning applications anywhere in the area. The Trust is elitist and unrepresentative but it enables a small group of affluent residents to keep control of town affairs, and over a large part of the surrounding countryside as well.

The Trust operates through a system of committees, each with its own remit. Between them they cover planning law, so-called 'green' issues, and any threat to the local environment, in particular to the town architecture. The heads of these committees are in permanent session by email, computer, phone and text messaging. They are able to respond instantly when danger threatens.

For example if a whisper reaches them that the county are seeking somewhere to build a new crematorium, to create a landfill site in one of the local villages, to allow something nasty involving research on live animals, or even more alarmingly to issue a licence allowing fracking for oil, their contingency plans snap into immediate operation. Literally within minutes an effective challenge is put together. And if it is something that meets with Amelia's disapproval her executive committee has it zapped at birth.

Ralph Chadwick knew from previous experience the power she was able to deploy, and the efficiency of her spy network. She has a stranglehold on local affairs that is hard to break. A long line of infiltrated Town Mayors have answered to her first and made sure that things stay the way she likes them. Most of the people chairing the main district council committees are her nominees which means there is no chance of any significant change to the town or its surrounding villages taking place without her approval. An approval that is only rarely granted. Mostly she says 'No' and when Amelia says 'No' that is the end of the matter.

I am not joking when I say that she commands an army of dependable spies. She does. They are not opportunist whistle-blowers of dubious motives but an information gathering nexus of reliable informers who report directly to her. She has agents placed at every level of local government from the humblest parish council right up to county hall. Their allegiance never falters and when danger threatens they report within the hour.

Amelia exerts discipline over her spear carriers, and inspires their devotion. In return she provides them with continuity. Continuity, vigilance, and a refusal to compromise. Serious-minded townspeople join the Trust and work for it because they know they are vulnerable. They are vulnerable to the whims of the electorate and to bright ideas from social science graduates taking up senior posts in the council departments and eager to try them out in a town which is seldom their own. They join and stay loyal because councillors and officials and their latest gee-whizz initiatives come and go but the Trust is here forever, and does not waver in its opposition to unwelcome change. They rely on Amelia to protect them, and she does.

I hope I have not given the impression that Amelia Ashby is an old harridan.

On the contrary she is an exceptionally good-looking woman who is always at her elegant best in public, and smells even better if you can get close enough to breathe her expensive perfume. In particular she has nice legs and likes to show them off at every opportunity. Her long slender calves always look good on a platform, with plenty of appreciative gentlemen seated in the admiring audience below.

She favours smart tailored clothes in bold colours, yellow for instance, which makes her easy to spot when surrounded by men in dark suits. She is one of those confident aristocratic women who look stunning at any age, and she has had many admirers. This is the secret of Amelia's success, her ability to get on with men and make them work for her. At any reception they can be seen clustered round her as she stands, wine glass in hand, accepting their homage. Men who have captained warships or commanded armies hasten to do her bidding. Perhaps all men secretly enjoy being ordered about by a handsome and strong-minded woman, who knows? Either way she speaks, and they obey.

Rumours of marriage were commonplace in younger days but none of them materialised. Although La Ashby is no virgin she is not the marrying sort either but has been able to retain her lovers as friends afterwards. The passing of the years has made no difference to her faithful admirers. They are utterly devoted to her and plead to be allowed to render whatever small service she requires of them.

If you said that she was a woman who did not scare easily you would be wrong. Amelia does not scare at all. She comes in a formidable package with her lovely legs and French perfume, her smart London clothes, her icy charm, her throat-slitting smile and her keep-you-in-your place manners. Plus the diamond-edged certainty of her opinions which she delivers with such courtroom skill and logic that you can see her curtain-twitching disciples nodding in agreement long before she has finished speaking.

What you cannot see is her playground vindictiveness, her corner-shop prejudices, her contempt for intellectuals and anyone of a tolerant or liberal nature, her suspicious mind, her bullying manner or her meanness of soul. From which you will gather that I do not much care for Amelia Ashby but it may help to explain her visceral distrust and dislike of Ralph Chadwick, an equally uncompromising character who has forced some changes through in spite of her fierce opposition.

Because farming was in recession and likely to stay that way for many years to come Ralph diversified first into property development and then into retailing as the best means of making money from the resources at his disposal. These activities brought him into conflict with Amelia who did not approve of his business methods and did her best to make life difficult for him, a situation about to get worse.

Amelia relished a battle, particularly one she was sure of winning. All successful commanders know the value of surprise and she wasted no time in launching the biggest protest campaign ever waged by the Beckles Valley Trust. Our local newspaper is the Herald and Amelia is not only a principal shareholder but installed her nephew as the editor. Even a newspaper as unimportant as the Herald embodies all the power of the universal printing press and Amelia was in no mood for half measures. It comes out on a Friday and hit the newspaper stands with a banner headline, SAVE PACKHORSE MEADOW.

Amelia's dutiful foot-soldiers went from door to door with a petition, and no one able to write their name escaped the trawl. Battle-hardened, buoyed up with the euphoria of many previous victories, and with complete and utter faith in the invincibility of their leader, they snapped into action like a panzer division sweeping across open desert. The gauleiters on her executive committee all had favours to call in and soon recruited their friends in high places to support the cause, starting with the Lord Lieutenant of the county and the local Member of Parliament.

Amelia's next door neighbour is a retired archdeacon whose name I can never remember, and he is her most loyal henchman. His brief was to persuade all the local clergy to offer up prayers for the wild creatures that lived on Packhorse Meadow, and which were now under threat of extermination. Also to prevent the Ancient Britons buried in the round barrows from having their graves desecrated.

Amelia Ashby's personal contribution was to write individually to the heads of every known ecological organisation. In recent years the enthusiasm for so-called 'green' issues has caused these to proliferate to such an extent that she soon had promises from dozens of Chairpeople and Spokespersons all pledging their wholehearted support for her valiant crusade to save a strip of precious heath-land from a vandal landowner. Admire her or not, Amelia was brilliant at mobilising public opinion.

Because farmers are allowed to put up large buildings on their own land without permission she sought an injunction preventing Ralph doing any such thing, and alerted the Environment Agency to the risk that he might try to divert the water courses without prior consultation. She applied for Tree Preservation Orders on all the freestanding mature timber and found out the penalties for destroying ancient monuments. She saw the Bronze Age burial mounds as her trump cards and was successful in obtaining some old photographs of them which she had reproduced in the Herald.

As a clincher Amelia arranged a public debate in the town hall and it was standing room only on the night. An exhibition was put together in the entrance lobby, supposedly by a group calling itself Friends of Packhorse Meadow, a new one on me but a smart idea by one of Amelia's lieutenants. The exhibition consisted of photographs of the prehistoric burial mounds and the rare plants and animals that lived in Packhorse Meadow, and whose existence was now at risk from wicked landowner Ralph Chadwick. A grasping uncaring farmer whose hobby was shooting harmless wild animals, a barley baron who drenched his crops with pesticide and kept broiler chickens by the thousand in darkened sheds. A man who had frequently expressed his wish to zap all the badgers, and who, if allowed to do so, would dish out a similar fate to the goldfinches and wild orchids.

Amelia was wearing a bright green suit appropriate to the occasion. On the platform she crossed one elegant black-silk thigh over the other, to loud applause. Called on to speak she explained that she had no personal vendetta against Ralph Chadwick but could not allow this desecration of all the Trust stood for. There must be no change from leisure to agricultural use. Packhorse Meadow had to be retained intact and unchanged for the community to enjoy as a precious wildlife habitat.

'Rare butterflies,' she intoned. 'Orchids. Newts. Toads. Wrens.' And playing her trump card last, 'Nightingales! Once common in this country but now only surviving precariously in a few treasured havens which we must defend at all costs. My mission is to protect and preserve our heritage. I know you will all support me in winning the battle for Packhorse Meadow.' She sat down to loud and prolonged applause.

Although Ralph Chadwick had been bracing himself for some adverse opinion he was taken by surprise at the savagery and speed of the onslaught. He was shaken to find himself so quickly outmanoeuvred and put in the wrong. Amelia not only punched above her weight but hit below the belt as well. The mailed fist and the big boot were her favourite methods of persuasion, and they seldom failed her.

'I wouldn't know a natter-jack toad if I trod on one,' he sighed in despair when I visited at Giants Farm to commiserate with him. 'Or a great crested newt. Would you?'

'Very possibly. Yes, I think I would.'

'It seems I now own quite a few of them. Not a very good reason for buying Packhorse Meadow, was it?' Before I could reply he held up his hand, and it was a big hand attached to a muscular arm. 'I know, don't tell me, I don't own them, they are precious wild creatures that belong to everyone. Even slowworms! The wretched woman says they are rare and need to be treasured.' He scowled. 'I know what Amelia needs. And don't think I wouldn't.'

He had my full sympathy. Amelia and her humourless eco-bandits were as impervious to reason as the puritan zealots who had trashed all the lovely medieval churches for miles around, stripping them of their monuments and whitewashing over the colourful wall paintings. To cheer him up I said, 'You're not the only one who knows what she needs. Someone ought to do something about Amelia. She's had her own way for too long around here.'

Ralph was indignant but also resigned to defeat. He said sadly, 'All I wanted the place for was to run a few tractors backwards and forwards to save going miles round the road. Now she won't even let me do that.'

'We could write a letter to the Herald. Would you like me to draft something out? Putting the case for a limited return to agricultural use. A few sheep, for example. No one could object to that, could they?'

'Walter Vokes rang me to say that the Meadow was continuously farmed for several centuries until quite recently. He could produce records of grain crops going back to medieval times when it was owned by the priory. A bit late, that sort of ammunition.'

'Amelia got her retaliation in first. As always.'

'Walter also said that expert witnesses never look quite so

expert when they're challenged. He seems to think the goldfinches and skylarks and rare orchids exist mainly in Amelia's imagination. I can't say I've ever seen any sign of them myself.'

'What will you do next?'

'I was hoping you would tell me.' He smiled encouragingly. 'Come on, Alan. You're the one with the brains and the education. Think of something.'

I spread my hands to indicate sympathy and helplessness. 'You need some respite from the bad publicity. The smart option would be to do nothing for a few months.'

'Nothing?'

'The Herald soon dropped it from the front page. People only have a limited attention span. If you're not provoked into a response I think the interest could die down quite quickly.'

Ralph rasped his chin with his hand. 'It doesn't come easily but that sounds like good advice to me.'

'People still visit the Meadow, dog walkers mostly. Christmas is always a big distraction. If you let things carry on as they are it will soon become old news.'

Still deeply troubled at the way his purchase had rebounded on him Ralph thought it over and finally agreed. 'Alan, you're right. I won't go near the place for six months, longer if necessary. And none of my people will set foot on it either. We'll let it all carry on as before. Let it all go quiet, just as you suggest.'

'And after that?'

'I'm still deciding. It was my idea to buy it so I can't complain about it going wrong. Packhorse Meadow has caused me nothing but trouble so far.'

'Amelia will never make the slightest concession. She likes to win all her battles twenty nil.'

'I don't want to placate her. She is going to cost me a lot of money whether I do anything about it or not. And I've parted with more than enough already.'

'What then?'

Ralph suddenly became less dejected. After weeks of

scowling and squirming uncomfortably while Amelia put the boot in I could see that a plan of action had started to form in his mind. 'Yes!' he said, jumping to his feet and striding up and down. 'I've decided. I'm going to put my hand up Amelia's skirt. She's rattled my cage once too often.'

9

'The Shorn Lamb'

Mardle has two public houses but if I need to take someone for a drink I always choose the Shorn Lamb, partly because it is nearer to where I live but mainly because it is a genuine country pub yet to suffer its facelift makeover. Long may that be delayed.

This story is about a young villager, a self-employed jobbing builder and unhandyman whose name is Jeff Goodey. When visiting the Shorn Lamb one quiet lunchtime during half term I had to step over him. He was on his hands and knees, wielding a trowel and scooping out earth to put in bedding plants along the short concrete path leading to the bar entrance.

'You're doing a good job, Jeff,' I said by way of conversation as I passed by. 'They look like prize specimens.'

'Polyanthus and winter pansies,' he replied politely, standing up to ease his back. 'They ought to do well, I've just put half a ton of horse manure underneath them.'

Jeff Goodey worked mostly for other members of his large extended family who were in the same line of business. He was dressed in a skimpy yellow T-shirt that did not quite reach as far as his tattered jeans. In between was a muscular beer gut, acquired by spending all his free time and most of his money in the Shorn Lamb. He was tending the landlord's garden as a form of penance. He would not be paid for his labour and had provided the bedding plants and the fertiliser at his own expense. Not as a community service, more as a ritual humbling to appease the landlord whose finer feelings he had offended.

I will explain.

Mardle's other pub is on the main road leading away from the village. It is tricked out with hunting horns, copper warming pans, carriage lanterns and red flock wallpaper. The restaurant wall is hung with a scythe, a pitchfork, a horse collar, an embroidered shepherd's smock and a corn dolly or two. You get the idea. None of the real country people who live in Mardle have ever set foot in this pub and would not be seen dead there. They all go to the Shorn Lamb which is inconveniently situated in a narrow lane behind the school. Not only is it small but it is dirty and dimly lit, with uncomfortable wooden benches. The walls and ceilings still reek of nicotine and the bare floorboards are ingrained with countless years of trodden farmyard muck and mud.

Only the most wretched food is served, and then grudgingly, and the customers local or otherwise are looked on as a nuisance to be endured rather than a source of income. Yet the Lamb has a loyal clientele who would not dream of drinking anywhere else. The credit for this must go to the landlord, Ted Hounsome. He is a man of principle who believes in treating all his customers equally badly.

Tales of his incivility are told in the playground. If offered a large denomination note in exchange for a glassful of beer he will glare and snatch it away rudely and hold it up to the light while complaining, 'Haven't you got the right money?' If then offered the right money he will count it suspiciously from hand to hand as though he is being paid in some obscure currency from a far-off foreign land.

A bigot is always popular. 'At least you know where you are with Ted Hounsome', people tell one another, apologising for his extremist views. He is genuinely admired for his contempt of the political correctness which constrains every-one else. Ted says aloud what others dare not even think. For those who are timid and fearful he is a hero.

To mark great state occasions he drapes a giant flag across the front of the pub, wedging it between the two bedroom windows on either side. There is no junior or distant member of the Royal Family so obscure that their birthday goes uncelebrated, no day of the year on which a battle anniversary does not fall, no patriotic event too insignificant to pass unnoticed. But it is no longer the Union flag he displays. He now flies the flag of Saint George, the English flag. Ted long ago lost patience with communities both large and small who clamour for independence. 'Give it to them,' Ted says. 'If they want out, let them have out, all of them. Dump the ungrateful bastards before they change their minds. We'll get on a lot better without them.'

Ted Hounsome is a small man, pale and thin. He has his own distinctive style of dress which is a grubby white shirt buttoned at the neck without a tie, and a black waistcoat. This gives him an austere judicial presence, and it is accompanied by a mirthless baring of yellow teeth by way of a smile. This chilling stare is used to kill stone dead any attempt at pleasantry on the part of a customer. Ted sees no need to be polite, still less to be welcoming. If people don't like the way he runs the pub they can go elsewhere for all he cares.

During the summer months motorists will occasionally stray off the tourist routes in the hope of finding some unknown picturesque village. This is not a description anyone would apply to Mardle, which is a plain working village. Their first glimpse is so discouraging that most of them drive away immediately, although a few persevere until they find their way into the cheerless interior of the Shorn Lamb.

Mostly they will be shirt-sleeved salesmen chinking their company car keys and brandishing their plastic. Ted does not object to these because they never stay long and are more interested in using their mobile phones than engaging him in conversation. But once in a while some slick weasel of a big city tax-dodge accountant will turn up complete with enamel-led girlfriend and expect to boss everyone around and order special drinks and ask to see the chef.

Intruders like these get short shrift from our granite-faced publican and are soon driving away again humbled and subdued. Just to hear people breezing in with cries of, 'How wonderful darling, a real spit and sawdust pub, so clever of you to find it,' brings out the worst in a man who does not believe in bandying words with people he does not know, or does not like, which means just about everyone.

The loud confident flow of introduction and small talk gradually dies the death when they meet his hangman's stare from behind the bar. No hotshot company director talks down to Ted Hounsome and gets away with it. His response is not so much hostile as a massive and genuine indifference. All he wants is for them to buy their liquor, consume it without bothering him, and then disappear from his life forever.

No one can turn their back on a customer with quite the same degree of contempt as our sour-faced landlord. His list of dislikes is too long to recite here but a random selection would include children, cats, do-gooders, fussy eaters, joggers, immigrants and foreigners. Especially foreigners. 'Don't mention the word Europe in this pub,' is Ted Hounsome's strictest rule. 'I don't allow it. Either we fought them and beat them, or we liberated them. Europe is nothing to do with us.'

If there is an industrial dispute anywhere in the kingdom he will pin a crudely printed notice to the door, *'Strikers Not Welcome Here'*. Anyone belonging to a trade union comes high on Ted's list of people he would not like to wipe their feet on his mat. His attitude to homosexual men is straightforward and predictable but his particular dislike is for students. In his simplistic view of society all students are classified as workshy scroungers. He thinks they should be made to leave school and start work immediately, and begrudges them a share of his income tax. He is not a nice man.

The incident involving the young man of the bedding plants, Jeff Goodey, began to unfold one hot summer Sunday at one o'clock in the afternoon. The bar was crowded as usual on a Sunday at midday, and there was so much clatter and chatter that conversation was difficult. A situation that suddenly changed. As though someone had pressed a switch the noise died away until there was almost complete silence.

Instinctively I looked round with everyone else to see what had caused the sudden hush, with many conversations amputated in mid-sentence. Moving towards the bar was a young man whose long blond hair was tied back with a ribbon. An exotic stranger in our midst. Ted Hounsome was reaching down to take a bottle from a low shelf and had not yet seen him but along with my fellow villagers I feared for his reaction. Ted was suspicious of any new face, particularly one intruding on a Sunday, and his reception was certain to lack warmth.

It was like one of those saloon scenes in old Western films where people edge away nervously to avoid the bullets that are about to be sprayed round the room. The young man with the hair ribbon suddenly found himself in a lot of space with every eye in the bar turned on him. Not only did he have a wispy little blond beard but he also wore blue-tinted wrap-round 'I'm an idiot' mirror spectacles. Ear rings and a man-bag carried on a shoulder strap were calculated to upset Ted's fragile constitution even more.

We waited with mounting apprehension. Ted became aware of the silence and slowly straightened. We watched his knuckles whiten around the bottle he was holding, then saw him stiffen and quiver, his eyes like the slits in a prison door. He began to move slowly forward with menacing deliberation, fixing the apparition at the bar with his most baleful glare. Then spat the word, 'Yes?'

At which point someone spoke up and offered to buy the young stranger a drink.

This came as a surprise because none of us imagined that one of the regulars would defy Ted Hounsome, or willingly incur his displeasure. He turned his head slowly, very slowly, looking at every face in the bar until he had identified the culprit. We all turned too, fearful for the chilling severity of Ted's reaction.

'You?' he snarled.

The culprit nodded. It was the young man of the bedding plants, Jeff Goodey. He said nervously, 'Steady on, Ted. This is a new mate of mine. He's an Australian over here on holiday. He's a student.'

This was the wrong word and triggered the landlord's most deep-seated prejudice. Ted whispered menacingly, 'A student? Did I hear you say 'student'?'

'He can be a student, can't he? Everyone's a student these days.'

'A mate of yours? Is that what you said?'

Jeff nodded miserably. He was the most harmless of villagers, an easy-going young man impossible not to like. He had Left and Right tattooed on the backs of his hands, and Rum and Gin above his nipples. These were on view because his shirt was unbuttoned to the waist, exposing his large sun-tanned beer-filled tummy. Permanently displayed in the window of his rusty van was a sticker with the words, '*Sex Appeal. Please give generously*'. A young man who saw life as rather a lark, or at least he did until now.

'Honest, Ted,' he said in a voice that trembled slightly. 'He comes from Ozzieland. Ask him.'

Ted Hounsome permitted himself a grim smile. He enjoyed watching people squirm and offer feeble excuses, none of which had the slightest effect on him. He was not a man who could be moved by an appeal to his better nature because he didn't have one. The Goodeys and the Hounsomes were the two most numerous families in the village, much inter-married, so Jeff and the landlord were well known to one another as well as many times related. It made no difference.

Sweating copiously now Jeff looked round the room for support. He had his own personalised tankard which hung on a hook behind the bar, in a short row of hooks reserved for Ted's most favoured customers. Winning the right to this hook had been his equivalent of securing a place in the pantheon. It was the greatest achievement of his life, and he could see it being taken from him.

Until this crisis point he was a favoured family member smiled on by the landlord, with his own set of darts on a shelf behind the counter, along with his Christmas Club savings card. A situation about to change, with all his privileges withdrawn. By bringing someone Ted disapproved of into the pub he had forfeited his insider status and as from now would be excluded from the elite group of most privileged customers.

He whispered to his friend, 'Sorry, mate. He doesn't like Australians.'

The young student with the hair ribbon and idiot glasses could see the way things were going and did not look pleased about it. Everything people back home had told him about the Brits was proving to be true. He said nastily, 'What do you mean, he doesn't like Australians? We're the world's favourite people. Everybody likes Australians.'

'Ted doesn't.'

'I've got an Irish granny, too. Does he have a problem with that as well?'

Licking his lips in desperation Jeff Goodey said, 'I'll get the bevvies. Come on, we'll drink outside.'

Slowly the bar returned to normal with much shuffling of feet by the embarrassed drinkers as Jeff stumbled through the door to begin his exile. He had been banished from court, or at least from favour, and could not pretend to be other than a broken man. I had seen enough, drank up and returned home. Although I knew it was none of my business I could not help feeling concerned for the young man who had just been stubbed out by our vindictive pub landlord.

From happiness to unhappiness took only a moment. To win back the lost happiness would take years. If Jeff was sick at heart it was because he knew that although he would eventually be purged and shriven it would never be quite as good as it was before. Ted would never forget that he had once brought someone unsuitable into his pub and then argued the toss when told to leave.

Ahead of Jeff was a long ingratiating process of rehabilitation. A process that is ongoing. Twice a day, early and late, he takes the landlord's dog for its walk, he nurtures his garden and tends the tap-room fire, stacking up great piles of weathered oak logs supplied and sawn to length by himself. When no one else is around he slips in by the back door to hand over a brace of pheasants poached from the estate, or a few rabbits, or a huge joint of illegal venison wrapped in newspaper. Loyally he supports the darts team, although he is now no longer picked to play himself. He contributes generously to the Licensed Victuallers Benevolent Association and collects up the empty glasses at closing time.

I am sure it has never once occurred to Jeff that the landlord's behaviour was unreasonable, that his likes and dislikes were arbitrary and capricious, and his malice inexcusable. The most Jeff ever wanted from life was to be part of the charmed circle, that tight-knit group of regulars who basked in the wintry sunshine of Ted's approval, and whose personalised beer jugs chinked side by side on a row of hooks over the bar.

I do not suppose it was Jeff's only pleasure but it was certainly his greatest pleasure. To be greeted by name, to see others ignored while his glass was filled, made him the happiest of men. Just to hear Ted say fondly, 'Same again, Jeff, me old mate?' was the only reward he had ever sought from life. He had lost it, and was inconsolable.

To be excluded from the group you most long to join is a depth of suffering hard for anyone to bear. And this was the real tragedy for poor Jeff, who all alone bewept his outcast state. Ever so gently he was eased aside by the other members of the charmed inner circle who wished to safeguard their own privileged positions.

Only in subtle ways but to the man who is no longer accepted where he was once welcomed these perceived rejections were knife thrusts of unbearable pain. The Shorn Lamb was Jeff's club, his church, more like his home than his home, the mug holders dearer to him than his family. It is easy to smile at the needless or imagined suffering of others but I did not smile as I watched Jeff Goodey on his hands and knees planting polyanthus and winter pansies for the ungrateful landlord.

He was watering them in with his tears.

10

The Batty Sisters

The Chadwick policy on employment is simple but effective. Ralph's father and grandfather employed good people, paid them well and left them alone, and he does the same. Farming is made up of many specialist jobs and those with acquired expertise never react kindly to intrusive supervision. Everyone who works for Ralph is considered to own their job, and encouraged to do it to the best of their ability.

In charge of the large herd of Holstein cows at Giants Farm is a man named Dave Batty. His is one of the top jobs in the whole Chadwick enterprise and he is very well paid, even by non-farming standards. Dave and his wife and four growing daughters enjoy a high standard of living and in return they contribute to the life and work of the village. Especially the four girls who do everything together. This includes close harmony singing and they are star performers at the annual village concert which takes place on the second Saturday in December every year.

Does a village as small as Mardle have the resources to stage an annual concert? No, is the short answer but there is an explanation. Our nearby market town has a Choral Society and every Christmas they put on a big show of songs and carols in the Town Hall. It has become their custom to hire Mardle Village Hall every year so that they can have a final rehearsal in front of an audience. As a return gesture some local talent is given an opportunity to shine and we all turn up and give them a sympathetic clap. Not necessary where the Batty Sisters are concerned because they are the big attraction and responsible for about half the audience, most of them admiring young men who have smuggled in cans of lager and congregate noisily in the back rows.

Our village hall is a substantial brick building with a stage and a large car park. The land and the building were donated by Ralph's father, Lionel Chadwick, the second of the Chadwick dynasty at Giants Farm. The hall pays for itself because it is the only such building for miles around and does well from charging rent, with three sessions for hire every day, morning, afternoon and evening. It is a prized asset, booked up for months ahead.

In addition to the main hall there is a committee room which many of the local clubs and societies use as their regular meeting place. Supply companies hire the hall for promotional events when selling to farmers. Children's play groups and the Women's Institute could not function without it and its well-equipped large kitchen. Because it is also licensed for a bar it is in demand for wedding receptions and anniversaries, significant birthdays or national celebrations.

The concert organisers have enough sense to keep the star turn till near the end, so the young men have to listen to much formal singing until the Batty Sisters can take the stage. They fidget restlessly while they wait, dropping their empty lager cans on the floor where they can be rolled and kicked around. Eventually their impatience is rewarded and the four Batty Sisters enter from the wings, all four wearing identical costumes made by their mother. There is an immediate roar of applause and a commotion from the back of the hall as they start their routine.

They sing a pop song in unison and do a little dance. Only a shuffling sort of dance with arms linked but they smile at the cheers of encouragement and their eyes sparkle with excitement. When they first appeared on stage they were in the junior school but now they go to the big school and are themselves bigger in every way, certainly in ways approved of by the boys in the back row. Theirs is not the most appealing of stage names but no one objects to this because they are healthy country girls and when they start kicking their legs in the air the audience goes wild.

Beside me I can hear Ruth being disapproving but the home audience is in no mood to be critical. The Batty Sisters as usual are runaway popular winners and get a resounding round of applause, plus whistles and ribald shouts from the drinking customers at the back. This year their mother kitted them out in Highland costume and they looked very sweet, even if their red tartan skirts were a little on the short side. On the very short side, in fact.

The four Batty Sisters are not just popular with the boys but well thought of at school and in the community. They love to join things and go everywhere together. See one of them and the other three are sure to be somewhere nearby. Four sisters growing up fast but who are still inseparably fond of one another. Although their father Dave Batty is well paid he needs to be, because his four lovely daughters are high maintenance. When they have a family expedition to buy new school clothes before the start of term his bank balance suffers a grievous wound from which it has barely recovered before the next term comes round and still more new clothes have to be bought. Sports and leisure outfits add to the expense, and the girls all expect to be treated the same.

Fortunately Dave's wife Sue is clever with a needle. Dressing the four girls is a big interest for her and takes up most of her spare time. She follows the fashion pages closely and is one of those gifted people who can sit down at a sewing machine and run up an outfit without needing a pattern. The four girls are always nicely kitted out for every occasion and the general opinion is that they are a credit to their parents, and to the village.

Even so things are not quite what they seem because Sue the expert needlewoman is Dave's second wife. His first wife took a midday job at the main-road pub on the far side of the village, mainly to help serve the food. Allowing your young and pretty wife to work in a public house is asking for trouble. For some reason a woman seen in a bar is more enticing than the same woman seen at home, in particular a bar where sales reps go to eat lunch. This is what happened to Dave Batty's first wife who ran off with a fertiliser salesman and never came back.

Unusually for a woman she left their baby daughter behind. Fortunately for Dave his widowed mother also lived in the village and she was able to look after the little girl until he could find a new partner. This he did very quickly and sensibly by joining a club in the town run for the benefit of single parents. There he met Sue, a young mother in similar circumstances, and rather than just live together they decided it was best for their children if they got married and all had the same name. This was because Sue had two baby girls to contribute to the new family, and not long after they were married they had a child of their own, also a girl, and the fourth of the Batty Sisters.

Far from being disappointed Dave was tickled pink and loved being the father of four pretty girls. With a wife, a mother, and four daughters he could see a very comfortable home life ahead of him. And so it proved. He never needs to pour himself a cup of tea or cut a slice of cake because there is always one of them willing and eager to do it for him. He goes off cheerfully to milk the cows every day thinking that things have worked out very nicely for him, thank you.

The Batty sisters and their parents are a modern family. I am sure there are many such.

Although Sue contributed two girls to the marriage only one of them was hers. The man she lived with had a baby girl from a previous liaison and he abandoned her along with their own daughter. Sue had brought the two little girls up as sisters and being equally fond of both continued to look after them until such times as she could find a man to support them again. Happily for all concerned she soon met Dave Batty and between them retrieved a difficult situation.

Even so it is worth reflecting that of the four girls in Dave's family one is his, one is his wife's, one is theirs jointly and the fourth is not related to either. This has not prevented the four girls from bonding closely. They love to go out together and do things together, and on suitable occasions to dress alike as well.

At the village concert last year the Batty Sisters wore daring Malaysian cheongsams, figure hugging dresses with split skirts, split almost to the waist I may add, which caused pandemonium among the back-row aficionados. The year before that they were kitted out in Tyrolean dirndls and looked very sweet.

As they did this year in their Highland costumes with white silk blouses and buckled shoes. They looked prettier than ever and kicked their legs up even higher, scandalising my wife who muttered disapprovingly that their tiny tartan skirts were much, much too short.

11

William Chadwick

To understand Ralph Chadwick it helps to know something of how his grandfather came to acquire Giants Farm.

People are intrigued by the idea of a dynasty, yet few families manage to hold a business together for very long. Something soon goes wrong. A dominant father is followed by a weak son, wills are contested, divorce settlements eat into the capital, the younger members of the family are either too well-educated, too genteel or too degenerate to work the necessary long hours and apply their minds. And a business that is not daily nurtured by the undivided effort of its owners will not stay solvent for very long. The Chadwicks of Giants Farm seem to have managed it and consequently they are the subject of much curiosity in the village, and indeed most of the surrounding area. This is how they did it.

The Beckles Estate goes back a long way. Money earned during the Industrial Revolution in the north was used to buy land and respectability in the south. It has been well managed over a long period, and it is still owned by descendants of the original family. At the time in question, about a hundred years ago, the estate owned fifteen farms of varying sizes with an equally varied assortment of tenant farmers. Economic recessions knock early at the farmer's door and the tenants either went under or pulled out in search of an easier way of life, and a better return for their money.

So being a landlord was a big headache for the owners of Beckles Court, who needed to fill their vacant farms with suitable farmers. Most troublesome of all was Giants Farm, so called as I mentioned earlier because it stood on a hill where there was a shallow depression known locally as the Giant's

72

Footprint. It was an apt name because it was the largest of the estate farms being eight hundred acres in size, and no one had yet farmed it profitably. In fact every tenant in turn went broke, and soon no one new could be found to take it on.

Giants Farm had been built at a time when land was cheap and labour cheaper still. The owners had plenty of money and hired a fashionable architect who conceived a grand design. The farm was built on the side of a hill where it commanded superb views but from its size, and the number of rooms in the farmhouse, it would have been more suitable as a hotel, or a convalescent home, or a posh prep school.

The farm buildings were on an equally massive and impractical scale. The barns were huge, four of them, arranged in a square with a vast paved quadrangle in between. They enclosed as much space as a cathedral. Indeed there was faintly ecclesiastical cast to the architecture, with gothic pointed windows and huge studded doors that would not have disgraced a medieval castle. A grand design, but hardly suitable as a farm. The addition of a byre and dairy built on a similarly ambitious scale, plus a matching four-sided clock tower, only made it worse. The owners despaired of ever finding anyone capable of farming it profitably and paying them some rent.

The shining example to offset all this gloom was right on their doorstep.

In keeping with tradition the land adjacent to the manor house was farmed by the family so that it could be kept permanently provided with food. The bailiff of their Home Farm was a sensible fellow named William Chadwick and he turned in a handsome profit every year with no more staff or capital investment than any of the other farms. Thus disproving the complaints of impoverished tenants that it was impossible to make money from farming on the Beckles Estate.

William Chadwick was a solid homespun character, a man of few words, much given to quiet reflection. In an unspectac-ular way he got the best out of the land, the workmen and the machinery at his disposal. He was both diligent and financially competent. He had the rare knack of making farming pay. So the owners and their agent came to a unanimous decision. They begged William Chadwick to stop working for them and to take on the tenancy of Giants Farm instead, knowing that he was their best hope of retrieving a desperate situation.

He was certainly surprised by the offer and promised to consider it seriously. Which he did, methodically treading every inch of the ground and costing with great accuracy how much money he would have to borrow to buy sheep, cattle and machinery. Even with a minimum labour force his fixed overhead costs would still be too high to pay rent as well so he came to the reluctant conclusion that he should decline the offer. Making it as polite a refusal as possible since he did not wish to upset his employers.

It must be remembered that farming was in one of its worst-ever depressions at the time, with falling land prices and little demand for home-produced food. So with good reason did William make up his mind to refuse and keep his well-paid job instead. With reluctance though because his wife and three lovely daughters were bursting the seams of his modest estate house at Home Farm, the house now lived in by Jamie and Agnes Paterson. The draughty splendours of Giants Farm would have eased the pressure nicely, to say nothing of the spectacular view from the biggest bedroom down through the Beckles Valley.

His wife was sorry too but consoled herself with the thought that Giants Farmhouse would have been a nightmare to keep warm. It was built on the lofty and expansive scale of a huge Victorian rectory, and the girls could have had three bedrooms apiece if they wanted them. But just as William was on the point of formally declining the offer something happened to alter the balance of his calculations. His wife who was pregnant with their fourth child suddenly gave birth to a son.

It was a quick confinement, over and done with in an hour.

Much to the surprise of William Chadwick who had gone off to work as the father of three daughters and came home at lunchtime to find himself the father of a son. Without further thought he sat down and wrote a note to the agent accepting the tenancy of Giants Farm.

Needless to say he succeeded where others failed. Eight hundred acres was a big spread to bring under production, given the machinery available, but he soon had a proper crop rotation going and subdued it faster than anyone would have believed possible. He could not afford a single mistake and so took care not to make one. He was a hard taskmaster who gave orders and expected them to be obeyed, but was calm in appearance and manner. Until the end of his long life he dressed every day in a cap and a stockman's fawn coat. With his sturdy build, ruddy face, steady blue eyes and big brown boots he was a formidable character as he stood in his yard overseeing the work.

Inevitably there came an economic upturn and for a while farming prospered again. William Chadwick did not relax his grip on the farm just because times were a little easier. He was always to be found standing foursquare in the middle of the huge yard directing operations. Wealth made no difference to his lifestyle. He still counted every penny twice and lived comfortably below his income.

Less fortunate were the owners who came badly unstuck in an insurance swindle and needed to raise some money quickly. They offered William the option of buying Giants Farm as a sitting tenant and this time he did not hesitate. He closed the deal at once before they had a chance to change their minds.

Farming was once again the wrong thing to be in. Land prices were falling fast, farmers everywhere were going broke or committing suicide in despair, the public were not sympathetic and cheap imported foreign food was flooding the home market. Everyone told William he was mad to borrow money at high interest rates to buy a property that was certain to plummet in value the moment he signed his name on the contract. He ignored them, having found out by this time that the only advice worth taking was his own.

He was seventy years of age when he purchased the farm, and lived another fifteen years to prove his critics wrong.

12

Lionel Chadwick

A betting man would have given you odds against a farmer of William Chadwick's calibre being succeeded by a son equally competent. But such was the case and from an early age Lionel was determined to secure his inheritance. He had no intention of putting a winning formula at risk and did everything his father told him.

He studied hard at agricultural college and applied himself to the farm with such steady effort and thoroughness that the Chadwick grip remained strong for fifty years, long enough for the changes to be irreversible. Lionel's contribution can be summed up in one word – consolidation. He improved and updated every section of the farm. Even a holiday motorist knowing nothing of agriculture could not fail to be impressed when driving uphill out of Mardle past Giants Farm.

The entire landscape bore the imprint of a masterly hand. The neatly trimmed hedges, beautifully hung gates and clean track-ways told their own story of a well-run farm. Even the cattle in the fields seemed glossier than elsewhere. The sheep were visibly woollier and the corn grew higher, the furrows were gun-barrel straight. Any tile that slipped was immediately replaced, every door had a latch that worked. The yards were hosed down every day and the implements were not put away after use until they had been cleaned to look like new, however long it took.

It was a bit like the army where anything that moved was saluted and everything that didn't was painted. Lionel was a perfectionist. 'Do things properly', was his motto and since he was the boss and insisted on having his own way, they were. The men respected him for it and took a pride in their work.

To have been employed by the Chadwicks was considered a sufficient recommendation in itself and the few men who left never had any difficulty finding a position elsewhere.

Although Lionel married late he married well. His wife had grown up in an English country house and knew what was what. She had also worked for one of the fine-art auction houses in London and developed an unerring good taste in furniture and furnishings. So what her husband had done for the land, Mrs Lionel was able to do for the house and its contents. With considerable wealth at her disposal, and a broad span of years in which to complete the work, she turned Giants Farmhouse into a kind of minor stately home and garden. It is still quite a showpiece.

Men always study their boss in order to understand his ways and it was not lost on them that for a decent chap with plenty of money Lionel never treated himself to a holiday. His wife went to stay with her family occasionally but he never left the farm. Why? He was not an overanxious workaholic, nor distrustful of his staff. 'He won't go because he's afraid it might not be here when he came back!' was the standard reply by farm staff to anyone who enquired.

A true answer and the exact reason why Lionel Chadwick never went on holiday. Until quite late in life he behaved with a sense of wonderment at his own good fortune, as though he could never quite believe it was all his, and would be snatched away the moment his back was turned. But he had a son, the formidable Ralph, who was treading hard on his heels. When he reached the age of sixty-five he suddenly packed it in, to general surprise. He took his wife to live in one of the exquisite town houses in College Close overlooking the college playing fields and embarked on a second career that would last for twenty years.

He had always been urbane and easy-mannered, with a natural aptitude for chairing committees. He enjoyed ceremonial occasions and soon became a local dignitary with an impressive string of honorary positions to his credit. He was president of the agricultural society, the rugby club, the golf club and at one time or another most of the other clubs and societies as well. He was also for many years an active and well-informed chairman of the College governors. He took a big interest in the daily life of the school, made easier by living on the doorstep so to speak, his house in College Close being just across the way.

He also served a term as Deputy Lord Lieutenant for the county, and took his duties seriously. These varied services to agriculture, education, and the general community, were recognised with an OBE in his seventieth year. 'Lionel fancies himself as a bit of a toff', someone whispered to me once and if he ever shook your hand you certainly had the impression that he expected you to be suitably deferential. So if Lionel had a fault it was perhaps that he took himself too seriously and had a fair notion of his own importance.

His photograph appeared regularly in our local newspaper, the Herald, usually in a dinner jacket as he and his wife attended yet another institutional dinner. In later life he became somewhat pink of face and tight of waistband as the wining and dining took its toll but he always looked the part and carried himself well in a silvery, ambassadorial kind of way. His eightieth birthday portrait will hang in the entrance hall of Giants Farm until the end of time.

Lionel lived to exactly the same age as his father, eighty-five, and was buried close to him in Mardle churchyard.

13

Ralph Chadwick

If the men on the farm hoped that affluence had softened up the Chadwicks they were in for a nasty surprise when Ralph appeared on the scene.

He was nothing at all like his father, the urbane and easy-mannered Lionel, still less like his quietly prosperous and unassuming grandfather William. They reckoned he had to be a throwback from some earlier generation of Chadwicks who must have earned their living in a tougher trade than farming.

As a young man Ralph had thick black curly hair, with a blacksmith's arms and shoulders. He looked and acted more like a fairground boxer than the heir to a farming fortune. He seemed to have a permanent scowl on his face and the older men on the farm soon learned to back down when he wanted his own way about something. From an early age he spent his spare time in the farm workshop and soon had his own bench and a small area to himself.

On any farm there are plenty of rough jobs that need doing, and on a farm as big as Giants Farm the need was multiplied because everything was on such a large scale. There are also dirty jobs, smelly jobs and dangerous jobs. The Chadwicks solved the problem by having a hard-nut general-purpose fixer on the payroll, a young man very good with an axe or a big hammer. He was a strong young man who answered to the name Hud. He had a scar, a broken nose and was plentifully tattooed. He liked a drink and solved arguments with his fists. Hud was tolerated because he was useful, because he was strong, and because he never complained at being given the worst and hardest work.

He also had an apprentice who hero-worshipped him –

Ralph.

Almost as soon as he could walk Ralph decided that Hud had the most interesting job on the farm and by the age of five began to follow him around. All through his schooldays this loyalty never wavered. Hud was rather tickled at having the young boss as his mate, and flattered that Ralph should model himself on him. Before long there was little to choose between them. However rough, dirty or awkward the job, Ralph and Hud never flinched. The moment there was trouble anywhere on the farm they turned up in a crumpled Land Rover and sorted it out.

Sometimes it would be to mend a puncture in a huge tractor wheel, or to rescue a cow that had fallen in a ditch, or to pull aside a tree that had blown down in a gale, and then to carve it up with chain saws. The tougher the job the better they liked it, whether it was digging deep drainage trenches or blasting out tree roots to widen a field.

Ralph was not academically inclined and gave higher education a miss, opting instead for a machinery course at the local agricultural college. He gave no sign of wishing to share his father's office and becoming part of the management, and in his twenties still continued to occupy himself in the farm workshop. All their tackle was big. They needed the largest combines, balers, ploughs and spray booms, an investment in machinery and equipment of several million pounds. Keeping all this expensive kit mended and in working order became Ralph's area of expertise.

If the Land Rover chauffeured by the faithful Hud clanked it was because it was permanently loaded with heavy tools and welding equipment. Machines were not supposed to break down but when they did it was not many minutes before Ralph and Hud were underneath with torch and goggles putting things right. There was nothing they could not take apart and put back together again. Between them they kept the farm operational.

Men always study their bosses and try to understand their ways, and it has to be said that Ralph's behaviour caused considerable disquiet among the staff. He still did all the dirty or dangerous jobs himself, never went near his father's office, never went to meetings, never wasted his time talking to reps, read only trade magazines advertising spare parts for machinery, and took advice only from his pal Hud. Who now hero-worshipped him in return.

So was Ralph up to the job? This was the big question they asked one another. Lionel was getting on a bit but instead of learning how to manage the farm his son preferred to do the evening milking from nine until midnight, or to help out in the lambing sheds, or to keep the combines rolling and the grain dryer burning through the summer nights. Bulldozing hedges with his mate Hud was all very well but how was he with a set of tax returns and a balance sheet? They had their doubts.

Not so his father Lionel who was delighted with the way his boy was shaping up. He could not have been more pleased and no doubt this influenced his decision to retire to College Close and leave Ralph to get on with it. He knew that what Ralph was doing could be explained in two words – problem solving. As a result he had become supremely self-reliant, the secret of Chadwick success.

His father knew that Ralph would never sit cowering in an office being ordered about by accountants or lectured by supply-company advisers. From hard practical firsthand experience he had learned how every part of a farm should be run. He knew to the minute how long it took to milk a herd of cows, to plough a field or shear a flock of sheep. While still at school he had mastered the tricky skill of how to reverse a tractor-and-trailer through a narrow gateway, and had yet to meet a chartered accountant who could do it at all, let alone do it better.

Ralph was thirty-two years old when he finally moved into the comfortable office vacated by his father. And with it came a new policy – expansion. Everything necessary to expand the business was safely in hand. They had no debts, plenty of collateral and a mountain of cash in the bank. The farm had been well run and profitably managed for many years. All they needed now was someone with the necessary guts, drive and ambition to make things happen. And needed to wait no longer.

During Lionel's lifetime Giants Farm had gradually increased in size from eight hundred to a thousand acres as adjacent fields were purchased when they came up for sale, a process Ralph continued. When an adjoining farm came on the market he snapped it up immediately. This message was not lost on the local land agents and any farm for sale was quickly put his way. Soon he had converted a thousand acres into a thousand hectares, three times the original size of the farm. And he was still eager for more.

Nor did he make money just from farming. Awkwardly situated plots of land that could not be farmed profitably soon had houses built on them. 'The last crop but a good one,' was his verdict on bricks and mortar. Planning permission was easy to obtain when the Chadwick millions were behind the application. Ralph had no qualms when it came to calling in favours he was owed, no scruples that prevented him from using his financial clout to bully, bribe or influence commit-tees, no conscience in bending rules that were not to his liking, no hesitation in kneecapping builders, town planners, councillors, architects, lawyers, government inspectors, or any other of the assorted officials and bigwig nobodies who were trying to slow down his race to the next million. With a few barn conversions thrown in and a couple of housing estates to his credit Ralph did very nicely from property development and used the money to expand his core business still further.

The fastest fortunes are made in retailing and Ralph was quick off the mark. He increased the size of his already huge Holstein herd and began selling the milk himself. He was soon able to buy out all the local small independent dairies and shortly afterwards opened a big farm shop. This was a supermarket type enterprise with a large car park and provided an outlet for his own products. These included butter, cheese and yoghurt, his own eggs and market garden produce, even thousands of needle-fast Christmas trees grown on the farm and a big annual money-spinner. This led in turn to opening a garden centre and nursery, which needed an even bigger car park.

Ralph made money from farming because he followed the example of his father and grandfather. Which was to produce what the market wanted, not what was convenient or easy to grow, taking care to protect the environment at the same time. He did not see vegetarians as misguided, he did not despise the low-cholesterol lobby or oppose those who campaigned for greater compassion in farming methods. On the contrary he saw them as valued customers with special needs and applied his mind to offering them the kind of food they wanted to buy.

He provided organically-grown market-garden produce and a range of low-fat milk products, naturally flavoured and attractively packaged. Meat was more of a problem but he offered it as a lean, wholesome product that found favour with his customers. Hygiene and animal welfare were paramount. There were no lame cows in Ralph's herd and he made sure that all the calves and breeding sows were decently treated. His policy was to study the market and go along with public opinion, not to resist it.

By the age of fifty Ralph had become a very rich man indeed. Not entirely unaided, his father and grandfather having set it up for him, but he had made his own fortune as a farming entrepreneur by a combination of business astuteness and skilful retailing. No one begrudged him his success which had been achieved with hard work backed by his own money.

After all this effort his hair was still thick and curly but now more grey than black. He no longer wore overalls but was seldom seen in a suit and tie either. The crumpled Land Rover had been exchanged for a shiny new one but he still liked to be driven round by his equally tough pal Hud, now a pensioner. He spent more time out of the office than in it and had the habit of turning up when people least expected him.

His was not a very democratic organisation. Ralph expected to get his own way, and invariably did so. He had a strong brooding presence that killed off objections long before people had the nerve to utter them. He carried with him a sense of urgency that brushed aside difficulties and went straight to the heart of any problem. He created an impetus that was unstoppable. From the moment he got up in the morning until he went to bed at night he drove his many business interests forward with relentless energy.

Rich men are always the object of curiosity, just as successful men command respect. On both counts Ralph was well known and admired. The boom years for farming had come and gone, times were hard again so anyone who could make money from agriculture deserved to be taken seriously. Whether he was aware of it or not he had become a celebrity in the farming world. His methods were widely debated and analysed in the hope that others could benefit from his example. They rarely could.

Being interested in such matters it impressed me that Ralph was always known and referred to by his first name only, as though he was a king from the dark ages. Local dairy farmers would enquire of one another, 'Which bull is Ralph using this year?' Name-droppers were quick to claim acquaintance. 'As I was saying to Ralph himself only last week…' Always a good way to begin a conversation. 'Ralph won't stand for that', was a commonly heard remark in the area, usually accompanied by a grim chuckle, knowing the vigour with which he protected his interests.

Yet he was not unpopular, having a bluff sardonic sense of humour that went down well in a hard-working straight-talking community. He was a man's man who was neither mean nor a snob. He reared a lot of pheasants and regularly invited his neighbouring farmers to the twice-weekly shoots, a gesture much appreciated. He was a good shot with a gun himself, something always admired in the country, and generous with hospitality. Farming groups came regularly to make study visits at Giants Farm, not only from this country but increasingly from abroad as well, and he always made them welcome and often showed them round himself.

Even so his physical presence created space around him. He was not a man you could get close to in any sense of the word, and Ralph was never crowded. He had been brought up from childhood to expect his own way and in the end this is what his money bought him. Instant obedience from his employees, deference from the lawyers and accountants and other professional people who looked after his affairs, the healthy respect of his neighbours and, less pleasantly perhaps, a lot of fawning from salesmen who wanted a share of his business.

As the virtual lord of all he surveyed from his bedroom window Ralph was much discussed in the village. Did he own a yacht and go sailing? Did he dabble in horse racing? How about a second home in Tuscany? A girl friend, perhaps? The answer to all these questions was 'no'. Ralph was interested only in his farm, and in making money, and allowed himself no distractions.

He adored his wife Beth but the general view was that he treated her badly, and their son Trevor, their only child, even worse. Far from spoiling him Ralph treated his son more harshly than any of his workers would ever have treated their own sons. Throughout his childhood and early adolescence Trevor was made to slave away on the farm as well as study hard for exams, and was shown little affection by his father. It was not something the people who worked for Ralph could understand.

As for Beth he allowed her only minimum help in the house. She drove a modest small car, did most of the gardening herself and dressed in clothes that were far from expensive. True, they had the splendid Giants Farmhouse to live in but Ralph seemed determined that they should live frugally with a lot more hard work than luxury. So all in all a complicated man, not easy to live with or work for, but the undisputed leader of the local farming community.

Holidays? Ralph seldom spent a night away from the farm, and for the same reason that his father and grandfather never left it either. The fear that it might not be there when he came back.

14

The Ablewhites of Godwins Farm

Although nothing is ever said at home I know that my wife Ruth is secretly proud to be a member of the principal farming family in the area, the wealthy and successful Chadwicks. My farming relations, the Ablewhites of Godwins Farm, occupy a more modest level of agricultural endeavour and their name dropped into a conversation does not have quite the same effect.

These Ablewhites are my cousins, and there are four of them. There are three brothers, Jim the eldest and Ken the youngest, both bachelors, and the middle brother Frank who is married to our cousin Emily, known to the family as Em. She is also an Ablewhite and so kept the same name after her marriage. It was a late marriage with no children, as is the custom between first cousins in the country. It solved the inheritance problem by keeping the farm intact and also provided the three brothers with home comforts. My father was born and brought up at Godwins Farm so I like to visit occasionally, and I am always made welcome.

Recessions come and go but pass by the rickety gate at Godwins Farm where fat years and lean years make no difference to their ordered way of life. As far as anyone can be immune from change they take little note of what happens in the outside world. They are humble and they are honest. They know their place and pay their bills on time. In return all they seek is privacy. They do not interfere with anyone else and all they ask is that no one interferes with them.

'They scurry,' my wife says. An accurate description of their behaviour when they try to avoid people who might know them and wish to speak. In the town's High Street recently she caught a glimpse of Frank the married brother, and his wife Emily. Ruth would have spoken but did not get close enough. Shy as forest animals Frank and his wife hurried away so that they could finish their shopping and return to the safety of the farm as soon as possible.

Godwins Farm is inaccessible to all but the most determined of salesmen. Getting there is like a commando assault course. It can only be reached up a long muddy track deeply cratered with potholes, with here and there a sly boulder to make unwelcome visitors in cars lose their nerve and turn back. The postman puts their mail into a box at the far end of the track where they collect it themselves. The Farmers Weekly and the Herald are rolled up and slotted into a drainpipe tied on the gate. Weeks pass without a single visitor, and that is the way my cousins like it.

They are fortunate in the local geography which allows only one view of their farmhouse across open fields. All the other views are blocked by trees or thick hedges, or by bends in the road. And the brief glimpse that motorists see is an ugly pebble-dashed house surrounded by barns made of asbestos sheeting, concrete blocks and corrugated iron. It looks awful and so they are never pestered by artists wanting to paint pictures, or by local historians in search of antiquities.

You would have to say that my cousins are good at dissemblance. As a member of the family I know what it is they are hiding, which is a lovely old farmhouse concealed beneath the coating of pebble-dash. Inside the house the floors are uneven, and the ceilings are made from great smoke-blackened rafters roughly hewn from the limbs of oak trees. The doors have all been individually made to fit their spaces and all are different. Some have iron latches that clank, others have brass handles worn smooth and lustrous with age. The narrow stone-flagged passageways are kept covered with long strips of brightly coloured coconut matting to absorb mud from boots. All over the house there are short flights of stairs because floors are on different levels, some up, some down, and the ceilings creak when anyone moves around overhead.

The special nature of the walled garden is equally hard to describe. The first effect is one of profusion because there is hardly a space in which to squeeze another row of vegetables or any more flowers. My cousins do not like supermarket fruit or vegetables and produce as much as they can themselves. Every patch of ground has something growing on it, with something else being brought on in the greenhouse to fill the space as soon as it becomes vacant. Figs, quinces and pears are grown along the walls and in every sheltered spot there is a cucumber frame, or a bed of herbs, or watering cans full of water warming up in the sun. There is no attempt to protect the soft fruit from birds which certainly eat their fill. 'The birds are entitled to their share', is Em's firmest rule and she always allows them first pick.

In warm weather a heady scent rises from the garden. If I ask Em to escort me down the long brick paths she will recite the names of the shrubs and flowers as we go: Aaron's Beard, Black-Eyed Susan, Bridal Gown, Columbine, Creeping Jenny, Goldenrod, Granny's Bonnets, Lady's Mantle, Larkspur, Love in Idleness, Love in a Mist, Night Scented Stocks, Phlox, Red Hot Pokers, Snapdragons, Solomon's Seal, Sops in Wine, Sweet Rocket. Their Latin names cannot be as nice as these.

Frank is the livestock specialist and Ken does the arable and tractor work. Jim, the oldest of the three brothers, handles the finance and business side of the farm but he also does most of the gardening, with Em as his assistant. In the summer months they are seldom to be found far away from this garden which absorbs all their spare time, even if it is only to stand around solemnly debating which cabbage to cut next. Em does all the cooking, the cleaning and mending and general housework. Looking after three working men in a big farmhouse is a full time job but it is not paid labour and she is happy all day long.

Farm animals respond to individual treatment and this is what they get from my cousins. Their main source of income is from beef cattle. These are fed on home-grown forage, mainly grass and maize silage plus a small amount of hay. The demand for top quality beef is constant year on year so my cousins have a guaranteed sale for their end product. They keep other livestock as well, a few pigs and some poultry, but all their animals thrive and there is rarely any sickness, still less a fatality. Although my cousins live without show they are quietly prosperous with plenty of money in the bank, often the way with old country families.

Ken, the youngest of the three brothers, is able to coax years of life out of moribund machinery, a great saving of money. He has a well-equipped workshop and such is his mechanical skill that they seldom if ever need to go outside for a repair. They never buy anything new and attend farm sales when an implement finally needs to be replaced, or to obtain spare parts.

When work is done and the table cleared my four cousins love to talk. What they talk about is not very important but they never tire of it, or of one another's company. In the summer they sit in the drawing room with the windows wide open. In the winter they sit round the fire, and it is a log fire in a stone hearth that gives out a gentle heat all through the night. Whether it is summer or winter they never want for a topic of conversation. They speak in turn without interrupting one another, conversing easily and literately, developing an idea at length until it has been thoroughly debated.

Sometimes when I am visiting and sit listening to their conversation a telephone can be heard ringing in the distant back room where Jim has his office, but they never answer it, indeed give no sign that they have even heard it. If they are all four together they are not interested in anyone else. As far as they are concerned a telephone has its uses but socialising is not one of them. It would never occur to them to ring anyone up for a chat, and they do not encourage anyone to ring them.

I suppose it has to be said that my relatives are somewhat unworldly, and their extreme shyness can be irritating at times. Yet for all that they are good people, appreciative of what they have and determined to hold on to it. All they ask from life is to be allowed to live quietly on their own. They have managed it up till now and I hope they always will.

I have two stories to tell about my cousins and apologise for this lengthy preamble.

15

The Hoard of Silver

On the Ordnance Survey map about a mile east of Godwins Farm appear the ominous words, 'Site of Roman Villa.' There is not much to see and does not detain visitors for long. There is a signposted path across a field to where a few foundation walls have been excavated.

This does not stop parties of students visiting the site to search for a more important building which they believe existed in the area, and for which there is some vague documentary evidence. They poke long rods into the ground feeling for buried walls, and there has been more than one aerial survey, although nothing was found.

Bounty hunters are also attracted to the site, furtive characters with metal detectors at work in the early hours of the morning, long before the honest citizen is awake. Lack of success in the immediate area of the villa has forced them to roam further afield, a development watched anxiously by my seclusion-loving cousins.

They have good reason to be worried. Their farm implements have been turning up Roman remains in the fields since they were children. In less leisured times, before the general public started taking an interest in archaeology, these objects were used to mend potholes in the track. Lumps of tessellated pavement for example, square hypocaust tiles and great chunks of mosaic flooring gouged out by previous ploughing. Even an elaborately carved frieze which was used to prop up a water trough in the corner of a field for as long as I can remember.

In the conservatory used by Jim and Em as a nursery for their seedling plants they kept an old Victorian tea caddy where they put coins dug up in the garden. Larger objects went into a wickerwork linen basket. These were mainly buckles, belt plates and cuirass hinges, most of them with shreds of blackened leather attached. I suspect that Em's garden fork turns up more Roman relics every year than you would find in a city museum. Eventually the bounty hunters with their metal detectors started to come too close for comfort and changed this casual attitude. The tea caddy full of coins and the basket of metal artefacts quietly disappeared from view.

Because my cousins knew only too well that their farm, situated on land which had once belonged to Godwin, the Saxon Earl of Wessex, was built over the site of the Roman building the students were looking for. They could only hope that centuries of ploughing, plenty of trees and grazing animals plus their untidy sprawl of ugly farm outbuildings had obliterated all traces.

Ken Ablewhite the youngest of the three brothers does all the tractor work. He has eyes like a hawk for any strange object thrown up by the plough. One evening when I was visiting at Godwins Farm he entertained me with his experiences of the working day, namely that the tines of the harrow had nudged an earthenware wine jar to the surface. He used his hands in an accurate description of a tall two-handled amphora which had once been filled with six gallons of Tuscan wine.

With an inward groan of despair I asked what he had done with it, knowing the answer in advance. Not hesitating for a second Ken had jumped down from the cab and smashed it into smithereens with a giant spanner, scattering the pieces far and wide. Prompt action that met with warm murmurs of approval from his two brothers and his sister-in-law.

'What else had he found lately?' I enquired, trying not to sound too appalled. 'Only one of those old breastplate things', Ken replied. And what had he done with it? Another silly question just as candidly answered. He had thrown it into the dell at the rear of the old dairy buildings. This was the farm rubbish dump where they disposed of empty oil cans and any old rusting machinery that made the place look untidy. Vicious stinging nettles and other rank weeds soon devoured this rubbish. The roots of bushes and small trees would complete the digestion process and I knew that the Roman breastplate had vanished for ever from human sight.

The legions left in too much of a hurry for my nervous and timid cousins, and left too much behind. It is a constant worry and the only shadow over their otherwise idyllic existence. So it is easy to imagine their horror when they came across some even larger metal objects.

A tree had fallen in a gale and damaged one of the old outbuildings. The pace of life is slow at Godwins Farm. Although they had every intention of removing the fallen tree, and making whatever repairs were necessary, several summers passed before the work was begun. And then only because Em was running short of logs for her winter hoard and the fallen tree was the easiest place to get them.

Ken the machinery expert busied himself with the chain saw, while brothers Jim and Frank began repairing the cart shed wall. To do this they first had to dig out a broken gate post, a five minute job that had taken them well over an hour, and they were starting to think it wasn't such a good idea after all. They sweated in their shirtsleeves until at long last they worked the gate post free and could begin rebuilding the wall.

The gate post had left a deep hole. 'Hello,' Jim said, on his knees. 'There's an old tin plate down here. Heavy though.'

At first the three brothers were only mildly interested and just moved it aside to dispose of later. Still on his knees Jim continued to feel around with his hand and found another heavy metal plate. Then another, then more, lifting them out one by one. Each plate had been individually wrapped in a coarse type of cloth and it became obvious that they had been carefully buried inside a hollow space built of square stones to protect them.

More alarmed now the three countrymen peeled away the disintegrating fabric and examined the plates more closely.

They spat on them and rubbed the dirt off with their hands and did not like what they were seeing.

'As big as dinner plates?' I asked when they told me the story in their usual slow manner. It was a warm summer evening and we were sitting in armchairs with the windows open, looking out into the garden. They took up the story in turn, each contributing their version of events while the others listened. They were vague about time but it would most likely have taken place while I was at university in London.

'Bigger,' middle brother Frank replied, in answer to my question. 'The two biggest ones were as wide across as a dart board.' He held up his hands to show me. 'Yes, as big as that.'

'How many?' I asked next, trying not to believe what I was hearing.

'Thirty of the small ones, maybe,' Frank said. 'We didn't waste time counting them.'

'Just plates?'

'No, there were some bowls as well and two jugs with spouts and handles. Quite big and elaborate they were.'

Such was their alarm that Em had been summoned from indoors. She bustled out wiping her hands on her apron to watch the hoard being retrieved from its hiding place. The smaller plates were plain but the two bigger ones had an inscription round the rim. Jim scraped the dirt off with his gardening knife so that she could see for herself what was causing them such concern.

Em took one look and confirmed what they were beginning to fear. The inscription was in the dreaded Latin and the heavy metal plates were made of solid silver, exceeding many times over the value of their farm. They stared at one another in horror, able to visualise all too clearly the avalanche of publicity that would descend on them if news of this discovery reached the newspapers. Their precious seclusion and settled way of life would be gone forever.

'You don't mean it's all in the dell, do you?' I asked hopefully.

No such luck. They knew that drastic measures were called

for and acted swiftly to dispose of the unwanted treasure, for good this time. At the back of the house was an old well that had been boarded up for years, and having removed the boards they proceeded to throw the entire hoard to the bottom. And it was a deep well.

Ken meanwhile had used his tractor-and-trailer and front-loader to bring tons of earth from the nearest ploughed field. All three men sweated in the evening sun shovelling the earth down the well, load after load, until not even the most powerful metal detector in the world would have registered a single bleep.

When the well had been completely filled in and sealed over again they went indoors for their reward. Em had cooked them a dumpling stew, their favourite of all meals. They ate it in celebration, full of relief at a danger narrowly averted.

16

An Invincible Innocence

The second story about my Ablewhite cousins concerns Ken, the youngest of the three brothers. But first I should like to describe their appearance.

Farming folk in general do not dress much differently from everyone else these days, and cannot be readily identified from their clothing as in the past. The young men I see around on the local farms favour brightly coloured overalls and zippered windcheaters, often the gift of the supply trade and bearing a company logo. Long-peaked trucker caps protect eyes from the sun, rawhide boots keep feet out of the mud and look snazzier than a pair of wellies. It is a comfortable and smart way to dress.

Trust my cousins to be different. This is because the town still has an old-fashioned country outfitter and Emily Ablewhite must be their best customer. If not their only customer, but while stocks last she will continue to shop there on behalf of her menfolk. This is where she buys their flannel shirts, serge trousers, patterned pullovers and hairy tweed jackets that last a lifetime. Jim, Frank and Ken go to bed in striped pyjamas and blow their noses on handkerchiefs as big as table cloths. They all have a pair of Sunday-best black shoes with huge polished toecaps, as a change from the hobnailed boots they wear during the week.

So their appearance is undeniably distinctive and the few people who visit the farm and catch sight of my elusive cousins go away with an impression of shy and backward countrymen wearing quaint old-fashioned clothes. And feel sorry for them, deprived of all the delights of modern living. Men who can have done nothing, and seen nothing. But wait.

Hadn't one of those funny old boys served in the army?

Local people took little interest in them and so could not be sure, they certainly could not have said which of the three brothers had been in the army, and who consequently might perhaps have seen a little of the outside world. It was Ken the youngest, the reason being that the farm could not provide a living for him while his father was alive, and they also employed a man at that time. From an early age Ken had been conditioned to the idea that he would go in the army and stay there until his father was too old to work, or died, whichever came first, and then rejoin his brothers at the farm.

Machinery was what he liked. Almost as soon as he could walk he was taking things apart and putting them together again, and there were plenty of old tractors and farm implements to learn on. He did well enough at school to enlist in an engineering regiment where his talent for repairing broken machinery was immediately recognised.

He had imagined, and no doubt expected, that he would spend his entire military career in some sequestered workshop giving the kiss of life to clapped out lorry gearboxes or rewinding burnt-out starter motors. The last thing he wanted was to see any action, being the most peace-loving and inoffensive soldier imaginable.

Unfortunately for him his great skill as an engine fitter determined otherwise. He had only to see a piece of machinery to know instinctively what it was used for, exactly how it worked, and if it was broken how to mend it. Others could do the theory, Ken could do the practical, and as a result company commanders wanted him on the payroll.

Army units far from home in hostile territory dread a vehicle breakdown more than anything else. Years of coaxing life into dilapidated farm machinery had been the best possible apprenticeship. Ken never complained that he did not have the tools or the right spare parts, he just made do with what he had and still got a result.

Just to see him advancing on a casualty vehicle with his heavy metal toolbox and slow country manners gladdened the hearts of his superior officers. Whether it was an armoured troop carrier or the adjutant's staff car, whether it was the hydraulics that had gone wrong, or the electrics, or a fuel injector needing to be replaced, Ken's air of calm confidence never wavered. Even in a battle zone with gunfire he remained as unflustered as he would have been in the workshop at Godwins Farm, methodically working his magic on every piece of broken machinery put in front of him.

With the unwelcome result that his army career was a lot more exciting than he would have wished. It guaranteed that he would always be heading for foreign climes, there to be greeted by explosions and the whine of bullets as he carried his toolbox down the aircraft steps. Trouble had only to break out in some distant land and within the hour Ken was summoned from his bench, given the necessary injections and sent on his way. There was no shortage of wars and he was first choice on every peace-keeping mission. While more ambitious soldiers desperate for excitement and glory fretted in barracks and married quarters at home, my guileless cousin Ken, the most peaceable of men, narrowly escaped death all over the world.

He was regularly shot at, twice nearly drowned, jolted across mountain passes in the back of ramshackle trucks, and flown over the ice-caps in wheezy old transport planes that should have been pensioned off a quarter of a century since. All without a word of complaint from this most dutiful and obedient of soldiers.

He witnessed famine, pestilence, refugee camps and the aftermath of earthquakes, saw a massacre at first hand and a dozen civil wars. Malaria one year made a nice change from frostbite the next. He sweated in the desert, was knifed in Africa, poxed and robbed in the Far East. Whether on or off duty the same inevitable mayhem attended his innocent excursions to the nearest bar for a quiet drink with his mates. A prostitute was sure to be murdered on the next stool or an armed insurrection break out the moment he set foot in town.

His knowledge of world geography was not good, virtually

nil in fact, so he had only a hazy idea where he was at any given time, still less what he was supposed to be doing there. But then one border checkpoint is much like another, see one bomb crater and you've seen them all. He had slept among sheep and penguins in the South Atlantic, scratched himself in flea-infested desert sands, taken cover in insanitary souks shelled by friend and foe alike, and was none the wiser. Baghdad, Basra? Bosnia? Darfur? Helmand? Kosovo? He had been there even if he did not know where to find them on the map. All he could remember of Afghanistan and Iraq was the searing heat by day and the freezing cold by night, the stench from makeshift graves and the constant danger from snipers, a horror story without end.

It was the stuff writers dream of, enough first-hand material for a dozen film scripts or action-packed novels. And all completely wasted on my mild-mannered cousin who toured the world's trouble spots for twenty years and remained as untouched by them as the day he set off for the recruiting office. No shortage of armed conflicts and no shortage of vehicles needing his attention. He just opened his toolbox, took out his ring spanners, and repaired them one after the other, for twenty years.

By this time both his father and the hired hand had passed away so the moment the army told him his time was up he returned to Godwins Farm to carry on where he had left off. For many country boys the army is a common escape route, and they are only too thankful to leave the farm, with no intention of ever returning to such a demanding and poorly rewarded way of life. Not so cousin Ken because I am sure it never once occurred to him, nor to his brothers, that he would ever do anything else.

During his army career I heard news of him from time to time, and kept track of his service abroad, and must confess that I feared for the effect these harrowing and brutalising experiences would have had on him. I need not have worried because literally within hours of moving back permanently into his own room it seemed as though he had already forgotten about the dreadful places where he had served sovereign and country. It was almost as if the twenty years of soldiering had been permanently erased from his memory.

His sister-in-law Emily had put together a complete set of new clothes in readiness for his return. From the moment he climbed up into the tractor cab to resume full-time work with his brothers on the farm it really was as if the twenty army years had existed only in their imagination. He has scarcely set foot outside the farm gate since.

Within weeks of his return I doubt if his neighbours could have picked him out of a line-up, the three brothers looked so alike in their old-fashioned country clothes. Not that the comings and goings of these quiet countrymen has ever excited much curiosity locally. Yet it is a paradox is it not, that my cousin Ken has probably seen more of the world than all the foreign holiday tourists who live here put together? And who had witnessed sights that they are never likely to see however many countries they visit, or however often they travel.

Personally I think Ken's behaviour before and since does him great credit. Miraculously he has not been coarsened by his experiences and is just as mild-mannered and modestly polite as he was before he joined the army. A remarkable achievement when you think about it. And the explanation?

He was protected by an invincible innocence that twenty years of grim soldiering had been unable to extinguish.

17

Scorched Earth

There is no sound quite as blood-curdling to the conservationist ear as the sudden roar of a bulldozer starting up, although the snarl of a chain saw must come a close second. The speed with which these instruments of destruction do their work is equally sickening. Such was the fate that befell Packhorse Meadow at the vengeful hands of Ralph Chadwick.

It was almost a year since Amelia Ashby had unleashed her storm-troopers to mobilise public opinion against Ralph's purchase of the fateful meadow. Winter had come and gone and it was once more Spring. The controversy over the change of ownership had faded into distant memory. It had all gone quiet. The dust had settled, the bugles no longer sounded, the Herald received no more angry letters. Everyone assumed that the scare was over, that things would carry on as before.

They were wrong. The day of the dog walkers had gone forever.

There were no houses overlooking Packhorse Meadow so it was a while before local residents realised what was happening. The clearance work had not started until the evening and the few people who gathered were horrified at what they saw. It had taken only two hours of bulldozing to alter the landscape beyond recognition. The tilt rams at the front and the rippers at the back removed the bushes and small trees with little resistance. The curved offset blades gouged through the earth and small vegetation at astonishing speed, carving wide bare tracks hundreds of yards in Length.

It soon became obvious that there was a whole fleet of bulldozers at work in a carefully planned operation. Going about their business with equal efficiency was a team of men in hard hats and goggles wielding the chain saws. Amelia Ashby was not the only citizen who could raise an army. Ralph Chadwick could too, and his battalions dealt death and destruction to Packhorse Meadow.

Voices could be heard above the din urging that crisis action should be taken to halt the bulldozers. Easier said than done. Ralph timed his assault to begin after the council offices had closed, knowing that the departmental chiefs would have long since abandoned their desks for the pleasures of hearth, home or holiday. The onslaught had started on a Thursday, the Thursday evening before the long Easter break. By the time the council offices opened their doors again on Tuesday morning Packhorse Meadow would have ceased to exist.

It was the first week of April and the evenings were light. More machines arrived and with them more men. When it finally grew dark headlights were switched on and it became apparent that they intended to work throughout the night. Which they did without ceasing and continued remorselessly for the whole of Good Friday, by which time all living vegetation above the ground had disappeared. Trees, bushes, thistles and all. Only churned-up mud was left.

A backhoe excavator began to carve out drainage channels at the squelchy east end while a compactor levelled all the humps and bumps, including the Bronze Age burial mounds, which vanished without trace in seconds. The trees were felled and trimmed and lifted on to low-loaders, then driven away to a saw-mills. Some of the machines belonged to Ralph himself, and about half the men. The rest he had hired like so many mercenaries and it was plain that nothing and no one was going to stop them before they had obliterated Packhorse Meadow and removed it from the map.

Ralph's plan of campaign began to emerge amid the chaos of noise and movement. The fences had been removed from the adjoining fields, one to the north, the other to the south, and it was clear that he intended to plough the three together as one big field, and to do it so deeply and so thoroughly that no one would be able to see the join afterwards.

It had been a dry winter and the tree roots and hedgerow rubbish were pushed by the bulldozers to the end farthest away from the town and burnt. These huge bonfires flared up at the touch of a match and as fast as they burned away fresh bucket-loads were tipped into the flames. Prudently Ralph had ordered the piles to be torched late in the evening so that the blackest of the smoke blew away during the night. Even so the tremendous heat ensured that the fires would burn for many hours and to the unbelievable volume of noise was added the lurid glow of flames and the swirling of smoke driven horizontally by a boisterous westerly wind.

And where was Amelia Ashby while all this was happening?

In Salzburg was the answer. Sitting in a concert hall listening to Mozart with a blissful expression on her face, her exquisite black silk ankles elegantly crossed. She was eventually contacted at her hotel and liked what she was hearing much less than the trio from 'Cosi fan tutte'.

She caught the first available plane home and was driven to the site straight from the airport, arriving early on Sunday morning. Easter Sunday that is, although long before the faithful began turning up at church for morning service. Never one to pass unnoticed Amelia wore a white belted raincoat with a bright blue scarf, the ends fluttering in the wind. She found herself a vantage point on some of the higher ground so that she could see with her own eyes what had happened to Packhorse Meadow the moment her back was turned.

I too am an early riser and because it was a public holiday I had been present on and off since the clearance started on Thursday evening. I was not going to miss this for anything and hurried along in the strange unearthly light of early dawn to witness the confrontation between Amelia Ashby and Ralph Chadwick.

When I arrived they were facing one another across fifty yards of churned-up mud and swirling bitter smoke. Amelia kept her hands in her pockets, for it was a cold morning.

Ralph leaned against his Land Rover and stared back impassively with his arms folded. Neither moved and neither spoke. What they would have said to one another had they crossed and met in the middle is an interesting speculation but they just went on staring at one another without either moving or speaking.

I stayed put too, fascinated by this highly personalised conflict. Everyone else was busy. The bulldozer drivers and the men with the diggers got on with their work and so were not aware of this silent encounter. Ralph's minder, the tough guy fixer known as Hud, sat reading a tabloid Sunday newspaper behind the wheel of the Land Rover. Eventually he too became aware of the woman in the white raincoat staring at his boss from the other side of the bulldozer tracks. He put his newspaper aside, opened the door and stepped down for a better look.

Ralph started to turn his head as though waiting for something to appear and soon we discovered what it was. Looming through the early morning mist and the licks of flame and smoke came a massive tractor with four huge wheels, each as high as a bus, bringing behind it on the hydraulic lift a giant sodbuster plough.

At Ralph's signal the plough was lowered, so in addition to the clanking of the JCBs came the throaty roar of the tractor as it took the strain and the huge plough bit into the earth. The task of bringing the land back into production had begun.

Barley grows quickly. In a few weeks the arrow straight lines of green shoots would stretch from end to end and fall to the combines in August. With millions of starving people in the world, and a net shortfall of grain, no one could reasonably complain at the sight of a field of waving golden corn. 'People listen better when they're hungry,' was one of Ralph's favourite sayings. Harsh but true.

It was such a huge field I doubt if even an aerial photograph could have detected where the old Packhorse Meadow ended and the new one began. New and many times as big. The law of possession is firmly on the owner's side so as victories go it was fairly comprehensive. And the lesson was there for all who wished to be instructed in the ways of the countryside.

Farmers plough fields. Always have, always will.

Even so I rated it as a savage response by Ralph to the annoyance Amelia's antics had caused him. I knew that he would be completely unrepentant, shrugging off any criticism that he had acted unreasonably. His resolve had been tested and his reaction had been brutal. If there was a price to pay he would consider it worthwhile.

The Chadwick millions carried more clout than a few petulant letters to the Herald. Ralph had just as many friends in high places as the old toffs on the Beckles Valley Trust. Farmers and landowners have their own professional bodies who would argue his case. The supply trade dependent on his custom and goodwill would likewise rally to his defence. Faced with such a decisive fait accompli few of the affronted pressure groups would feel strongly enough to parade their indignation through the courts, and even if they did the Chadwick coffers were deep enough not to suffer unduly.

So Ralph was able to stare back at Amelia Ashby without too much concern for the consequences of his action, either financial or ethical. The sun was unable to break through the cloud cover and as it grew light still more machines started up until the noise level was almost unbearable. It was a cold morning with spits of rain on the wind. Little wisps and scarves of smoke drifted like a pall over the scorched earth of the battlefield.

Which is exactly what it was, a field of battle between two strong-willed people who liked to have things their own way and rejected all forms of compromise. This meant that one of them had to lose and in this case it was Amelia who had suffered the defeat. And a dire defeat too, her reputation for invincibility gone forever. With his sleeves rolled up to display his muscular arms, with his iron-grey curls and splendid boxer's head Ralph looked like a winner without even trying.

Never again would pensioners air their dogs on Packhorse Meadow, no longer would the nightingales chirp or the frogs spawn, the last pair of lovers had roamed in the gloaming. Because it was so overcast the dying flames still burned brightly to accompany the smoke and mud and the infernal noise of the machinery. It was the worst possible outcome which reflected no credit on either of the two people most closely involved. But I suppose all human activity is conflict at one level or another, and whether we like it or not we slot into a league table of winners and losers. And in this unhappy affair it was Ralph Chadwick who stood with the folded arms and steady gaze of the victor routing an enemy.

He knew it, I knew it. Amelia Ashby knew it best of all.

18

Living Ghosts

Few days pass without a sighting of our mother and daughter neighbours, Molly and Polly. We see them so often that it is hard to believe a time will come when we no longer see them.

In the summer months they amble without haste down the long field-edge path that leads into the lane below our house. It starts on the steep back slope of Beckles Hill and gives descending walkers a panoramic overview of the village, the reason perhaps why it is one of their favourite routes. Mother and daughter will always smile and wave if they see us, and if Polly has picked a bunch of flowers she will hold them up to show us as they pass by in the lane.

During the winter months I sometimes see them in the headlights of my car when I am returning home in the evening. They always seem to know when it is me and will wave and smile. Even when it is raining they beam cheerfully, and never appear to notice the cold. They wear so many clothes that rain never penetrates very far, which means they are warm and dry underneath. Layers of dresses and aprons and old raincoats reach to the ground, the ones on top thrown round their shoulders like cloaks.

These clothes give them a distinctive shape, and it is a shape I recognise from old engravings of rural life in earlier times. Cloaked and hooded, leaning forward against the rain, their faces hidden, Molly and Polly come straight out of another century. Their lives would have been little different two hundred years ago, nor are the fields and hedgerows and hills among which they wander greatly changed. So for me Molly and Polly have slipped a stitch in time, I view them as living ghosts from an ongoing rural past.

This is Molly's story.

Her father was a tenant farmer on the Beckles Estate, a surly character with an equally unpleasant wife. Molly was their first and as it turned out their only child but instead of being cherished they seemed to resent that she was not a boy and said in that case she must do a boy's work. The harder she worked the more ungrateful they became. They treated her so badly that the village people tried to intercede on her behalf, but to no effect. On one occasion the rector plucked up courage and suggested they should treat their daughter a little less badly but was roughly told to mind his own business. And if anything Molly was treated worse afterwards rather than better.

It is a common story. The folklore of every village in the land could produce similar examples of female ill-treatment.

Why did she put up with it? Why did she not escape? Surely anything would have been better than this virtual slavery? To make matters worse her monsters of parents fell ill, requiring her to cook and care for them, as well as doing all the farm work. They were demanding and ungrateful invalids. Her father suffered from bronchitis, her mother from arthritis, neither of them life-threatening conditions, which meant many more years of drudgery in the years ahead. Molly never complained and endured her lot with a dutiful submissiveness that drove more spirited women to despair on her behalf.

Her youth had long since passed her by and it seemed impossible there would ever be any romance in her life. Yet miraculously this happened. There was an ageing bachelor who lived in Mardle with his mother and he took a liking to Molly, although the implacable hostility of her parents made it a difficult courtship. Molly had hardly any free time, and no money with which to buy clothes or cosmetics or have her hair made pretty.

She was just on forty when fate gave love a helping hand and disposed of both parents within a few months of one another. Walter Vokes the family solicitor made sure that what little money was left after the sale of machinery and livestock came to her. It was enough to provide a modest dowry and the marriage soon took place. Molly was blissfully happy, even more so when she became pregnant.

Alas, women of forty run a greater than average risk of having abnormal babies and so it proved in this case when she produced a severely handicapped Down's syndrome child. The father took one look and promptly abandoned his wife and baby daughter. He had been a feeble character throughout. He had made no attempt to take Molly away from the farm and merely waited on events. His departure came as no surprise and he was never heard of or seen in Mardle ever again.

Village communities act swiftly in an emergency. Molly's life history and pathetic circumstances were well known. Everyone rang everyone else and an approach was made to the owners of Beckles Court. They received a sympathetic hearing and a small cottage on the estate was made available so that Molly and her daughter had a home for the rest of their lives.

Every creature on earth responds to affection and Molly displayed the most surprising skill and patience in bringing up a handicapped child. So although it came about by default she did finally have someone of her own to love and look after, and devote her life to, and was very happy as a result.

Mother and daughter have never been separated, either in distance or time. Since the birth they have never been more than a few feet or a few seconds apart. As soon as Polly could walk they became a familiar sight in the village and neighbouring countryside. This is because they love to be in the open air, in the winter just as much as in the summer. Polly is now over thirty years old and it is how they have lived out their lives. Mother and daughter spend all day every day roaming the ancient track-ways that criss-cross the area, but do so happily, and from choice.

Ruth and I have grown accustomed to seeing these two short substantial figures, wearing hats and layers of cardigans and coats as they pass by in the lane. Sometimes we only half see them, at night for instance, or if they are cloaked and hooded with their faces closed in against heavy rain. Similarly in the early morning. They loom out of the mist and then disappear again so quickly that sometimes we cannot be sure whether we have seen them or not.

It would be hard to find two happier people than Molly and her daughter. They are gatherers. Sometimes it is blackberries, or hazel nuts, or mushrooms, and they always know where to find such things. We see them most often in the summer and autumn months. A glance out of the bedroom window and there they are, meandering without haste down the long field-edge path that leads off the hill.

When they turn into the lane and pass the house they will always smile and wave. Polly loves to pick flowers, the more colourful the better. She is never without a bunch and will hold them up to show us as she passes by in the lane. At which my wife Ruth always shakes her head and makes the same heartfelt comment.

'What will become of poor Polly when her mother dies?'

19

Hans the Old Soldier

When I left for university at the age of eighteen my parents gave up the tenancy of their farm on the Beckles Estate. Sales of machinery, milk quota and livestock plus their savings and some inherited family money allowed them to buy a nice home in the village for their retirement. This was the Glebe House, situated on the other side of the church from the former rectory. After university I obtained a teaching post at the College and being unmarried stayed on with my parents in the new family home. I looked after them until they died, my father first, my mother many years later, and as their only child I inherited the house. Although I began a relationship with my wife Ruth soon after finishing at university, she too was looking after ageing parents elsewhere in the village and we were not finally free to marry and live together until we were almost forty.

Although Mardle has a church it no longer has a rector. For many years we have been part of a joint ministry with its headquarters in the larger village of Long Beckles, three miles to the south. Long Beckles is not only larger it is more prosperous and certainly more picturesque, a real biscuit tin village with thatch and cobblestones, two charming old inns, polite society, and tubs of flowers everywhere. Photographs of its handsome medieval church with a tall pinnacled tower appear in all the tourist brochures. Mardle does not even rate a mention.

In the years leading up to the first world war Mardle was a fast-growing village with so many big families that it needed a new school and an extra aisle built on to the church to squeeze the faithful in on Sunday mornings. The effects of farm mechanisation and falling school rolls brought an end to this expansion. Later, the coming of the motorway system played a part in Mardle's gentle decline. The network of roads linking us to the nearest motorway were changed to divert traffic in the opposite direction, for good or ill depending on your point of view. Either way Mardle became a quiet backwater village, not much visited. No one pretends it is an exciting place in which to live.

We receive a monthly copy of the group ministry parish magazine, although there is seldom anything written about Mardle. So it came as a surprise one day when Ruth drew my attention to an item in the latest issue of the magazine. This stated that our village war memorial, a Celtic cross in grey granite, was dilapidated and in need of attention. My first reaction was one of indignation, followed by guilt and then by shame. Of all the houses in the village the Glebe House is the one closest to the memorial cross. It is visible from all our front room windows and so I should have noticed that it had become overgrown and was indeed in need of some urgent attention.

The granite cross, now much weathered, is enclosed by a low ornamental rail and recessed into a shrub covered bank. It stands opposite the church, separated by a small area of grass which serves as the village green. There are two long bench seats near the memorial, and because our infant and junior schools are close at hand, these seats are conveniently placed for the many young mothers waiting to collect their children when lessons have finished for the day. Summer or winter it makes for a pleasant village scene as mothers and aunties and grannies are rejoined by jostling and noisy children tumbling out of the school gates.

In common with most village war memorials it was put up after the war of 1914–1918. The holocaust of young men was frightful in this war which was supposed to end all wars, and the long tally of local names still has the capacity to disturb. Not being a rich village the sum of money raised was just enough to pay for a cross six feet high, and set within a low railed square. The 1939–1945 war reaped a smaller harvest but still robbed the village of some good men, each one a personal tragedy for the family bearing the loss.

It is hard not to sorrow for them after a glance round the nearby churchyard. The headstones of women surviving as widows for fifty years and even longer is a poignant reminder of the futility of armed conflict between civilised nations. Wars fought in the last century have little relevance for the young people who live in the village today. Even those whose family names appear on the list of war dead seem indifferent to the fate of the memorial.

It is now several years since we saw the last gathering of elderly servicemen and women in Mardle, wearing their poppies and medals for the Armistice Day service. This is now held at Long Beckles every year but tends to be a low key affair. The young priest who heads the group ministry makes no secret of his distaste for war and military parades, a common view these days. The Remembrance Service, that most sombre of occasions, passes almost without notice.

Having made a close inspection of the memorial I reported back to Ruth that much work needed to be done, mainly to cut away the large encroaching shrubs. Failure to rake up the fallen leaves over many years had resulted in a thick black unsightly mulch underfoot. The low ornamental rail enclosing the memorial was rusted and bent. Lichen had established itself on the plinth and set like concrete. The more I looked, the more I could see needed to be done. Who was supposed to look after it? Who was responsible for the neglect? Who would have to pay to put things right? I was sure Ruth would know.

'Hans,' she said. 'Hans used to look after the war memorial. Don't you remember? He planted the shrubs, and the bedding plants, and kept it looking nice.'

The moment she said it, I did remember. 'Of course. And obviously no one has done it since.'

This set me thinking. Hans was an old soldier but as you can tell from his name he was a German old soldier, and he died many years ago. So why should a German soldier have concerned himself with a British war memorial?

Hans came to live in the village after the end of the 1939-45 war, a young refugee still in his twenties. Only the middle-aged and above will have any memory of Hans, and as time passes the number of local people who remember him will be very few. The second world war is distant history, I cannot imagine that our young people would be remotely interested in hearing anything about a German prisoner of war who lived in the village so long ago.

No sooner had Ruth reminded me than I was able to recall seeing Hans on his knees with a pot of black paint and a brush painting the low ornamental rail that surrounds the memorial. It has a barley-sugar twist and Hans kept it black-enamelled and shining new. All communities honour their war dead so the timely rebuke in the magazine indicating that we had failed the fallen was a bugle call for some prompt action.

Hans did not have a good war and was reluctant to say anything about either his early life, or his experiences in the German army. Only when he had lived in the village for a few years, and had become fully assimilated into the community, could he be persuaded to say anything at all. As a young person eager for knowledge of any kind I tried harder than most to coax him to speak.

Hans told me that he was the youngest of six sons, their father owning a small farm east of Dresden, close to the border with Poland. One by one his brothers had been conscripted to fight in Hitler's army, or to work in the mines. In vain his father had pleaded to be allowed to keep his last remaining son to help run the farm but the Germans were losing the war and took him just the same. He was sixteen years old.

By the time I asked him to tell me more about his exper-iences Hans had taught himself to speak reasonably good English. With a little prompting he told me about his service with the Afrika Korps in the Libyan desert. It was not a nice story. He remembered with acute feeling the unbearable heat, the constant thirst, the vile food, the desert flies, the teeming lice, and above all his fear when he heard the guns firing and saw the shells landing close by. No hero, Hans. All he wanted was to make it safely back to the farm in one piece.

No such luck. When he told the story you could almost experience the bombs and shells falling, the panic and wild rumours, and worst of all the bad news from home. One by one his brothers had gone to fight, one by one they had died. The first in a submarine, the second in a shot-down bomber, the next in an explosion deep in a coal mine. Even for a young man it was unbearable. Then one day he and the other conscripts were lined up while a strutting officer stepped down from a staff car to address them as follows. 'Gentlemen, my congratulations. Soon you will have the honour of fighting for the Fatherland on the eastern front.'

At first Hans had been pleased. This was because his knowledge of geography was good enough to know that Russia was nearer to Dresden than Libya, and better still it was joined on. Feeling quite cheered he climbed into a rickety old transport plane that headed north over Greece and the Black Sea until eventually the soldiers on board joined the beleaguered army that was laying siege to Stalingrad. On arrival it did not take him many minutes to change his tune and he soon began to feel much less cheerful.

He and his fellow soldiers now regretted complaining about the desert heat because Russia in winter was infinitely worse. It was a living hell that lasted for over two years, with every hour of every day a struggle for survival. Hans counted himself one of the lucky ones because he escaped capture by the Russians. Starving and demoralised the German army was slowly driven out of Russia. All Hans could remember apart from the mud and the cold was the deafening noise of the artillery and the cries of the wounded pleading not to be abandoned.

As the war neared its end he and his remaining comrades sought above all else to escape from a vengeful Soviet army that was advancing on them faster than they could retreat.

When his boots wore out he took a pair from the nearest dead soldier until he and a few thousand broken and defeated survivors stumbled towards the safety of the American lines and gave themselves up only hours ahead of the pursuing Red Army.

Hans told me that he thought his troubles were over and that he would soon be returning to the family home on the Polish border. He was mistaken. Anti-German feeling ran high and for nearly two years he had to continue to fight for survival in camps not much different from those run by the Germans themselves. Thousands of men died in them from malnutrition and disease but Hans was young and strong. He wanted very much to stay alive, and did.

Because his home was in the partitioned East Germany he was not wanted in the west. He waited patiently in a series of transit camps hoping for a new life in sunny Australia. He was sent to Canada instead, his only memory of that country being that it was even colder there than it was in Russia.

The war had been over a long time but he was interned once more, this time sent to a camp in Northern Ireland pending a decision on his future. Eventually released he was given a pass to England. It had been a long circuitous route from Dresden to Mardle but former prisoners of war were soon found jobs in the agricultural industry, the country being in desperate need of food at the time.

Which explains how he came to be milking cows on the Beckles Estate. Hans could hardly believe his good fortune after so many years of hardship and rejection. In the opinion of local inhabitants Mardle is a place where nothing exciting has ever happened in the past, or is likely to happen in the future, but to the war-weary soldier it was little short of paradise.

Within a year he had married one of the village girls and soon had a family of his own to replace the one he had lost. Two daughters, blonde and blue eyed, and after quite a long interval, a son. By this time Hans had become a naturalised citizen and his children were born British, a matter of some pride to him.

From the start Hans found that he was accepted without resentment, in fact most people went out of their way to be friendly to him, knowing that the only choice conscripts had in wartime was to obey or be shot. Hans was an exemplary worker, industrious, reliable, and above all clean. He had the old soldier's love of order and tidiness. The equipment he used looked like new because he took such good care of it. He was always smartly dressed, even in his working clothes, and carried himself with the square-shouldered bearing that can only come from military service.

He was respected as a good family man, and also as a keen gardener who grew some prize vegetables in the large garden of his estate cottage. Off duty he was relaxed and clubbable, accepted as a Friday night regular in the Shorn Lamb. I was too busy studying to spend much time in the Lamb myself but went occasionally with Tom Mundy until I left home for university at eighteen.

This was where I heard Hans repeating his story of how he had been sent to the Russian front. If he overheard anyone grumbling about something unimportant he would always admonish them for complaining, and then tell his story. I think we all realised that every time he did so he could see it happening in his head. He would have been a teenager himself at the time so it was understandable that it had made a terrible and long-lasting impression on him.

'I mean it,' he would say earnestly in his heavily accented English. 'Never complain. Never! Because you could end up being worse off. Did I ever tell you how I got sent to the eastern front?'

'Yes, Hans,' everyone in the bar would reply. 'You did. Lots of times.'

But once started he could not be stopped. 'Listen, there we were sweating it out in the desert, forty Celsius in the shade, not that there was any shade, half a litre of water to wash in, shave in, and make coffee with afterwards. It was terrible, you can't imagine it. Then one day up drives this fat Major, sitting in the back of a Mercedes staff car. "Gentlemen," he says. "My congratulations. Tomorrow you will have the privilege of fighting the Russians on the Fuhrer's behalf. Take some warm clothes with you, it's cold over there." Cold? It froze our bollocks off. So never complain. It could always be worse, believe me.'

The story varied slightly each time, although not by much, and in the village it was rated as a good story with much truth in its message. Hans could be coaxed to talk about the war but never about his home in Germany, or the family he had lost and left behind. He never once went back and if anyone commented he said simply that he had spent most of his life in Mardle, considered it to be his home, and had no interest in foreign travel, having seen more than enough of the world in his youth.

Which brings me to why Hans fussed over the war memorial and joined the dwindling band of old soldiers who bared their silvery hair to the winter wind and stood to attention for the Armistice Day parade. It was not only to honour the memory of his own old comrades but also that of his only son.

A fair-haired son, probably not much different in appearance from Hans himself at the same age. A son who had joined the British Army and been killed in the South Atlantic during the Falklands conflict. His name was added to the roll of honour on the war memorial, the reason why Hans gave it such loving care and attention until his death. He said it made him feel closer to his son, and that he was proud he had fought and died for his country.

The young soldier's body had been brought home to be reburied by Tom Mundy in a secluded corner of the church-yard, another long circuitous journey ending in the same place. Because Hans lies there too in the long sleep, and no doubt others of the family he founded will join them in the fullness of time. His two daughters both married locally and there are children and grandchildren who come out of school and play on the seats by the war memorial.

Which is, I regret to say, still in need of some urgent attention to rescue it from its present neglected condition. The appeal for action in the parish magazine was an uncomfortable reproach and it must have stirred a few consciences apart from mine. I promise that something will get done, and most likely will end up doing it myself.

Meanwhile life goes on. Wars are best forgotten.

20

When Dougal Needed the Doctor

I hope you remember the earlier story about Dougal and his education. Dougal is doing well at Oxford but I think I should explain why Jamie Paterson and his wife Agnes were such neurotic and over-anxious parents

As a baby he was long awaited, in fact the Patersons had almost despaired of having a family when Agnes finally became pregnant. She had arranged to stay with relatives in Dumfries when the baby was due, not because she wanted them to be present at the birth but to ensure that the baby was born in Scotland. It was as unthinkable to her, as it was to Jamie, that their child should be born in England. The inexorable law of mischance decided otherwise and the baby announced its arrival long beforehand.

Cursing loudly Jamie bundled his wife into the Land Rover and they set off north in a race against time, labour being already far advanced. Although she was in great pain Agnes gritted her teeth with true Braveheart courage and held on until they reached the border. They made it if only just, Dougal being born in the home of a rural policeman, with his wife delivering the baby.

After this it was not surprising that the Patersons became anxious and over-protective parents. Fortunately their young son Dougal proved to be a healthy child who did not give them a moment of worry until one night when he was three years old. Agnes called her husband upstairs for a second opinion and Jamie did not like what he saw. There could be no doubt the boy was unwell, being deathly white and feverish. Having no experience of childhood illness, and fearful that it could be meningitis, Jamie and Agnes overreacted and began to panic. It was ten o'clock at night at the start of Christmas week and raining heavily, definitely not the best time to try and contact a doctor in the country, even in those distant days when doctors made house calls, however reluctantly.

The Patersons were registered with the local group practice and on telephoning heard the inevitable taped message. This gave the number of the agency doctor who was already out on other emergency calls and it was almost daylight before they could speak to him. Jamie Paterson did not care for this much and his notoriously short fuse had long since triggered an explosion of violent temper.

But irascibility is not confined to harassed farm managers. The duty doctor had also endured a fraught and busy night and was not a youngster who could be bullied. He was an equally awkward customer so before long he and Jamie were rubbing each other up the wrong way and making a bad situation worse.

The doctor was professionally detached, making plain his belief that the furious farm manager was exaggerating the child's condition, which from the symptoms described was not serious and certainly not the meningitis his parents feared. He assured the angry couple that toddlers often fell ill suddenly and exhibited alarming symptoms, recovering just as quickly.

'Your first child, I see,' he said over the phone, obviously having their details on a screen in front of him. He advised them to get in touch with their own doctor when the surgery reopened, predicting that he would tell them much the same.

By this time Jamie Paterson was livid with fury, and also quarrelling with his wife, who was all for wrapping their child in a blanket and taking him to a hospital and waiting until a doctor could see them. It had escalated into a battle of principle. Their child was ill, he had been trying for many hours to get a doctor to call, and he was not going to give up until a doctor did call. More frustration followed, the surgery number being permanently engaged when he rang at opening time. Eventually he got through and started doing battle with the receptionists.

This is where I became involved. Ruth and I were not married at the time, I had only just returned to the village and did not know either Jamie or Agnes very well. On the other hand Ruth had regular contacts with Jamie because of her job, her firm being agents for the Beckles Estate. By chance she had called on him at Home Farm on the morning when all this was happening, and having grasped the seriousness of the situation telephoned to ask me if I would join her at the farm. The College had broken up for the Christmas holiday so I was available to stand by in case Agnes and the baby had to be rushed to hospital.

This explains how I heard the details of Dougal's illness at first hand, and I must confess that my sympathy was for the receptionists at the surgery. Jamie was in no mood to be placated and described each one as more obtuse and bloody-minded than the last. They told him that his doctor's list was full for the day and refused to put him through so that he could speak to the doctor himself, insisting on relaying messages to and fro. Eventually he was put on to the practice manager, a sensible woman but whose attempts to help only made matters worse.

'What exactly is wrong with the child?' she asked him.

'Hell's teeth, woman,' Jamie answered back. 'Isn't that what I'm ringing you to find out? How should I know, I'm not a doctor. That is a bloody silly question, if you don't mind me saying so.'

She did mind, and matters rapidly went from bad to worse. By this time his Scots blood was well and truly boiling, the level of invective continued to rise and the surgery got the full treatment from a man whose language was forceful even on a good day. Perhaps a little tact and diplomacy might have served his cause better but the furious Scot was in no mood to back off.

'Deference?' he enquired of his wife who was urging him to be less aggressive. 'Is that the price I have to pay to get a sick child looked at by a doctor? Do I have to act all humble and grateful before one will even speak to me? Do I have to plead cap-in-hand for some medicine? Certainly I'm making a fuss, they haven't seen anything yet. They'll be sorry they played me up, I can promise you that.'

But even Agnes was incensed when the receptionist failed to remember the gender of their precious infant. 'The doctor says have you taken its temperature? Have you tried giving it half an aspirin?' In the end the woman gave way and put the Paterson's farmhouse on the doctor's visiting list for that day.

'When?' Jamie enquired. A foolish question which received the stinging rebuke it deserved. 'When the doctor can get there, of course!' Which made it game, set and match to the triumphant receptionist who asked him not to keep ringing the surgery with reminders because it prevented them from receiving urgent calls and would not get the doctor there a minute earlier.

So, a very unhappy story in which none of the people involved behaved well. The doctor came eventually and young Dougal's childhood ailment was soon put right by the standard remedy. Although even this proved irritating since it involved a last-minute dash into the town to have the prescription put up before the pharmacy closed.

Although their son soon recovered it was a childhood episode that rankled with Jamie Paterson for many years afterwards. He and his wife Agnes would tell the story to anyone who would listen, taking it in turns to speak. Both were equally bitter, and for the following reason.

Because at the very same moment when his wife called Jamie upstairs to say that Dougal was ill their head herdsman had knocked at the back door to report a sick cow. He was dressed in dripping waterproofs, torch in hand, and said that he suspected mastitis, the acute kind, and asked for the vet to be sent for immediately.

Which was done, and this is the reason why the Patersons remain indignant many years after the event. Simultaneously with trying to obtain medical counsel and treatment for his sick son Jamie had rung the veterinary surgery to seek help for the ailing cow.

How different this was! No pleading or wrangling was required. The veterinary surgeon promised to leave at once and arrived within fifteen minutes. Not cursing at the inconvenience of a ten o'clock call on a dark night in pouring rain but full of concern for the fevered cow.

Veterinary medicine is hands-on work, and often dirty work, when big animals have to be examined inside and out. The duty vet was soon booted and gowned and on the job, confirming the fears of the herdsman that it was indeed a case of acute mastitis. The diagnosis was immediately followed by the appropriate treatment, the vet filling a syringe from the wide range of medication carried in the boot of his car.

'This should do the trick,' he said confidently, promising to return early next morning to resume the treatment. A promise he kept, and he followed up the sick animal's progress for several days until she made a complete recovery and was able to rejoin the herd.

This dramatic gap in attitude between private veterinary practice and state funded medicine was not much to the liking of the aggrieved parents. 'You remember all about it, don't you, Alan?' Jamie asked me more than once in later years, and I assured him that I did.

'There's a lesson in it for all of us,' Agnes added, still equally angry. But at least it solved a problem for them, namely choosing a profession for their son. They had originally intended to send Dougal to Edinburgh to become a doctor but changed their minds after this. Their hearts were now set on him being an Edinburgh trained veterinary surgeon instead, a worthy ambition.

As I told you earlier this was not how it worked out for the unhappy couple, nor are they reconciled to the direction in which Dougal's education has led him. Theology and Holy Orders in the Church of England are not what they had in mind for his future when they brought him back in triumph to Home Farm in Mardle. But babies grow up and want to take responsibility for their own lives, a hard lesson that all parents have to learn sooner or later.

Jamie and Agnes are still hoping for a miracle, they pray that Dougal will suddenly come to his senses and switch to a more manly profession, engineering if all else fails, taking up golf at the same time. They will it to happen. Their disappointment is as hard to understand as it is to bear.

21

Uncle Sid

One cold day during half term in October I went to a farm sale where my wife's firm were the auctioneers. Pulling up next to me in the field used as a car park was a shiny Japanese land cruiser, a most prestigious vehicle. A nattily dressed gent swung his glossy brown shoes down on to the grass and graciously passed the time of day with me. He was a senior member of the large Hounsome family, and he eyed me with deep suspicion.

'What are you after, Alan? Nothing I want, I hope.'

I replied, 'You needn't worry, Sid. I left my cheque book at home. I'm not buying.'

'I've got my eye on a hen coop.' He favoured me with an autumnal smile. 'A nice soft-boiled egg for breakfast. That's how I like to start the day.'

'Only one?'

'Used to be a two-egg man. Old age, Alan. Catches up with us all.'

I think he would have preferred me to go on ahead but I lingered. This was because I knew what he was going to do next, and although I had seen him do it before I still liked to watch while he disguised himself.

Wincing slightly with displeasure at my continued presence he removed his smart tweed hat. It had a salmon-fly decoration and the distinctive checked design pattern of a smart Bond Street label. He replaced it with a flat cloth cap. Next he removed his expensive suede-leather driving jacket and pulled on a threadbare raincoat. Then unlaced his glossy brogues and slipped his feet into a pair of filthy wellington boots. A piece of farm string as a belt for his raincoat and a woollen scarf that looked as if it had been used to mop floors completed the poverty-stricken outfit he wore to attend farm sales.

By way of explanation he said, 'If they think you've got a bob or two they run you up.'

'I know they do.'

'You wouldn't run me up, would you, Alan?'

'No,' I said, but it wasn't true. If I could have squeezed an extra pound from him I would have sung with joy all the way home. Well, almost. But I sighed in advance, knowing it to be a lost cause. When it came to screwing the last penny no one ever got the better of crafty Sid Hounsome. He was without doubt the meanest man I ever knew.

Ted Hounsome the landlord of The Shorn Lamb was his nephew, and would often jest that he expected his Uncle Sid to put in a good word for him when the time came. This was because Uncle Sid was a chapel man on first name terms with the Lord. As a non-swearing non-smoking teetotaller he had never set foot inside The Shorn Lamb himself but mention of his name there was always good for a laugh. In Mardle if you referred to 'Uncle Sid' everyone would know who you meant.

I let him walk on, watching with grudging admiration as his posture adjusted to the new persona. The confident swagger was replaced by a stooped and humble shuffle, his hands deep in the pockets of his tattered raincoat and his cap pulled down low. Humble and deferential, appealing to the better nature of the auctioneer in the hope of a quick knock-down. He could afford to pay and so got things cheap. Always the way.

He had a whispering voice, an unctuous manner and a limp clammy handshake. He neither gambled nor fornicated and paraded his clear conscience as an example to us all. He let it be known that he lived a frugal life but prayed regularly. Just what he prayed about no one was ever quite sure, least of all his family, but he was a pious man who took care that you should be aware of his piety and treat him accordingly. I have to admit that Sid Hounsome was not one of my favourite people. I left him to bid for his hen coop while I took a look round to see what else was on offer.

Personally I do not care for farm sales much, and there are far too many of them in these hard times for agriculture in all its many forms. At this sale the smaller incidental items for sale were set out in rows in a paddock. There is something tragic at the sight of things which were once in constant daily use, and had value and purpose, being picked over by scavengers like Uncle Sid. Not long ago they had helped to make the farm a going concern, and were now junk. An empty dog kennel with its length of chain is a pathetic object when seen out of place in the middle of a muddy paddock, forlornly awaiting a buyer, and there were many similar items. The punters studying the various lots, catalogue in hand, were all looking for a bargain, while the farmer selling up was hoping to raise enough cash to help pay for the retirement bungalow. Incompatible aspirations.

Farms are special places. Nothing grows on its own, not even grass. Cows do not 'give' milk. Only constant daily toil can make any sense from the chaos of nature and produce things for people to eat, drink, use and wear. And farmers by the same definition are special people.

Even Sid Hounsome, who rather liked being called Uncle Sid. It made him feel genial and avuncular when in reality he was neither of those things. He was aware of his reputation for being mean but did not see it as a valid criticism, pointing out that he had survived comfortably in the rough trade of farming while many of his posh and better-educated neighbours had gone under.

He owned and ran Skinners Farm in Mardle, not far from where I live. No great leap of the imagination is needed to wonder why it was known locally as 'Skinflints' Farm. The line between thrift and meanness is too close to call but for Sid Hounsome it was his preferred way of life. His detractors, and they were many, said that his tumbledown farm was a disgrace. And so it was, for the simple reason that he refused to spend any money on it. Equipment and machinery designed to work well for five years and with care to last for ten were still in use thirty years later, and no nearer being replaced.

'Everything on this farm is either broken or covered in muck,' his son Terry told me candidly when we had a chat one day. He was one of my wife's car park volunteers on Show days so I always heard him out, although there were no prizes for guessing his favourite topic of conversation, which was grumbling about his father. 'You know Dad. He would sooner break his leg than pay for a new broom. Of course the place is filthy, we haven't had anything to sweep up with since my Chloe was born. And she's in the junior school now.'

This reminded me of another of Uncle Sid's little economies. One day in the town's main car park I came across a thin melancholy child standing close to the large new four-by-four I had seen at the farm sale. The child was Terry's daughter Chloe, just started at the junior school in Mardle. She recognised me and I suppose felt that an explanation was necessary.

She said, 'Grandad has left me on look-out duty, Mr Ablewhite.'

It was a Pay and Display car park so I knew what she meant. Grandad had gone off into the town about his business and left this young girl clutching a couple of low value coins. Coins which she would only put into the meter to buy a ticket if the car park attendant came close and started checking. This was because Uncle Sid did not believe in paying money into the coffers of the district council and knew all the dodges. When he came back he would retrieve the coins from the girl's hand and return them thankfully to his pocket.

In modern management terms his approach to cost cutting was laudable for its extreme simplicity, a stubborn refusal to part with his own money. Captains of industry might do the same thing on a commercial scale, and invent business-speak terms for it, but Uncle Sid had always thought of it first, and did it better. Being called a worse miser than Scrooge did not offend him, nor references to getting blood out of a stone.

Such words were music to his ears, they told him that his policies worked. It was stinginess of an inspired nature, imaginative and ingenious penny-pinching.

At another farm sale he once bought a tray of day-old chicks but not wanting all of them gave Tom Mundy a telephone call to ask if he would like to buy half. Tom accepted, and the sale price was quoted and agreed on. Except that when he went to collect them the next day he found it had increased, although only by a few pence.

'I've added on a bit for the food your half have eaten,' Uncle Sid explained in his whispering voice. 'That's fair, isn't it?' Tom Mundy told me the story with grim amusement. Well, yes, day-old chicks peck a few crumbs in the course of twenty-four hours but not many people would have thought it worth the effort of calculation, to say nothing of upsetting Tom Mundy by asking for it in cash.

I had few occasions to call at Skinners Farm myself but remember going there once during a heavy downpour of rain. Through the safety of my car window I watched as Uncle Sid toiled in the deluge, wrestling old rusty churns and water butts into position to catch the water as it gushed off the barn roofs and cascaded down through the gaps in the broken guttering.

He came to the car window and greeted me with the words, 'You wouldn't laugh if you had to pay my water bill.'

I assured him that I had not been laughing. It was the truth.

Sid had two sons and two daughters, and he also owned four cottages, a convenient arrangement. The cottages had once been occupied by farm workers but Sid preferred cheap family labour and soon moved them on. He encouraged his four children to form relationships at an early age so that they could move into the four cottages with their respective partners. He was offering free accommodation in return for a modest amount of work, and they did not need asking twice.

It was a shrewd calculation on his part because the temptation to sell his cottages must have been compelling. Country cottages with big gardens sell for high prices in this part of the world but he took the long view and laid up treasure for the future instead. He did so by allowing nature to take its course. Young people engaged in busy sexual activity soon start to produce babies, and babies grow up healthy and strong when they are surrounded with plenty of scenery and healthy country smells. Crafty Uncle Sid was thus ensured of a self-perpetuating and renewable source of labour to run the farm for him at the lowest possible cost. And it did, for the whole of his life.

He provided what everyone most wants, something as good as wages, and that is somewhere to live. In due course there came changes of partners, even a marriage or two and more children, plus the children that the new partners brought with them. Sid had no objection because they augmented his docile workforce. His sons he reckoned not to pay at all but when they threatened to take him to a tribunal he obliged with the legal minimum, reminding them of their free accommodation and eventual prospects when they inherited the farm from him.

Why did they put up with it? Why did they stay? Because they liked it was the answer. Life was pleasant and easy-going at Skinners Farm. It was a strange set-up but it worked, mainly because Uncle Sid was indulgent and never interfered, still less criticised. Skinners Farm lay well back from the road and the rest of us who lived in Mardle wisely left them alone to live their lives as they chose.

The numerous inhabitants of the four houses all had a very agreeable existence. Uncle Sid might have been a tight-arsed old so-and-so but he was not a landlord dunning them for money and left them alone to regulate their own small community. For one thing they had plenty of parking space, as much as they wanted, and that is something not lightly given up. Being well off the road and away from prying eyes they were able to do pretty much as they pleased.

There was no one to complain about noise, bonfires, washing lines, junked cars, unruly children, too many pet animals or immoral goings-on. The older and more settled family members who wanted to take up gardening for a hobby could have as much ground as they wanted to grow flowers and vegetables. Others preferred to keep rabbits or poultry, even a goat or two if they wished, and they often did. The free-range geese that were always wandering about doubled up as an alarm system, certain to honk and hiss in unison if a strange face appeared. As for the young female members of the family they had free livery for their ponies and that kept them happy.

To keep the men happy Uncle Sid turned a blind eye to ferrets, shotguns, lurcher dogs and poaching so long as the guns were also used on pigeons, squirrels, crows, foxes and other farm pests and predators. It was a village in miniature, a settlement made up from Uncle Sid's large extended family, a self-regulating commune where everyone was poor but happy.

It was also Uncle Sid's captive work force. Between them they grew a range of market garden crops exactly suited to their preference for piece rates and cash in hand. And since it was in their own interests to keep the farm going as a profitable concern they worked hard, and mostly with skill. Uncle Sid was not generous when it came to pay so what they lacked in wages they had to make up in benefits.

Between them they mastered a difficult brief. There was no allowance, entitlement, grant, or any other benefit of which they were unaware and had not successfully claimed. Collectively they could summon up as much expertise as a big Citizens Advice office. The babies, the children, the pregnant females, the lactating mothers and the men with bad backs and hernias all had the very best treatment and medication the nation could provide.

These considerable benefits in cash and kind from a benevolent government bridged the financial gap between their meagre wages from Uncle Sid and what they needed to survive. A sizeable chunk of these generous state benefits were spent in his nephew's popular establishment, the Shorn Lamb public house, and although Sid frowned at too much drinking he approved of keeping their money in the family.

There are men, and some women too I suppose, but mostly

men, who enjoy aggregating around themselves an entourage of hangers-on, many of them either vulnerable or inadequate in some way. Uncle Sid certainly did and never allowed his indigent relations to wriggle off the hook of dependence. They had no escape route because they had no money and no means of getting any, or at least not enough to save up for a mortgage and an independent life. They would always be poor and by being poor they kept him comfortably prosperous until the day he died.

Sid had the opposing character traits of meanness twinned with self-indulgence, and as he aged both traits became more extreme. He would wait in the barber's shop for an hour to get a pensioner haircut and then buy himself a new wristwatch, or an overcoat, or a pair of binoculars, or treat himself to a slap-up feed in the Bear Hotel. He believed in rewarding himself, not other people, and grieved for weeks if he was ever careless enough to pay the full price for anything.

By law all farm chemicals and pesticides have to be kept in a separate building under lock and key. They are expensive items and the dilution rates printed on the side of the containers repay careful study if the job is to be done properly and the intended benefit gained. All wasted on Uncle Sid because nothing would convince him that the recommended dilution rates were in his best interests.

'They just want you to use more of the product,' he explained to his sons and anyone else who might be listening. 'Of course they do! You don't need it as strong as that.' His sons hid the keys but Sid was artful and always managed to get in somehow. His purpose in doing so was to add a judicious quantity of water to every chemical container so that it stretched that little bit farther. It was his nature, he would always do such things, and his family gave up trying to stop him.

Sid's wife died at a comparatively young age and afterwards his funny little ways became steadily less amusing. She must have been a restraining influence on him because his refusal to spend any money on building maintenance was now causing considerable annoyance to the rest of the family. The bad feeling intensified, made worse by their frustration at not being able to do anything about it. Sid had the whip hand, with no intention of softening up in his old age.

He had always been pious but after his wife died he began to spend more and more time at the Primitive Methodist chapel which was conveniently situated at the end of his farm track. There was only a small congregation, all of them elderly and most of them women, but as it dwindled he made up the numbers by recruiting members of his family to fill the empty pews. Uncle Sid could be persuasive but he also wanted bums on seats. Acting on behalf of the Lord he had no hesitation in using strong-arm methods to press-gang his poor relations inside. They did not like it but soon learned that if you wanted a favour, meaning a hand-out of money, you had to put in a few appearances at the chapel first. Which meant the pews were full more often than not, particularly with children who were sent as unwilling proxies.

'We were all Prims on my side of the family,' Sid told me. 'I bought the chapel five years ago. There's a seat for anyone who wants one, and that includes you, Alan.' An invitation I declined.

The last minister had been long gone and when no one else came forward he took over the preaching duties himself. One of the original members could paddle away at the harmonium to lead the hymn singing, leaving Uncle Sid to do the rest. He had a jumbo-sized large-print Bible, a fondness for the sound of his own voice, and a readymade congregation. Everything he needed for running a successful gospel hut.

I suppose it was a paradox that the devout and abstinent Uncle Sid's liver should fail and bring about his death. And a painful death, too, although fortunately for him he did not linger. When he knew he was going to die he called on all the people who owed him money and asked them to pay up.

'Wants to take it with him,' Tom Mundy my neighbour said by way of explanation. 'Wouldn't put it past him neither.' I was inclined to agree. Nothing could be taken for granted when it came to separating Uncle Sid from his money.

True to form he visited the undertakers in College Street to plan his obsequies. Nothing but the best would do. Real brass handles for his casket, as coffins are called in these transatlantic times, and the finest silk lining. Anticipating a goodly congregation he decided against holding it in his own chapel but negotiated a keen price with the largest of the non-conformist churches in the town. He wanted his funeral service to include a sermon, the organist and a full choir. 'He'll be asking for the Salvation Army Band next,' his son Terry told me with some amusement.

Yes, Uncle Sid wanted a memorable send-off with no expense spared, although leaving it for his nearest and dearest to pick up the bill. He wrote out in laborious capital letters a glowing address of his life's work and achievements for the officiating clergyman to intone aloud in his honour. He ordered a new polished red granite headstone for his burial plot, complete with a long inscription. It was all planned to the last detail but omitted any mention of hospitality after-wards. Uncle Sid wasn't paying his poor relations to mourn him with a drink in their hands. They would not have expected otherwise.

But they had the last laugh, as the living always can. His grieving sons and daughters and their many children and assorted relatives dispensed with the formalities and had Uncle Sid cremated in the cheapest possible plywood coffin, and after the briefest of plain funerals. It may not have been the right thing to do but it made them all feel better. And better still when they took a tractor to the chapel and knocked it flat. Then had an almighty booze-up at the Shorn Lamb afterwards by way of celebration.

And that was the end of Uncle Sid.

22

Shoehorn Cottage

I have told you the story of Jeff Goodey, the young self-employed jobbing builder who supped his ale at The Shorn Lamb and incurred the landlord's displeasure. This story is about Jeff's father, who has always been known in the village as 'Banjo' Goodey. Apparently because as a youth he announced his intention of saving up to buy a banjo. He wanted to pay for lessons so that he could play in a group. It was obvious to everyone else that he meant a guitar and this knack of never getting things quite right has been the distinguishing feature of his life.

Banjo is one of those sublimely inept men who have only to go near something for it to malfunction immediately. His garden is littered with disembowelled machinery that he has taken to pieces and been unable to put back together again. These repeated failures do not dim for one moment his unshakeable belief that he is a skilled engineer.

'I'll mend that for you!' is his battle cry. 'Nothing to it. Bring it round to my workshop, I'll soon have it going again.'

Poor unhandy Banjo cannot be trusted with the simplest job that requires accurate measurement, or the ability to follow an instruction manual. He has a limp from falling off a ladder, numerous scars, a big chunk of thumb missing after testing a grain auger to see if it was running properly, something embedded in an eye and welding burns on both arms.

Never mind, Banjo Goodey is one of my favourite people, someone I have known since childhood. If our cars pass in the narrow lane leading to the main road out of the village we always stop and chat for a moment through the windows. He and his wife Nina have brought up a large family in the

137

smallest of country cottages. A sense of the absurd is an appealing human trait and Banjo has an affinity with the dafter side of life. Screwed to his front gate in crude poker-work on a piece of wood was the name Shoehorn Cottage. It was apt and it was funny. I appreciated it even if his wife and seven children didn't.

For several years Banjo had a pet pig, a black pig kept in his back garden. He would take it on a lead for a walk as though it was a dog and leave it tied on outside the Shorn Lamb while he joined his sons for a drink inside. He was devoted to this pig which he would help up on to his garden seat so that they could sit side by side on a summer evening and enjoy the view.

In middle age he took up moto-cross, a particularly testing form of motorcycle racing which is performed on an undulating muddy track. He spent money he could not afford on a succession of expensive competition machines. However often he is ambulanced off to hospital with broken bones or concussion he still comes back for more.

Banjo will always remain a delinquent teenager at heart. He embraces each new day with an unquenchable zest for mischief. His longsuffering wife Nina, who is some five or six years younger than he is, makes no secret of her lot. Which is that she has an extra grown-up child to look after, counting him as more trouble than the other seven put together.

Banjo would often wink and apply a hand to one of his wife's very squeezable haunches and boast, 'We're going to have our own football team.' To which Nina always made the same heartfelt reply. 'Not if I can help it, we're not.' Even so seven children wasn't bad and Banjo was proud of his stock-getting record as evidence of manly virility.

For birthday parties and barbecues he plays his guitar far into the night, and sings and capers with his children and their friends. Balding and beer-bellied but still a fourteen year old teenager between his ears, endlessly good-natured and full of harmless fun. It is impossible not to like him. In the story about the Shorn Lamb I said that his son Jeff Goodey saw life as no end of a lark, and I think you can now see where he gets it from.

Even so Banjo has his serious side and is keen to do his bit every year when the Show comes round again. Although volunteers are welcome on show days, and in the hectic days of preparation beforehand, we need to prevent poor Banjo from wrecking weeks of work, if possible without hurting his feelings. He is always sure that he can improve on the public address system, or plumb in the water troughs for the live-stock tents, or mend a broken traction engine.

He can't, and everyone knows better than to let him try. Banjo can make machinery go wrong just by looking at it. He could put our showground generator permanently beyond use if we were foolish enough to allow him anywhere near it. My wife has a soft spot for Banjo, saying that she spends much of her life coaxing reluctant volunteers to help with the Show while at the same time refusing the one person who pleads to be allowed to offer his services.

'We just can't risk it,' Ruth will say. 'Poor Banjo, it hurts his feelings so much but he's a liability we can't afford. No insurance company in the world would cover us against the havoc he could cause if we let him loose.'

Once when he was laid up with a broken leg, after yet another moto-cross accident, Ruth persuaded me to take him a jar of Joan Mundy's home-made jam as a little get well present. This was because she suffered a permanent sense of guilt where Banjo was concerned, and was always looking to make it up to him. The pot of jam was kindly meant but I took him a bottle of vodka as well and called on him at Shoehorn Cottage to deliver the gifts in person.

Which I did, although not without some difficulty. His cottage really is small, with tiny low-ceilinged rooms, all cluttered with furniture. And not just furniture. I had to step over large chunks of motorcycle in the narrow passageway, avoid a bowl of sump oil and various other booby traps artfully placed on the stairs, including a broken television set that Banjo had taken apart but failed to mend. Just getting to his bedroom was like surviving an assault course but I managed it and eventually fought my way to his bedside.

He was pleased to see me and when I asked him how he was feeling he responded cheerfully, 'Nothing that a length of rope and the kitchen chair won't put right. How about you, Alan?'

'I don't go round falling off motorbikes.'

He ruefully admitted that it was time he gave up motor-cycle racing. 'Nina says she's going to leave me otherwise. Do you think she means it?'

'Undoubtedly.'

'That would be one way of getting rid of her, I suppose. A pity you can't trade wives in and get a new one like you can a bike.'

'You wouldn't want to do that.'

'In America they let a man marry his motorbike. Couldn't happen here, could it?'

'No.'

'You can't make a motorbike pregnant though. At least I don't think you can.'

It took me a few moments to work out the implication of what he was telling me. Although slow on the uptake I got there in the end. 'Banjo,' I said in admiration. 'You don't mean...?'

He nodded proudly. 'Yep. Nina's got one up the spout again. Number eight by my reckoning, although I lose count sometimes. Nina would know.'

'I'm sure she would. How did this come about?'

'There was a big darts match at the Lamb. Our Jeff was playing and Nina came with me. We both got a bit tiddly. It was a halfway up the stairs job. I blame it on all the white wine she drank. That stuff makes my missus as randy as hell. She couldn't wait, the silly cow, and that was the result.'

To change the subject to less personal matters I pointed to a large portrait on the wall facing the marital bed. It was of a large black pig. 'Who painted that for you, Banjo?' I asked him.

'My pet pig. You remember him, don't you?'

'Of course. Patrick the Pig. One of the sights of the village.'

'Better trained than most children. I could take that pig anywhere.'

'And you did, Banjo. You did.'

'Nina made me give him up. I cried like a baby when he went off to the pork pie factory.'

'Anyone would have done the same.'

'There's a man who advertises in the market. Does pet portraits. You take him a photo and he makes a painting from it. I had the large size, it cost me plenty but I didn't begrudge the money. I reckoned I owed it to Patrick. After doing the dirty on him like that.'

'He was a pig with character. You can see it in the painting. I should say you got your money's worth from that artist.'

Banjo beckoned me to come a bit closer. 'I tried to do a deal with Nina. Offered to give up the motorbikes if she would let me have another pig. She said she would leave me straight away if I did. Reckon she means it and all.' He heaved a despairing sigh. 'Would I sooner have a pig, a motorbike or a wife? That's what I lie here trying to work out. Can never decide which.'

My high opinion of Banjo Goodey was not changed by meeting him at home, even if in bed with a leg in plaster. He bore his injury with commendable stoicism. Cheerfulness in adversity is always to be admired and on returning home I asked Ruth if there was not some small task he could be entrusted with at the next Show so that he could feel loved and wanted rather than rejected. We discussed it at length but could not think of a single thing and reluctantly agreed to stop being sentimental and keep Banjo and the showground equipment as far apart as possible.

Banjo and Nina have a teenage daughter named Kerry. A pretty girl, still at school.

She was soon into fun, which in her case meant boys and

under-age drinking. When we next met in the lane and exchanged a few words through our respective car windows Banjo informed me that Kerry's latest boyfriend was getting up his nose. This was because he came back to share her bed on Friday evenings, but unlike all her previous boyfriends he then expected to spend the rest of the weekend at Shoehorn Cottage as well.

Banjo was annoyed. Not because he minded them sleeping together but because by a gradual process of encroachment the young man stayed longer and longer after every weekend until finally there could be doubt that he had moved in permanently. Shoehorn Cottage was so full already that one more mouth to feed made little difference but to my surprise Banjo exhibited the first stirrings of adulthood I had ever detected in him. He told me that he did not think this particular boyfriend was good enough for his daughter.

He summed him up like this. 'Appetite – very good, always clears his plate. Sleepytite – would stay in bed all day if I let him, the idle sod. Talkytite – the bugger never stops. But Workytite?' Banjo spread his hands dismissively. 'Doesn't want to know. A pretty girl like Kerry could do a lot better for herself in my opinion, and I told her so.'

A few months later Banjo very kindly invited me to his fiftieth birthday rave-up which was held at the Shorn Lamb one warm Saturday evening in May. I was pleased to be asked but sensible enough to arrive late so that I was not tempted to drink too much. It was a memorable occasion, not just for the noise and the oceans of booze being consumed but because Banjo's wife Nina and their teenage daughter Kerry did a little dance together. Rather a sedate ballroom-type dance with clasped hands but their efforts were loudly applauded.

Not that they were able to get very close to one another because mother and daughter were both terminally pregnant. They revelled in the clapping and laughter that accompanied their somewhat awkward attempts to dance together, pleased to share the moment and be the centre of attention. Nina gave birth safely not long afterwards, her daughter Kerry obliged two days later, so it made a nice epilogue to the fiftieth birthday revels.

'It was that same bloody darts match,' Banjo explained, the next time I met him in the lane. 'Nina and me weren't the only ones to get caught out. Kerry and that stupid boyfriend of hers were all worked up and excited after the match and must have forgotten to do the safe and necessary. It was the white wine. I blame both babies on the white wine. I reckon Ted Hounsome must have put something in it to get the ladies going like that.'

'Perhaps I should buy a bottle.'

'Don't risk it, Alan. Don't risk it.'

I laughed as we began to move apart. But felt concerned enough to enquire after his daughter's plans for her future. 'Will Kerry go back to school? You ought to encourage her. Girls need all the education they can get these days.'

'No, she's finished with school now. She's seventeen. Well, almost. That's quite enough education for anyone.'

'Perhaps you're right.'

'Nina was the same age when she had our Jeff. Must run in the family.'

No doubt he was right about that as well. People should be allowed to lead their lives as they please, without unwanted advice from well-meaning neighbours. I drove on, reflecting that two more babies would make little difference to daily life in Shoehorn Cottage.

Better two babies than another pet pig.

23

Keeping it in the Family

My wife and I are both related by marriage to Ian Maynard, one of our younger farmers. Ian owns Bellwether Farm and lives there with his widowed mother, his charming wife and his four children, these being two growing sons and two infant daughters. Bellwether is not a large farm by the standards of the Chadwick holdings, or the Beckles Estate, but it is prime farmland with a big modern farmhouse, and they live comfortably.

Ian is the fourth generation of Maynards to hold the farm so you would have to say that life has dealt him a good hand. Not that anyone need be jealous because he works hard and is a solid citizen and foursquare family man. When there is a local event such as the annual ploughing match, or bonfire night, or the point-to-point races, you can be sure the whole family will be there in force. Ian is an indulgent father, patient and calm when things go wrong. He is idolised by his four children who love these family outings.

He inherited the farm as a comparatively young man because his father, Nigel Maynard, had died a few years ahead of time at the age of sixty, which is considered to be early middle-age in this part of the world. Until he fell ill Nigel was Ruth's most reliable helper, and a longstanding member of her showground committee. He was also the chief livestock steward, a key post.

I was as surprised as everyone else when Nigel fell ill and was taken to hospital, and even more surprised when it became known that his condition was serious, with not long left to live. I visited him more than once before he died, a sobering experience. The people who run hospitals know

144

when someone has the sign of death on their forehead, and Nigel was discreetly moved into a secluded side ward for those who would soon die.

He knew it too and made a wry face when I told him how much better he was looking. It was warm in that small ward, warm and very still, so we hardly needed to speak above a whisper. At my previous visit he was propped on pillows, this time he was lying down, an indication of his deteriorating condition. It was July and he was concerned about the show in August, anxious that the stewarding and judging should go smoothly in his absence. He wasn't sure if his deputy would remember where the water troughs were stored, or how to connect them up, or where the posts were kept to mark out the judging rings, and the sledgehammer to knock them in, and the yards and yards of rope to go round them. I assured him that his fellow committee members had rallied, and that it was all under control, after which he became less agitated.

He drowsed for a while and then suddenly clutched my arm. In a small voice he whispered, 'Come a bit closer, Alan. I want to tell you something.'

'I'm here. Go ahead.'

'It's about Ian.'

'Something serious?'

'Yes.'

Nigel liked to discuss family matters. In common with all farmers he was concerned about money and property and the importance of keeping them in the family. He was becoming agitated again so I guessed it was something of a personal nature involving money, most likely jealousy over a legacy, or envy at the success of Ralph Chadwick's nursery and garden centre, one of his favourite topics of conversation.

I whispered back, 'I'm listening, Nigel. About Ian, did you say?'

'Do you remember that day when you came to see me and Dot was in a temper?"

I did remember, and nodded agreement. Nigel's wife Dot and my mother Enid were first cousins, both being Lintotts before they married. One of Ruth's uncles is also a Lintott so I know the family well. Nigel was an amiable and uncomplicated man, in contrast to his wife who had a more forceful character. A battle-axe and a slave-driver might have been a more accurate description. She was always chivvying Nigel to work harder, or to do things to improve the farm.

I said, 'It was some time ago now. But yes, I remember.'

'Dot and me didn't quarrel much. We had a girl working for us at the time. That's what it was about.'

'I know. She told me.'

'I've been lying here trying to think of the girl's name. Can't remember her name but I can remember what a goer she was. A right little sexpot. Marvellous.'

'Perhaps you should have introduced me.'

He shook his head. 'She was trouble, that one. Be grateful I didn't introduce you.'

'Dot forgave you though. At least I assumed she did.'

'It was touch and go for a long time but it worked out all right for us in the end.' He still kept hold of my arm as though afraid that I might leave. 'I'll tell you what happened. Pull your chair closer, I don't want anyone else to hear.'

Approaching death is the traditional time for intimate disclosures. I expect that the effect of the drugs he was receiving also helped to bring long suppressed memories to the surface. I don't suppose that Nigel was the first farmer to misbehave with a young female employee but it soon became obvious that in his case it had far-reaching consequences. His voice was barely above a whisper and he unfolded his story in such a disconnected way that it was hard to understand exactly what he was telling me.

I shall have to retell the story in my words rather than his. He began by saying how proud he and his wife Dot had been to have a son, always important in a farming family. He was their only child as it turned out but young Ian grew up to be a likeable and untroubled young man who never gave them any cause for concern. He got up early in the morning and beavered away cheerfully on the farm all day. Ian was fair of face and amiable of nature, in fact very like his father in appearance and temperament. He kept himself clean without being nagged by his mother, and had never had a day's illness in his life. He cleared his plate at every meal and contentedly watched television every evening until it was time to go to bed – alone.

This began to trouble his mother who was anxious to have grandchildren. When he reached the age of twenty-eight she raised the matter with her husband. She had done so before but this time she insisted that he put his mind to solving the problem.

'Girls,' she said. 'He's not interested in girls, Nigel. What are you going to do about it?'

'Give him time, Mother,' Nigel pleaded. 'He's just a slow developer, that's all. He'll get round to it when he's ready.'

'That's what you said a year ago. If he was interested in girls he would have asked one to go out with him. Why doesn't he?'

Nigel could only squirm in embarrassment, unwilling to face up to the alternative. 'He couldn't be a homosexual, could he? Gay, as they call themselves. Not our Ian.'

'I don't know,' she admitted. 'I honestly don't know. He doesn't seem interested either way, that's what puzzles me. You're always pleased to tell everyone it's a family farm. Now's your chance to do something about it.'

'It will be four generations when Ian takes over. Not many farmers can say that.'

'No, but it's going to be four and last unless Ian gets married and has a son of his own. We're not getting any younger and I should like to have some grandchildren before I'm too old to enjoy them.'

'Me too, of course I would. But how do you propose to go about it? We can't force the lad, can we? Have you got a plan?'

'A helping hand is all he needs, Nigel. He won't go out looking for girls so we've got to bring the girls to him.'

'To work on the farm, do you mean?'

'There are always girls from the agricultural college wanting a year's practical for their course. We could have one a year for as long as it takes. One might be enough if we can get a suitable girl first time round.'

'Do you think Ian will suspect anything?'

'We can tell him that you're feeling your age and want to ease off a bit. That's true enough, I don't see he need be suspicious.'

Dot Maynard was right in predicting there would be no shortage of applicants and they soon found a young lady student who was just right in every way. She came from a farming family and could not only drive a tractor but she was also strong, healthy and well-behaved. A ready-made daughter-in-law.

Without making it obvious they organised the daily routine so that the two young people spent as much time together as possible. If Ian had to go into town to buy supplies for the farm they always sent the girl with him in their Land Rover. In the evenings, if they were in the same room together, mother and father would exit discreetly so that they were left on their own.

At first their plan seemed to be succeeding. Ian and the girl laughed a lot and got on well together, but that was as far as it went. He showed no inclination to invite her out for a drink or a meal, still less for a close encounter in the back of his car afterwards. When asked to comment on the young lady student he spoke about her with enthusiasm, although only to say how good she was at looking after the animals. She left at the end of the year when her time was up, and Ian still spent his evenings placidly watching television on his own.

So it was try again time, another eager student but with the same result. Ian worked with her companionably for a year but of sexual interest there was not a flicker. Being an intelligent woman Mrs Maynard soon worked out where they had gone wrong. They had selected nice girls from good families, girls for whom feeding animals and clearing up behind them just seemed to come naturally. She decided it was time to widen the goalposts a little and chose the prettiest applicant next time round, irrespective of whether she could tell one end of a cow from the other.

They had dropped into the habit of calling the girls by numbers when discussing them in private and had no difficulty in picking Number Three. She was not only better looking than the first two but had a splendid pair of breasts which she liked to show off by wearing figure-hugging tight sweaters.

Lorry drivers delivering to the farm winked, leered, whistled or tooted their horns in admiration and there could be no doubt that Number Three had what it took to make men notice her. If Ian liked what he saw he gave no sign. His parents provided him with every opportunity, even going out in the evenings and leaving him alone with the girl for hours at a time, but he never had so much as a grope. A dispiriting experience from which Dot Maynard drew the conclusion that her son was a neuter who had no sexual feelings of any kind.

She was not the sort to give up and Number Four duly arrived to take her turn. Number Four was different again, a punk rocker with green hair. Her appearance might have been against her but she proved to be a willing worker, chatty and cheerful all day long. Ladylike she wasn't. On view in the warmer weather were her tattoos and her pierced navel, nor could she help her naturally flirtatious manner. She was not quite what Dot had in mind for a farmer's wife but since Ian was not tempted by her either the problem seemed as intractable as ever.

There had been a change though, and an important one.

Until the girls arrived Nigel had slopped around in shape-less old overalls but before long he began to take more care with his appearance. By the time they were on Number Two he had his straggly grey hair razored down into a wiry crew-cut, and he began to wear smarter and more youthful clothes. He was only in his early fifties, still in his prime you might say. He was lean and strong after a lifetime of hard work and began to walk with a spring in his step again.

Soon it was Ian who worked on his own, which was how he preferred it, while Nigel instructed the girls in their duties, which was how he preferred it. He had certainly enjoyed instructing Number Three, the girl with the big breasts, but got away with it, his wife not finding him out until she caught him misbehaving with Number Four. It was Number Four, the girl with the beringed navel and the green hair, who had been responsible for the spot of bother Nigel had referred to when I visited him in hospital.

His wife Dot had not been amused when the incident took place. I had called to see Nigel in his capacity as chief livestock steward at the Show but when I stepped out of my car and approached the back door she greeted me with the words, 'He isn't here, Alan.'

'Not here?'

She could see that I was surprised, having arranged a time to call. To explain herself she said, 'I mean he's not in the house. He's out on the farm somewhere. I'm not sure where exactly.'

'He knew I was coming. He must have forgotten.'

'That isn't the only thing he's forgotten. Lost his senses, more likely.'

'Oh?'

She said viciously, 'We've got a girl working for us, a student, although just what she's a student of I'm not quite sure, and I don't think she is either. You're welcome to go and look for her because when you've found her my fool of a husband will be about three feet away. And if they are any closer I suggest you throw a bucket of water over them!'

Advice I was bound to ignore. All I could do was disappear quietly and hope that this little footnote of domestic bother would quickly sort itself out. I never referred to it again and had forgotten about it until Nigel reminded me. While sitting at his bedside in the hospital he told me that this spat with his wife over Number Four had brought matters to a head. Her time was up and Dot Maynard decreed that after this scare with her husband there would be no Number Five.

She was soon forced to change her mind.

Work on the family farm had become geared to another pair of hands and they could no longer manage without the extra help. Even so Nigel's wife was not going to be caught out like that again and personally chose the next candidate. Number Five when she came was even more prim and proper than Numbers One and Two. Her parents were also in farming, chapel-goers from a strict non-conformist tradition. Dot was satisfied that she could be relied on to keep her husband in his place, and at a safe distance.

Once again she had miscalculated. Not only under-estimating Nigel's sex drive now that his appetite had been whetted but forgetting that other people could also scheme and lay plots. This was because Number Five was smarter than all the others put together and soon worked out what they were up to. And just as surely worked out the correct solution. She could see a secure future for herself if she played her cards right, and made sure she did.

Before many weeks had passed she coolly announced that Nigel had made her pregnant and enquired what they proposed to do about it. The pregnancy was confirmed as genuine, and Nigel admitted to being the father, so the first requirement was to keep the news within the family while they debated what to do.

Number Five had her solution ready and it met with general approval. This was for her to marry Ian Maynard and regularise the situation as soon as possible. Everyone was happy with this arrangement, none more so than Mrs Maynard who wanted above all else for her son's status in the farming community to be normalised. Within weeks he became a respectable married man and a few months later a good family man as well, when his wife produced the long-awaited grandson.

Ian was happy too because he had no wish to be a lonely bachelor and thought it had worked out nicely for him. Nigel was happiest of all because Number Five wished to consolidate her position with a bigger family and allowed him to father a second son followed by two lovely little daughters. When I challenged him at this point in his story he nodded brightly.

'Are you telling me those children are yours?' I whispered. 'All four?' He beamed proudly, as well he might.

Nigel died a few days later, a sad loss to the farming community, but with his duty to the family having been done he died a contented man. He had been waiting for my reaction and I can still remember his triumphant smile when he saw the surprise on my face. People who have done something clever or unusual always want someone to know, they rarely take their secret to the grave. Nigel's funeral took place on the day the elder of the two little girls started school. I was sorry that he had missed out on this important rite of passage for his young daughter.

Number Five was equally happy with the way things had worked out for her. She soon became a respected member of the village sisterhood, on the flower arranging roster for the parish church and a noted doer of good deeds. She had no intention of compromising her comfortable situation with little adventures and settled down to enjoy the tranquil pleasure of twin beds with a husband interested only in having a good night's sleep.

I think it is a story which does everyone credit since it was a tricky situation that needed imagination and tact to bring about a successful conclusion. I would rate it as a typically English way of resolving a delicate sexual and social problem, achieved with the best of good manners and the minimum of expense.

The Maynards are a model family, much admired. Old Mrs Maynard loves being a granny and Number Five enjoys being a wife and mother with a nice farmhouse to live in and a settled way of life. Better still she shares an affectionate relationship with her husband and there is no doubt they have become very fond of one another and work hard to bring up their family. The two girls love helping to keep house and the two lusty lads need no encouragement to help on the farm. As proud parents Ian and his wife can look forward to a very comfortable future in the years ahead.

I do not see them regularly but I see them often enough to marvel at how quickly children grow up. And I too share in the general admiration of such a happy and well-adjusted family. Ian loves taking the children into town for a treat on market days. He is endlessly tolerant and generous, keeping them supplied with burgers and fizzy drinks, or the latest must-have possession.

He never refuses, and it seems to keep him young at heart himself. He loves to hear so many children all calling out, 'Dad, can I have an ice cream?' 'Dad, I want to go to the lav.' 'Dad it's broken, can you mend it for me?' He always obliges, never scolds them for misdemeanours, and is rated by every-one as the sort of patient good-natured Dad they would have loved to have themselves.

More like an elder brother really. But his secret is safe with me.

24

Dawn Chorus

This story is about my cousin Derek Lintott. He owns Trusslers Farm which is half in Mardle and half in our next door parish of Long Beckles. My mother Enid Lintott was born at Trusslers Farm, I have visited many times and know it well. Although I am on cordial terms with Derek our paths do not cross much. In recent years we only seem to meet at funerals or the occasional family get-together. I regret this because our wives are also distantly related to one another, we are all in the same age group, and have known one another for most of our lives. We should be friendlier than we are.

I think the main reason we are not close is because Derek and his wife Bridget are rather holy. They are High Church Anglicans and attend a congregation in the town favouring incense and rich vestments. Bridget is a churchwarden and Derek is big in the town's Christian Fellowship. These and other good works take up most of their spare time. They are the most sincere and decent people imaginable.

When the economic screw began to turn on conventional forms of agriculture Derek was one of the first to see the potential of organic farming methods. Although it took him several years to set up, and a lot of investment to make the necessary changes, he now has an established and prosperous business. He is noted as an exemplary employer who works hard himself and is scrupulously fair in all his dealings.

Derek is also an old boy of the College and as a lay reader officiates at our chapel. He likes to be involved in College activities, mainly to encourage Christian worship and regular church attendance. He certainly encouraged and befriended young Dougal Paterson and has had a big influence on his life. Thanks to my cousin Derek he is now in his final year reading Theology at Oxford and has never wavered in his intention to be ordained as a priest in the Church of England.

Nor is this the only association between myself, my cousin Derek and the College. We have an even closer link through a student named Aurora.

Aurora is an outstanding young singer, just seventeen years old. I should like to tell you about the short recital she gave the teaching staff in the music room at the College. This was by way of saying 'thank you' for their help in arranging for her talent to be professionally developed. Our head of music and the teacher who specialises in careers advice investigated the opportunities open to her, looking first at choral scholar-ships. They came to the conclusion that Aurora's talent lay beyond the scope of university education and sought specialist advice. An audition was arranged with an opera company, the quality of her voice was recognised, and the problem taken off our hands.

The recital took place after school. It was an afternoon of golden sunshine and this helped in making it a memorable occasion, for me at least. Aurora was sensitively accompanied by her music teacher on the piano and delivered a carefully arranged programme of songs that were ideally matched to her wonderfully expressive young voice. It began with songs by John Dowland and ended with Brahms, taking in a difficult but intensely moving song by Hugo Wolf on the way. For me, it went straight to the heart.

'Sings like a bird,' the head of the science department whispered to me when there was a break in the music.

I was not pleased to have the spell broken by such a banal remark. We were sitting side by side so to discourage any further attempts at conversation I whispered back, 'Yes. She does. Just like a bird.'

Banal or not this casual remark triggered my memory and started a chain of thought. I folded my arms and finally shut my eyes tightly. Not to drowse but to help me remember more clearly the details of Aurora's conception. Once again I must apologise for going backwards in time and recounting a story partly at second hand. My excuse is that I had forgotten about it completely until Aurora's wonderful singing voice came to our attention. Sitting on a comfortable chair in our pleasant music room at the College gave me time to put it back together while she sang.

The link between us is that Aurora was conceived at Trusslers Farm, the farm belonging to my cousin Derek, and where my mother was born. Trusslers is not easy to find unless you know where to look, being situated halfway along a narrow winding lane which is not signposted and does not actually lead anywhere, eventually rejoining the same road a mile further on.

The incident relating to the way in which Aurora was conceived took place when Ruth and I were still not married, although we had become a couple. I was still looking after my mother in the Glebe House, Ruth was still looking after her father in a more modern house in a different part of the village. We had been invited to take Sunday afternoon tea with my pious relatives and on arrival found them in a mildly agitated state.

We soon learned why. Derek and his wife Bridget had returned home after attending morning service at their High Anglican church with its choir, incense and colourful ritual to find a glossy top-of-the range BMW car parked outside their farm gate. Inside the gate they found a young couple trespass-sing in their farmyard. The intruding couple were staring up into the farm's hay barn, they had their arms round one another and jumped guiltily and were more than a little embarrassed and disconcerted when Derek and Bridget arrived.

They tried to make a run for it but their car was awkwardly parked, forcing them to stay put and account for themselves. Derek said that the couple were well dressed, and not particularly young, being in their early thirties at a guess. The woman was heavily pregnant and wore a wedding ring so at least they were a respectably married husband and wife couple, and neither vandals nor thieves.

But equally they had to be there for a reason. Even though godly, Derek and Bridget were just as curious as anyone else would have been in a similar situation. The couple were well spoken but reluctant to give any details about themselves. The English are awkwardly polite on occasions such as these. The Lintotts felt obliged to offer coffee, the intruding couple would have preferred to decline and leave, but felt equally obliged to accept.

The kitchen at Trusslers Farm is blissfully warm and quiet. Derek and Bridget keep a good table and offered a delicious walnut cake as well as freshly ground coffee. The atmosphere began to thaw and with it the story started to come out. And although it had been slow arriving it speeded up once it got going.

The trespassing couple explained that they had met at a party nine months previously and liked one another very much. So much in fact that in the early hours of the morning they went for a drive with the intention of looking for a secluded lane where they could make love. The party had been held in the neighbouring village of Long Beckles but neither of them knew the area and just kept driving until they found a quiet lane where they could stop the car and have their kiss and cuddle.

By this stage in the story Derek and Bridget were too embarrassed even to look at one another and stared at the table while the younger couple chattered away happily about their lovemaking in the most uninhibited way imaginable. I fear that my prudish cousin and his wife had never discussed such intimate matters even between themselves. They listened with deepening dismay and anger as the story unfolded.

Their visitors had a habit of finishing sentences off for one another and sometimes of saying the same things at the same time, both talking at once. They explained that it was mid-June and as it grew light they could see that they had parked in the gateway of a farm, close to a barn full of invitingly soft bales of hay.

They took one look then jumped out of the car and climbed up into the freshly baled sweet-smelling hay so that they could make love lying down. It was almost as if it had been arranged for them in advance. It was wonderfully warm and still, they embraced in the soft light of a summer dawn, one of those enchanted occasions which come only once in a lifetime.

They had been up all night, they had both had too much to drink and after making love they drowsed for a while. Only to be awakened by deafening bird song. They were a town couple with no experience of the countryside and had no idea that birds could sing so loudly. 'So this is the dawn chorus!' they said to one another, sitting up to listen in wonderment at the effortless outpouring of bird music coming from all round them. Although they could not see any birds they chirruped from every roof and twig, an amazingly beautiful sound they knew they would never forget.

Hardly surprising after such a passionate encounter the woman found herself to be pregnant. At this point it could have gone wrong, in the way of most party babies and one night stands, but instead there was a happy outcome. The man was from London, he had moved down with his firm to the town's small industrial estate. The woman had been a holiday visitor but they were put back in touch with one another by friends. When he offered marriage she accepted and agreed that she should be the one to move. They both liked the area so it was an easy decision to buy a house and make it their permanent home.

To pass the time while they waited for the baby to arrive they went for Sunday morning drives to try and find the hay barn where they had made love and conceived the baby, but were unable to find it. They found the house in Long Beckles where the party had been held, and used it as a starting off point to try and retrace their route, but many Sundays went by without success.

In the end they were starting to wonder if they had only imagined the barn, the soft bales of newly-mown hay and the joyous outpouring of bird music. Until this morning. They had tried a new route, found the isolated lane, rounded a bend and called out in unison, 'That's it!'

They watched for a few minutes but could not see anyone. They guessed, correctly, that there was no one at home and could not resist the temptation to get out and have a look. And were only sorry to have been caught before they could drive away again. Derek and Bridget tried hard to conceal their severe displeasure when the recital of this episode came to an end. Their farm was a private place and they felt that it had been violated. They were outraged on several counts and were about to show their guests the door when the pregnant woman softened them up with a request.

She had seen them return in their Sunday best with Derek carrying a prayer book and hoped it might solve a problem for her and her husband. She said they did not know the town very well and had been looking for a church to join so that their baby daughter could be baptised. Could they perhaps join theirs?

Derek and Bridget softened their attitude on hearing this. They could see that the parents were deeply in love and well suited to one another, which mitigated the hurt. Their joint mannerism of speaking in tandem showed that they shared the same thought processes, which augured well for a harmonious married life. They laughed a lot and seemed happy, gazing into one another's eyes and clasping hands when describing their romantic encounter in the hay, serenaded by bird music.

'Our daughter will like it here,' they said confidently. 'There are some really good schools and we're keen on education.'

'How do you know it's going to be a girl?' Derek asked, an innocent in these matters.

The woman said, 'Oh, we asked for a scan so that we could buy all the right clothes and things. We've even decided on the name, haven't we, darling? We're going to call her Aurora.'

'Goddess of the dawn,' her husband added by way of an

explanation. 'We thought it would be appropriate. They won't object to that at the church, will they?'

Derek assured them it would be a pleasure to welcome any new baby into the church. The parents joined as promised, becoming regular communicants and active members of the congregation. Bridget stood as godmother when Aurora was baptised and they have been friends ever since. Theirs is an Anglo-Catholic congregation. Not only do they like their vestments and ritual but they also insist on the highest possible standards in church music. They have a first rate organist, an uncompromising choirmaster and a large disciplined choir. This is where Aurora learned to sing properly from an early age. Nothing happens without an explanation and it is an easy link to make. The strict choirmaster deserves much of the credit for her early success as a well-trained singer.

I asked Ruth later if she remembered the story too, and she did, in every detail. So for more than one reason it was a pleasurable occasion for me that afternoon in the college music room. Success comes early to those who are going to be successful. Aurora was already launched and on her way, and I claimed her as one of our own.

Singing is a linear art and although my musical knowledge is not great I knew enough to recognise the accuracy of line I was hearing. She hit the right key at the start and never deviated from first to last. She managed it without apparent effort and this convinced me that she was a natural singer. However hard soloists try to conceal the effort there is always some gulping and straining and facial contortion but Aurora smiled happily with relaxed shoulders and her lovely light clear voice was completely unforced.

Although she is now assured of professional training that will lead to a successful platform career she will have to cope with a prodigious amount of work before it finally happens. Not just extending her musicality and learning the repertoire but honing her diction in French, Italian and German and learning acting skills as well. But that is in the future and just for the moment I am happy to sit back and listen while she sings.

The dawn chorus can reach almost deafening proportions when in full blast on a June morning and by their own account Aurora's parents had sat up listening in wonderment after making love. All of which made me extremely thoughtful as the child conceived during this bird music sang her heart out in front of me.

'Sings like a bird,' the science teacher repeated to me in a whisper. This time I was inclined to agree because she had just thrown off a run of trills that reached us as liquid and flutelike, as though it really was a bird singing.

'Yes,' I whispered back again. 'So she does. Just like a bird.'

Was it really possible, I asked myself, for such a talent to be hard-wired in at the instant of conception? However fanciful the notion I rather thought that in this case it might have been. The intense emotion shared by the girl's parents must have triggered a re-programming sequence in the gene pool, just an extra little music chromosome to hitch a lift on the DNA exchanged between them in an enchanted summer dawn.

What the hard-headed science man would have replied if I put this proposition to him I dared not think. So wisely I said nothing and kept the idea to myself, but hoped it might be true.

25

Major Crosbie-Farrell

Our neighbour Rupert Crosbie-Farrell lives on his own in the Old Rectory. This is situated on the other side of Mardle Church from the Glebe House where I live with my wife Ruth and four cats. No explanation is necessary for a happy face but if someone is always in a bad mood there has to be a reason.

The Major, as he likes to be called, is in a permanent state of ill temper, with a sarcastic remark never far from his lips. He can be shockingly rude to people and seems to take a grim pleasure in being disliked. He is also a snob, and glories in being a snob. He loves his rank, his considerable wealth, and above all he loves his ancestry. More than anyone else I have known he is an elitist, proud of belonging to that fortunate group of people who own and run the country, or behave as if they do. From the moment he wakes up in the morning until the moment he goes to bed at night he is conscious of this deep and abiding sense of caste, and conducts himself accordingly.

Genealogy might have been invented for him as a consuming interest. He researches his family tree with obsessive zeal, and he likes what he finds. He has never been slow in coming to see me when he wants some Latin translated but he is also eager to share freshly garnered titbits of his family history. He follows up every new trail with unflagging enthusiasm and usually finds something that meets with his approval. 'Service,' he told me proudly. 'We Crosbie-Farrells have always served our country. And served it damned well most of the time.'

I cannot really afford the time to humour him over his

162

ancestors but living as close as we do it would be unkind to refuse if he has found something new and wants to show me. Within minutes of my arrival he is spreading out his charts to bring me up to date with the latest recruits. Some are Crosbies, some are Farrells, some are both and many are neither, being related by marriage only. It is in the nature of genealogy as a hobby that family trees spread ever further backwards and sideways into the dim and distant past, as evidenced by my neighbour's pasted together charts.

Even so his was an impressive list I have to say, particularly during the nineteenth century with so many large Victorian families to trawl through. He netted a judge here, a general there, a bishop somewhere else, and was well pleased. A bit short on titles and just off the pace where the aristocracy was concerned but taken all round a good solid batting order of public school alumni and their womenfolk.

The Major does well to take pride in the dogged respectability of his ancestors. Whether or not you think the Empire was a good thing, these people and others like them, were the men and women who helped to put it together, and to keep it together. They were dutiful and they were incorruptible, strivers and achievers one and all, with not a slacker among them.

Hardly surprising then that as a young man he did not see himself as the end of his line. So strong was his sense of continuity that he considered himself to be comfortably situated in the mainstream of an evolving and ongoing family. This being so he knew that his first duty was to ensure the succession in his turn. No royal spouse could have taken his procreative duties more seriously. The Major married early and landed an equally young wife with impeccable middle-class credentials, the daughter of a rural dean, and you can't get much more respectable than that.

Three boys they considered a nice little family and with the hard part done Major Rupert and his lady wife settled down to inculcate their offspring into the family traditions of service and duty. All three sons imbibed these superior notions with their mother's milk, and with it the absolute knowledge and certainty that they had indeed drawn first prize in the great lottery of life by being born an Englishman and a Crosbie-Farrell.

Alas for the Major his three sons did not do the business in their turn.

His eldest son grew up and married a career lawyer who announced firmly that she did not like children, could not spare the time and would not be having any, thank you. Nor did she. The second son and his wife tried hard to oblige but soon ran into fertility problems and gave up at an early stage. They wanted a family and adopted two lovely little girls. Unfortunately these did not count for the succession and were only grudgingly entered on the joined up charts so laboriously compiled by my grumpy neighbour.

As for the youngest son, Neville Crosbie-Farrell, he gave university a miss and went straight into a firm with financial interests in the Far East. He soon vanished into the Asian business community where Mandarin was useful as a second language for Europeans on the make. He never wrote, never came back and disappeared without trace, swallowed up somewhere between Shanghai, Hong Kong and Singapore, cities that he visited regularly to pursue his money-making career. The Major had never liked him particularly and news of his death some years later did not distress him unduly. But as he drifted towards old age it began to sadden him intensely that he had no grandsons to carry on the name. What depressed him even more was to discover that all his cousins were similarly placed. There was not a single male heir among the lot of them. What had once been a thriving family tree with cadet branches in all directions had suddenly started to wither.

Worse was to follow. His eldest son was diagnosed with a severe form of diabetes, with complications that hastened his death. His second son was drowned in a yachting accident, and with his third son long since dead in the Far East this left my unhappy neighbour high and dry as the sole male survivor of his dynasty.

To have outlived three sons was bad enough but then his wife died as well, leaving him stranded to face a bleak old age on his own. By now he was sixty and he flinched from the ordeal of seeking out a compliant woman of child-bearing age and starting all over again with a second family. And abandoned the idea altogether after a scare with suspected prostate cancer, which fortunately for him proved non-malignant, although he underwent some treatment, including an operation. He was not at all reconciled to this sad state of affairs but had no option except to make the best of a bad job and put away his genealogy charts and computer printouts, even to abandon his website in despair.

Disappointment of any kind is hard to bear and although he has never been one of my favourite people I have to confess that in my heart I felt something of his sorrow. Researching his family history had become the most important activity in his life, central to his health and wellbeing. A big room in a big house was dedicated to the purpose, filled with shelf after shelf of books on the subject and festooned with charts taped together. A knowledge of costume, heraldry and medieval scripts is essential for the dedicated amateur genealogist and Rupert Crosbie-Farrell studied until he became an expert in many fields. He could quote dates and facts with the authority of one who does not expect to be challenged, and carried in his head a massive quantity of information which he would recite at length to anyone foolish enough to enquire.

Only to end up beached as the end of a line with no descendants. I did my best to console him, saying that it was not his fault, but was unable to lift the bleak sense of failure that was blighting his old age and making him even more disagreeable than usual. He felt that he had let down all those ancestors whose names and deeds he had compiled so meticulously. 'My forebears', as he always referred to them. He could not be comforted and was utterly miserable for so long that it seemed impossible he would ever be happy again.

I hope this in some way explains the morose ill-humour

that has made him such an unpopular local resident in recent years. An acquaintance of mine who had once got on the wrong side of him, not difficult where Major Rupert Crosbie-Farrell was concerned, said to me afterwards, 'I never fully understood the meaning of the word "obnoxious" until I met that awful man.' Which gives you some idea of his behaviour and how he was generally perceived by other people.

Do miracles happen? For my churlish neighbour they did. One day he received a letter from Singapore. It began 'Dear Grandfather' and ended 'Simon Crosbie-Farrell.'

Was it possible? A grandson? One he had not even known existed? It took him an hour and a couple of brandies to recover from the shock. He read and re-read the letter to make sure he had not misunderstood. But no, the message was clear. The writer of the letter introduced himself as the son of Neville Crosbie-Farrell, explained that he was coming to London on a business visit after which he would like to make a courtesy call on his grandfather.

The Major wanted to tell someone this amazing good news and hurried the short distance from the Old Rectory to call on me at the Glebe House on the other side of the church. 'Can it be true?' he whispered, wiping away tears with the handkerchief from his breast pocket. 'What do you think, Alan? It's not a hoax, is it?'

'Seems genuine enough,' I replied cautiously, after reading the letter and handing it back to him. I was almost as surprised as he was.

'I ought to check though. I'll get Walter Vokes on it straight away, this is a job for a solicitor. I didn't even know that Neville had been married, let alone that he had a son.'

Well he did and in due course, after an anxious few weeks of waiting, the mystery grandson duly arrived and called on his grandfather at the Old Rectory in Mardle. Simon Crosbie-Farrell turned out to be a charming young man who was instantly likeable. He had the distinction of manner appropriate to a Crosbie-Farrell, hardly surprising with so many distinguished forebears, and he made a favourable first impression on the little gathering invited as his reception party. Although it must have been a strange environment for him he had the self-assurance and unaffected good manners that can only be acquired from growing up in a large cosmopolitan city.

I was pleased to be on the guest list and took my turn for a short conversation with him. He smiled all the time but I soon discovered this was to disguise the fact that he was a young man who took life seriously. The smile was disarming and diverted attention from a considerable intellect and a strong sense of purpose. I was impressed, as I am sure were the other people gathered to meet him.

So how did the Major react when he finally met this surprise grandson who had materialised in such miraculous fashion from an exotic faraway city? His pride and delight can only be imagined.

There was just one slight problem. The sleek and charming Simon with his ready smile and confident manner, dressed in his cool linen suit and dark blue shirt with matching tie and handkerchief, also had rich raven hair and almond eyes. It was explained that his mother had been a Malay Chinese, and a beautiful woman she must have been too, if her elegant son was anything to go by. To give the Major his due he behaved impeccably. If he was in any way surprised or disappointed he never, to his credit, allowed it to show.

We had all assumed that Simon was only passing through. But no, Simon liked the area so much that he announced his intention of staying. In short to make his home here, although by living and working in the town, rather than imposing on his grandfather's hospitality at the Old Rectory in our humble village of Mardle.

It soon became apparent that Simon was not an indigent poor relation who had made the long journey in search of a meal ticket. On the contrary he proved to be a young man of considerable means, with a very deep pocket indeed. He was brimming with energy, full of ideas and obviously not short of business acumen. He soon found himself somewhere pleasant to live, a small south-facing apartment, after which he spied out the land and snapped up an old building ripe for development. It had once been the warehouse depot for an agricultural supply company but had long stood empty. It was a tall building, several storeys high with many rooms, and fronted the river not far from the town centre. There was an immediate concern that he would use it for some unsuitable purpose.

Not so. To the general astonishment he announced his intention of transforming this large property into a gallery selling fine art and furniture. Those of a sceptical nature doubted if he would get the project off the ground, or predicted failure even if he could, but were proved wrong. The building was renovated and redecorated to a high standard and came into commission room by room. It was an immediate success.

The townsfolk had never cared much for Simon's grand-father, the self-important Major with his bullying manner and the philistine tastes appropriate to his education and upbringing, but they flocked adoringly to his grandson's gallery and jostled one another in their eagerness to buy his pictures, objets d'art and exquisite small items of furniture. It was the place to see, and to be seen. In an upstairs salon small but select audiences found it very agreeable to listen to a recital of the Songs of the Auvergne, or a string quartet playing Beethoven, when seated on comfortable chairs and surrounded by beautiful works of art. Coffee and croissants in the ground floor restaurant tasted even better when served in such elegant surroundings, and for many people it added glamour to the daily round, and was considered to be a great asset to the town.

One thing more. Simon was a gay man and this was a further complication for his grandfather, a former tank commander, whose robust attitude to male homosexuality was tested to the limit. Not that Simon was the sort who scared the cavalry. He was gentle and sweet-natured, completely unthreatening, and no one else seemed to mind one way or the other.

He was a gay man who loved the company of women, and the embroidery ladies and the water-colour ladies loved him in return. They knew he would never offend them with coarse remarks, never squeeze their bottoms or lure them up to his bedroom. On the contrary his happy disposition and unfailing politeness were much to their liking, and his ability to get on with women of all ages contributed to his success as a fine arts entrepreneur.

Where did all this leave the Major?

Perplexed, I think it would be true to say. He was bemused by these surprising events one after the other and solved the problem by staying safely in Mardle for a couple of years while he waited for things to sort themselves out. The last time he showed me the family tree he had compiled with so much labour I noticed at the bottom the name SIMON CROSBIE-FARRELL written in capital letters. Underneath he had ruled two black lines right across the sheet, from one side to the other. It was an emphatic and symbolic act indicating that his life's work, like his family, had come to an end.

He did so without bitterness. It no longer troubled him. He muttered a few remarks by way of explanation, unnecessary in my case because I understood perfectly well what he was saying. That there is a beginning and an end to everything, and having researched backwards as far as he could go he was now satisfied that his knowledge of the family was complete. By drawing a line under Simon's name he was relieved of his responsibilities as curator of the family history and the flag-bearer of its future.

In the end blood was thicker than water, to use one of his favourite expressions. Even if his grandson was half Chinese and a homosexual he was, when all was said and done, still a Crosbie-Farrell. My neighbour decided that this made up for any other shortcomings so after a long stand-off he began make occasional visits to his grandson's gallery, and when they met to treat Simon with a little more warmth and affection.

One day he rang to ask if I was at home and once more made the short journey from the Old Rectory to Glebe House. He said he had something to say to me and wanted to talk. I led the way into a small room with chairs and a table where it was convenient to speak with anyone who called. Although he had not told me in advance what he wanted to discuss I guessed that his grandson would be top of the agenda. So it proved.

He said, 'There's been a development.'

'Oh?'

'Simon is looking for a bigger place. His apartment is too small for him.'

'Does he have somewhere in mind?'

'Yes. There are some new houses being built on the other side of the town. He told me he was planning to buy one.'

'I'm surprised he stayed in his flat for so long. Is there a problem?'

'There didn't seem much sense in him spending out money to buy a place when I'm living here on my own. I asked him if he would like to move in with me instead. Plenty of room for both of us in the Old Rectory. What do you think about that, Alan? Am I doing the right thing?'

'Simon is family. Of course you're doing the right thing.'

'It would be very quiet for him here.'

'He'll come, I'm sure of it.'

'Do you think so? It would be a big step for both of us.'

'A logical step though. May I tell Ruth? We shall enjoy having Simon for a neighbour. Good all round. I'm pleased for you.'

A few weeks later Ruth and I watched the furniture van arrive and so Mardle had a welcome addition, a stylish new inhabitant for the Old Rectory. We were pleased and hoped that it would be a permanent arrangement, that Simon would make his home among us and in the fullness of time end his days here.

Either way his grandfather's life has now entered its final

phase, and fortunately for everyone concerned it is a lot happier than it had been for a long, long time. The Major had never minded being unpopular but he cannot have liked it much either. He had become lonely and embittered but now lived again through his grandson. Simon's courteous good manners and willingness to please had an immediate influence. Almost overnight the Major began to mellow. His angry expression disappeared, no sarcastic remarks crossed his lips, and he was even seen to smile occasionally. Life was good again, and continues to be so.

I see them together in the town from time to time. The curmudgeonly old soldier with his neatly clipped moustache and neatly clipped parade-ground vowels is not quite as upright these days but is gruffly affable and contented in his old age. It has become his custom when eating out or attending a function to enter the room holding on to his grandson's arm, a gesture which does not go unnoticed. His smiling raven-haired grandson is equally attentive in return. He has become devoted to his grandfather and their genuine affection for one another is plain for all to see.

So it is a story with a happy ending.

26

'I'm Howard Noyce'

Mardle church stands on a mound and from almost any point in the churchyard there are good views over the surrounding countryside. The churchyard itself is large for such a small village, mainly because the church commissioners owned some adjacent glebe land which was developed as a cemetery. There is one big yew, reputedly older than the church, and several smaller yews. There are lime trees on one side and horse chestnuts on the other, so there is plenty of shade in summer and plenty of leaves for Tom Mundy to rake up in the winter.

Mardle is a quiet village, too far from the nearest motor-way to be troubled by traffic noise. Nor are we near an air force base, a rifle range, a railway line or any factories. Although visitors are few and far between there is a book inside the church where they can write their names and add a comment. Those who do so usually say how peaceful it seems to them. I guess they come mainly from places with more hustle and bustle and so are more aware of the silence than those of us who live here permanently.

Not that it is ever completely silent. The infant and junior schools are nearby and at playtime the children can be heard all over the village. Sheep bleat on the hill, tractors come and go all day long, and in the trees behind the church there is a rookery which provides a constant background accompani-ment to the daily round. But the visitors count these as peaceful sounds and do not consider them to be noise, as such, and write little notes in the book to say how much they enjoyed their brief moments of tranquillity in a country churchyard.

So taken all round it is as good a place as any to be buried in. A funeral has just ended, the mourners have gone off for the eats and only two people remain. These are myself and my pal Tom Mundy, the grave-digger.

'Poor old Howard,' Tom mused as he began the melancholy task of shovelling earth on to the coffin and filling in the grave. 'Cut down in his prime. Could have been any of us the way people drive these days.'

Our neighbour Howard Noyce had died in a crossroads accident at the age of forty-six. Like us he was a native of Mardle. He had been born here, worked all his life here, and he had certainly died here. He was a pig farmer and since pigs need tending every day I am sure he never spent a night away from home in all his life.

'Made his mark though,' Tom continued, leaning on his spade. 'Even the Member of Parliament used to send him a Christmas card. Strange really, when you know that he could hardly read or write, poor old Howard. He loved hanging out with the nobs and they treated him as one of their own. Could never think why.'

It is not given to everyone to die a fitting death but Howard Noyce managed it better than most. Watching a grave being filled in is a grim spectacle but did not take long and while I admired the view uphill through the Beckles Valley to Giants Farm and beyond I pondered on Howard's eccentric double life.

There is a fat boy in every village and in Mardle it was Howard Noyce. He was stout and red-faced with wispy fair hair. There were a few jeers but they were half-hearted, the other children being wary of upsetting Howard who was strong as well as fat. By the age of ten he had developed the personality that was to stay with him for the rest of his life. This was a kind of aldermanic presence, an unshakeable self-importance that set him apart.

He was the only child of doting middle-aged parents, which may explain his good opinion of himself. Not that he had much to swank about. He made no effort at school and left at sixteen almost as illiterate as when he had started at age four. He was hopeless at sport and too fat and pustular to be attractive to girls. The family pig farm was only a bungalow smallholding so he was not rich either, apart from smelling strongly of pigs.

His father soon died but his mother lived on and made sure Howard had the best of everything. In fact too much of everything for by his late twenties he carried a lot of weight, most of it round his middle. Not that he was lazy. He worked steadily all day in overalls encrusted with pig manure, topped off by colourful woollen bobble-hats knitted for him by his mother. Scarcely a heroic figure but he stuck at it and made a modest living. He was a diligent stockman with low piglet mortality who seldom needed to send for the vet, being able to treat most conditions himself.

Had it not been for his double life he would not have been worth writing about. He would have lived and died unnoticed like the rest of us. But when work was done Howard liked to dress up and go to meetings. In our nearby country market town there are a great many meetings, in fact there are so many clubs and organisations that anyone who wishes to do so can find somewhere to go on every night of the week. Howard could, and did. While still a young man he became a familiar figure in the town, and no gathering was complete without him.

He carried with him an impressive aura of solemnity and gravitas. By the time he was thirty he had an equally impressive wardrobe to go with it. In his dark blue suit with a waistcoat and tie he looked like a banker, in his tweed suit he looked like a duke, and had the bearing to match. It was his custom on entering a room to look round until he had identified the highest-status person present and then move forward with hand outstretched saying, 'So glad you could come. I'm Howard Noyce.'

He was an active member of the Conservative Party, a loyal constituency man who never missed a meeting. He was big in the National Farmers' Union, the Growmore Club, the

Grassland Society, the Rabbit Clearance Task Force and the Drainage Action Group. He was also a Life Member of the Agricultural Society and never missed the annual show. He became a stalwart of the Beckles Valley Trust where he passed muster as a good committee man. This was because he had enough sense to agree with everyone, a sure way to earn a reputation for soundness of judgement. Having little to contribute to a discussion he always gave the impression of listening attentively, murmuring every so often, 'How interesting', or, 'You're so right'. It was nicely done and he got away with it.

As a member of the Lions he helped to raise money for charity. These efforts included two main events, a summer production of Songs from the Shows and the annual Christmas concert with carols. Howard liked a bit of culture and graced the foyer of the town hall in his dinner jacket, shaking hands with the men and bowing the ladies in with all the aplomb of an impresario.

No deception was involved. Howard never pretended to be anything other than he was, nor did he try to obtain any financial advantage from hobnobbing with the local great and good. Nor to my knowledge was he ever challenged. No one accused him indignantly of being an impostor, although I fancy that one or two wondered just where in Mardle his large estate was situated.

He always seemed to be taking part in a ceremony, as well as looking pleased with himself at all times. He carried a slight smile at the end of his nose as though he knew something good that you didn't. Perhaps he did, who knows what goes on in the mind of another? The lesson being that we are all taken at the estimate we place on our own worth, and Howard loved himself dearly.

My last glimpse of him was at the Show, shortly before his untimely death. He was wearing a linen jacket with his member's badge dangling from the lapel. He had a straw hat on his head, carried a shooting stick in one hand and his show catalogue in the other. He had a portly presence that was worth anyone's entrance money as he meandered in a one-man procession towards the Secretary's tent where I was helping my wife Ruth to cope with all the last-minute emergencies.

Not that he could spare many words for us. He had spotted the Lord Lieutenant who had opened the show this year and bore down on him and his lady wife. 'So glad you could come,' he said as they shook hands. 'I'm Howard Noyce.'

Soon they were chatting affably as though they were old friends. Perhaps they were, but it was this easy assumption of social equality and the effortless small talk which went with it that finally decided me. Howard deserved his success because he had perfected a difficult art form, that of inventing a persona for himself and then starring in his own life. He may have been only an illiterate swineherd but he had found a way of forcing people to take him seriously, and they did. Had he been born in slightly more advantageous circumstances, for example if his parents had been prosperous city shopkeepers, he might have made it big in local politics and become a lord mayor instead of just acting like one.

And the fitting end to which I referred earlier? Howard was a poor driver, short-sighted and overweight with slow reaction times. His ramshackle old van was scarcely roadworthy either, the result being a gruesome crossroads accident in which he had been killed outright.

Anyone else would have been flattened by a lorry, but not Howard. He had made the headlines by overshooting at a road junction and having an almighty pile-up with police outriders and a chauffeur-driven limousine containing royal personages. The road was blocked for hours with ambulances, television crews and a helicopter circling overhead.

After all that the royal personages were unhurt, apart from a princeling who had suffered minor injuries. Much ink was spilled on him but very little on poor Howard who had caused the accident and got the blame.

I was sorry, and said so 'The Show won't be the same without him.'

'Parading round as if he owned the place, you mean?' Tom Mundy replied as he finished filling in the grave and arranged the floral tributes on top.

'It was a fitting end. I think he would have approved.'

Tom scraped the mud from his spade. 'You're right there, Alan. It took royalty to finish him off. You can't take that away from him. Howard only mixed with the best people.'

27

A Dying King

I have some bad news to tell. Bad for me and bad for a lot of other people as well but even worse for Ralph Chadwick who has been diagnosed as having an inoperable brain tumour and who will shortly die. At the time of writing he is fifty-five years old and he is understandably shocked by this dreadful stroke of misfortune.

Not being fond of doctors he put up with a year of headaches and nausea before his wife Beth succeeded in obtaining medical advice. Ralph is a tough guy of the uncomplaining school who had enjoyed robust good health all his life and never expected to have anything wrong with him. Eventually he had a blackout after which Beth insisted that he swallow his pride and consult a doctor.

Wifely intuition told her that the condition was serious. She accompanied him to see his doctor who referred him immediately to a London clinic where the specialist's report confirmed his diagnosis. Ralph has a tumour inside his head. It grows in size daily and even in these days of miracle surgery will soon bring about his death.

And not a nice death either. However gently the bad news is spelled out to him Ralph is not stupid and can only hope that the gradual loss of faculty will not be too distressing for his family. And that his death will be arranged as decently as modern pain control methods allow. He is not a coward so it is not the manner of his dying which bothers him but the thirty years he is going to miss out on. He is fifty-five years old and knows that he will not see fifty-six yet both his father and grandfather lived to the age of eighty-five. Thirty years of life is a lot to lose. He too had confidently expected to sail on

into his hale-and-hearty mid-eighties and is not at all reconciled to this gross affliction.

Beth Chadwick's counselling guideline from the specialist
was that his death could come in weeks rather than months.
Because she knew her husband's strength of character, as well
as his immense physical strength, she saw it the other way
round as months rather than weeks. Two months anyway,
which will prolong his life into the autumn, and it is already
July.

Beth knows exactly which date he has set his mind on, and
is determined to reach. It is the Show in August. She has
discussed this with me, although not in Ralph's presence. She
has calculated that he will make it to the Show, if only just.
And I know that she is as anxious for this to happen as he is.
Practically everyone they know in the world will be at the
Show, certainly all the people whose opinions they value or
care about. It will be her last chance to be seen in public as his
wife and the two events have become linked in all our minds.
The Show and Ralph's death, both rapidly approaching.

Women cope with life's emergencies better than men.
They never fail to impress me with their resilience and
resourcefulness. So it is with Ralph's death sentence. Beth
immediately severed his links with the outside world so that
she can have him to herself in the time remaining. She sits
with him in a small downstairs room where he cannot so
much as hear a telephone and refuses to let him see casual
visitors. Apart from the immediate family I am the only
visitor she will allow him to see.

She said anxiously, 'You won't stop coming to see him,
will you, Alan?'

'No, of course not. All the time you think I should come.'

'He looks forward to your visits. I don't suppose it's much
fun for you, just sitting with a sick man. I try to spend as
much time with him as I can. He doesn't say much.'

'I can still hardly believe that it's happening.'

'Nor me. Poor Ralph, he does so hate being dependent. I
try to avoid treating him like an invalid, or talking as if he is

already...' She smiled briefly. 'It would upset him dreadfully if you stopped coming. The doctors have warned me that the later stages might be upsetting. Head tumours are not nice things to have wrong with you.'

'All the more reason for me to keep coming to see him.'

'He would never tell you himself but I know he loved having you for a friend.'

'Don't distress yourself, Beth.'

'He never made many friends. Never wanted them, I suppose. Or was too busy.'

'Always the way.'

'Ralph was brought up to be self-reliant. He was afraid of being influenced and didn't like anyone getting close to him. A lot of people would find it hard to believe but in some ways he has been a very lonely man.'

'I know.'

She smiled again, near to tears. 'Such lovely weather for the harvest. And all he can do is watch it from the window.'

July is drawing to a close with hot dry sunshine, ideal for the grain harvest. Ralph watches it unfold day by day from his armchair in the room where Beth has set up her headquarters. She had a sofa bed brought in, plus all the requirements of a sick room including his medication and food. Because the strong summer daylight was beginning to hurt his eyes she put up heavier curtains with thicker linings. In the evening she positions his armchair so that he can look out over his cornfields and down through the Beckles valley, much of which he owns.

His son Trevor has kept him informed of progress as the combines roll. The barley is safely in and the wheat will soon be ready. Once again it will be a record crop and he is pleased to have seen it, since it will be his last harvest. His first question to me when I call is about the Show. I assure him that Ruth has it all under control and that the entries are up again.

'Too many damned horses,' Ralph grumbles. 'Every year more horses and fewer cattle. What are you doing about that?'

'It is only the dairy cow numbers that are down. The beef classes are up. We need additional stalling in fact.'

'Which costs money. Just a post and rail will do nicely. Anyway what do you mean, only the dairy cows? You won't get the trade stands without dairy cows. Ring round a few more farms, don't take 'no' for an answer.'

'The disease regulations are so strict. Farmers are reluctant to send cows to shows in case they catch something.'

'How many has Trevor entered?'

'Quite a few. Holsteins in the dairy classes and Simmentals for the beef.'

'Our Simmental bull must be in with a chance. Remind me to tell Trevor to keep its weight down. Most of the beef animals carry too much condition these days. Judges like a leaner beast.'

'They do. Yes.'

'Still too many horses though.' He smiles ruefully. 'Horses get better treated than people. If I come back to life in another form I hope it's as a horse.'

'I can arrange most things but that might be difficult.'

He smiles again, only fleetingly, soon changing it to his more normal glowering scowl.

'Beth is afraid I might not make it to the Show. I'll be there even if Hud has to push me round in a wheelchair.'

For several weeks Ralph has not looked much different. His forearms are just as thickly muscular, his boxer's head still aggressively thrust forward, but he cannot face food any more and in spite of all Beth's coaxing he has virtually stopped eating. Which means his death is fast approaching and his eyes stare at me with an uncomfortable brooding intensity that tells me he knows it too.

However hard Ralph tries to accept his fate he still considers it very unfair. With the benefit of hindsight it is likely that his tumour has been there all along, in some way fuelling his drive and ambition and limitless capacity for work. With luck it would have continued to be dormant but for some reason it suddenly lurched out of control, and so the same agency responsible for his success is bringing about his downfall by destroying his brain. Every day, every hour even, the malignant cells multiply and invade, causing damage which cannot be seen but is deadly for all that.

What is worse than watching a proud man brought low? I am desolated to see Ralph so listless and subdued, coaxed to eat by his wife at a time when he would normally have been on a daily tour of his farm and other businesses. For a man always confident in his opinions, in his judgement, and the rightness of his actions, I was greatly surprised when he began to exhibit a gloomy introspection about his past behaviour.

This was something I had never expected. One evening in late July he beckoned me to lean closer. He said, 'I keep thinking about Packhorse Meadow. Did I do the wrong thing in bulldozing it like that?'

'Too late now.'

'Of course it's too late. I asked you whether I was right to do it.' He pointed upwards and gave a brief wincing smile. 'Judgement Day. It will count against me, won't it?'

'Growing corn is what farmers do, Ralph. You have no reason to apologise.'

'I could have handled it differently. Done a deal with the council and helped them to turn it into a Nature Trail. Putting up a good substantial building, that would have been the right thing for me to do. An Information Centre. Toilets. Car parking. A restaurant. A lecture room for the local schoolchildren to come and learn about tadpoles and wild flowers. That's what I wish I had done instead of destroying everything. Leaving something like that behind would have been good, wouldn't it?'

'These are the sort of thoughts people only have long after the event. Never at the time.'

'Pride, Alan. I couldn't bear to be seen as a loser. I acted because my pride was hurt. Not a very good reason, was it? No wonder it's listed as one of the seven deadly sins.'

'There's no need to upset yourself at this late stage. Growing food for people to eat makes up for what you did.

We live in a hungry world.'

'Even so.' He forced another smile. 'Blame it on Amelia. She needn't have taken me on over Packhorse Meadow, not in the way she did. It was personal, wasn't it?'

'Very much so. On both sides.'

This cheered him up. 'It certainly was. Did I ever tell you what I would have liked to do to her?'

'Frequently. But not when Beth was around.'

'I should have done it when I had the chance. Can't even cross the bloody room without holding on now.'

'Someone should have given Amelia a good seeing-to long ago. None of us were up to the job. I guess that explains why she's had her own way all these years.'

He chuckled grimly, then gestured to the window. 'Pull the curtain over, there's a good chap. I think I'll lie down for a few minutes.'

I did as he asked and moved to the door. 'Is there anything else you need? Shall I ask Beth to come back?'

'Yes. You might remind her that Trevor hasn't been in to see me lately. There's something I need to discuss with him.'

I promised to deliver the message, knowing as I did so the hurt that lay behind it. Ralph and his son Trevor have never been on affectionate terms with one another, a situation made worse by his approaching death. Ralph begrudges his son the thirty extra years of his inheritance and finds it impossible to hide his feelings. No doubt the reason why Trevor does not come to see him more often.

There is another problem also, a sensitive problem which lies awkwardly between them every time they meet. The fact that Trevor has not provided him with a grandson.

Trevor is the fond father of two young daughters but his wife found childbirth an uncomfortable experience and let it be known that she considered her family complete. Which means that Ralph might never have the grandson he longs for above all else. It grieves him bitterly to think of dying with no male grandchild to carry on the name and the farming dynasty, and he does not keep his feelings to himself.

At first Trevor's wife Vicki was unmoved. Boys were noisy and dirty, the two girls suited her very nicely as a family and she saw no reason to get pregnant again just to oblige her father-in-law. However she changed her mind when his illness was made known to the family. She suddenly realised that her husband would be inheriting thirty years ahead of time and that a son might be very handy later on from her own point of view.

Ruth told me about this change of heart and said that Trevor and his wife Vicki have now begun trying to increase their family as a result of Ralph's impending death. Sons are never easy to come by but there is an inheritance to be secured, a powerful incentive. As a highly intelligent couple accustomed to having whatever they want I am sure they will soon succeed.

It is unlikely that Ralph will live to know one way or the other but the absence of a grandson deepens his unhappiness. He is not dying in tranquil resignation, he is deeply miserable and cannot pretend otherwise. He miscalculated badly and for this reason is incapable of consolation. He structured his life in the expectation that he too would live to a ripe old age, and have a long and congenial retirement, exactly the same as his father and grandfather before him. He had looked forward to a long golden evening of travel and eating out and enjoying time together with his wife.

Now he knows that none of these things are going to happen. For such a wealthy man he has led a dour existence with no luxuries for himself and precious few for his wife. He seemed afraid to relax and enjoy the good things in life. He drove himself as hard as he drove the people who worked for him, only to discover that when it came to it his money could not buy the one thing he now wanted above all else – time. No one likes to be caught out and Ralph knows he is the object of pity, something else he hates but is powerless to alter.

As I pulled over the curtains in his sick room I could see the spire of Mardle church picked out in strong evening sunshine. Ralph's parents are buried in the churchyard, as indeed are his grandparents, and quite a few other relatives as well. Soon he will be joining them there in the long sleep and he likes the idea even less the longer he has to think about it. He is not at all resigned to the idea of death, even if it could be arranged a merciful death, and I am finding his doomed gaze hard to bear.

'Do you feel sick?' his wife Beth enquired, coming in to rejoin us. He shook his head and gestured his thanks when she arranged a travelling rug over him. It was a cool evening and he was becoming sensitive to changes in temperature.

'Only a month to the Show,' he whispers to me as I move towards the door. 'Who did you say was judging the Simmentals this year? Tell Trevor to keep the weight down. Our bull won't win if it carries too much flesh.'

'I'm sure Trevor knows that.'

'He won't tell me how much the bull weighs. Because it's too heavy, that's why.'

'It will be in peak condition on the day. Trevor will see to that.'

'Has Paterson cut the grass yet? Keep after him, Alan. The trade sponsors won't cough up year after year unless the showground is properly prepared. I know Paterson is an awkward customer but so am I. Refer him to me if there's any trouble.'

His wife replaces the rug which he has thrown off in agitation. She catches my eye but I am leaving anyway, wishing that he did not keep counting off the days. A month to the Show means a month to his death, and we all know it.

Beth spends much of the night with him now, sitting close where he can be aware of her presence, even in the dark. It is a long vigil by the bedside of a stricken king. For such Ralph would have been in former times, or at least a feudal overlord obeyed by all. Now he lies dying, his strength gone, a man of tragic complexity and pathos.

28

Trevor Chadwick

This time it is Trevor Chadwick sitting with his dying father. But not sitting very close. Hardly surprising since they have never shared a close relationship.

Trevor has been to a livery company luncheon in London with his father-in-law, a merchant banker who holds several directorships in the City. It is a summer evening, he has just returned, and is still wearing his dark suit. There are gold cuff-links peeping from the sleeves, a blue handkerchief nestling in his breast pocket, and on his feet are the most wonderful pair of black shoes, hand-stitched and with a lustrous shine. He is at ease in these clothes of the City establishment, indeed hardly seems aware of having them on, or of being dressed differently from his rough-hewn father.

Nor does his body language express concern.

His posture is comfortable, lying back in an armchair with his ankles crossed. He is explaining some financial trans-actions to his father who listens intently. Ralph sits more awkwardly, half twisted in his chair as though to ease pain, but still managing a scowl. A man still powerful, still formidable, but with no future. Whether he likes it or not, and he clearly doesn't, he will soon be leaving everything behind for his son to inherit. His unwillingness is impossible to hide.

So he keeps his dark brooding gaze fixed on his son, a son who closely resembles his father Lionel. This resemblance has been apparent for many years, indeed is unmistakeable for anyone who knew the grandfather. The older members of staff remark on it frequently, although never when Ralph is around. Trevor has the same urbane easy manners as his grandfather, and the same absence of tension in his body. With the insight of the dying Ralph knows with utter certainty that he is looking at a man with another fifty years of life in him. Trevor has the air of calm durability that characterised the earlier Chadwicks. It is a safe bet that like them he too will sail on into his hale-and-hearty mid-eighties. As the generation that missed out Ralph is incapable of consolation.

From where he is sitting Trevor can see a photograph of himself taken at the age of five. It is one of his mother's favourite photographs and he knows she will take it with her wherever she goes, and always display it prominently. It shows him holding a red rosette while leading a calf on a halter, having just won a class at the Show. Even at the age of five Trevor could claim to be a veteran of the show ring since he had been competing seriously since the age of three.

It is not a photograph Trevor cares for himself and he would not be sorry to see it disappear. The face of himself as a five year old child is grim and watchful, staring sideways out of the photograph to where his father is waiting on the other side of the ropes ready to criticise him for the slightest handling error. It was not meant to be fun, it was preparation for doing things properly, and winning.

For Trevor Chadwick childhood had been over at the age of two. The moment he was strong enough to carry a bucket his father gave him a dozen hens to look after. It was called work, and work was meant to be taken seriously. His father counted the eggs daily, scrutinised the cleanliness of the water bowls, and would accept no excuses for anything not done as it should be.

In fact no sooner had his son been born than Ralph started anguishing about how best to prepare him for his inheritance. No easy solution presented itself. Modern farming had become such a complex business, and his own enterprise so large, that nothing short of a university education followed by an appropriate professional qualification would equip his son to run it successfully. Yet Ralph had always been contemptuous of college-trained farmers who never got their hands dirty. 'Too much education makes boys soft,' was one of his frequently uttered remarks, closely followed by, 'Too much education makes boys lazy.'

He was haunted by the fear that if his son had too much education he would lack the practical skills necessary to manage the farm profitably. The men would not respect a boss who could not do the work himself, who was unable to plough straight or calve a cow. So after much anguished thought Ralph came up with the answer. Trevor would pursue a twin-track objective. He would follow a rigorous course of academic study while at the same time learning how to do every job on the farm. Having little option except to comply with his father's wishes this was how Trevor spent his childhood and precious teenage years, in unremitting toil from early morning until late at night.

He was assistant shepherd at age six, expected to stay up all hours in the lambing sheds before going to school. He was milking the cows at age eight when scarcely able to reach their udders from the floor of the herringbone parlour. At age ten he was staggering around in the workshop, carrying huge tractor parts and fitting them with giant spanners. At twelve he was a dab hand with the arc welder, and an expert in building maintenance by fourteen.

His skills as plumber and electrician were often put to the test. Every so often he would return home from the College and be immediately sent out to one of the farm cottages to mend a burst pipe or investigate a power fault. One freezing winter night his father had him digging a trench back to the road because he had made a mistake over something and had to put it right the hard way.

If Trevor thought life would be easier once he went to university he was mistaken. His father was waiting for him on his return at the end of his first term, not for a welcome but to push him up into a tractor cab to begin work immediately. The paid workforce knocked off at five o'clock but Trevor was lucky to finish before eight and was then encouraged to put in a few hours of intensive study before going to bed.

The general opinion was that Ralph enjoyed bullying his

son and thinking up new things for him to learn. 'You'll thank me one day,' was his response when Trevor objected at being made to fell a stand of timber while studying for his finals. As soon as these were over his father had a treat in store. His holidays were to be spent in the local slaughterhouse on a butchery course. 'You start on Monday,' Ralph informed him. 'Seven o'clock. I'll make sure you're not late.'

By this time Trevor could inseminate cows and pigs by AI, serve customers politely in the farm shop, load a lorry with sacks of potatoes so that they did not fall off, trim a hoof, shear a sheep, plough an arrow-straight furrow, interview sales reps and come off best, programme the farm computer and design new software when needed, as well as sweep the yard, a daily penance imposed by his father in early childhood. When it came to leisure activities he could gallop a horse, row a boat, hit sixes at cricket, was an even better shot than his father and able to hold his liquor when they went drinking afterwards. While at university he found time to swim and dance and speak in public. He was a young man rapidly running out of things to learn.

Both proud parents turned up on graduation day when he was awarded his BSc Agric, second class honours upper division, a most creditable performance under the circumstances. But Ralph was not letting him off the hook yet, not by a long way. A year at the Royal College of Agriculture at Cirencester studying estate management was followed by a year putting it into practice. Ralph fixed him up with a placement on a spread of comparable size in the next county, the landowner being a shooting friend of his.

After this Trevor was rewarded with a trip abroad to work with a top Holstein herd in Canada. He enjoyed this but finally asserted himself and slipped the leash. He travelled all over the USA and then spent six months in Australia, ending up on a cattle station in the Northern Territory. The jackeroos were used to young Pommy toffs sent out to be made a man of but found there was not much they could teach Trevor and considered him an all-round good bloke.

When this fun was over he had a nasty surprise in store because once again his father was waiting for him on his return. Only this time not to push him up into a tractor cab.

'Accountants rule the world,' Ralph told him by way of a fatherly greeting. 'I hate them all the soulless bastards, even more than I hate lawyers, and that's saying something. Any fool who allows them to tell him how to run his business deserves to be ruined, and usually will be. Accountants are the curse of mankind and you can have that in writing if you like. I don't know why you're laughing because you're about to become one. I've fixed it all up, you start on Monday morning. I'll make sure you're not late.'

By this time Trevor was ready to settle down and took readily to accounting, having a natural aptitude for finance. He saw the wisdom of his father's advice and soon found that accountants really did rule the world. Since qualifying Trevor has attended follow-up courses on computer fraud, tax law, property trusts and similar weighty matters, with the result that he begins to look much like any other accountant. Except for his hands.

Some things cannot be hidden, coughing, poverty and love among them, according to the saying. Big hands are another, and Trevor's are huge. Not only are they huge and strong, they are weather-beaten, knotted and scarred, the result of too much hard manual labour at a young age. They are a farmer's hands, he has them for life, and they are just as valid a qualification as the string of letters he can put after his name. Any stripling ploughboy who thought to take advantage of a greenhorn boss needed only one look at those powerful hands to know better.

'Is Vicki well?' Ralph asked suddenly.

Vicki is Trevor's wife, the mother of two well-behaved little girls. The implied message behind Ralph's enquiry is that if Vicki is a healthy young woman why is he dying without a grandson to carry on the name and inherit the business? Trevor wisely dodges the question by telling his father that she is well and happy and coming to see him some time soon.

He and Vicki had been the beneficiaries of some slick matchmaking. Her father turned out to be Ralph's shooting buddy, the merchant banker who owned the estate where Trevor spent his training year. Trevor was an only son, Vicki was an only daughter, so the two sets of parents had arranged it cleverly to provide suitable partners for their children without making it too obvious.

When Trevor leaves he is replaced by his mother. I stay for another few minutes and then leave husband and wife alone. The Show draws nearer every day and the evenings are long and sunlit. From time to time Ralph mutters in a gruff voice, 'Sorry, Beth,' to which his wife always makes the same calm reply. 'You don't need to apologise for anything.'

It would take a long time to unravel this condensed under-statement but fortunately they both know exactly what the other is trying to say and so do not need to have it spelled out at length. Ralph stares morosely at the view through the window, and it is a spectacular view with rectangles of golden stubble among the dark green of the trees, above which can be seen the spire of the church and its waiting churchyard. Beth Chadwick ignores the view. She keeps her eyes fixed on her husband as though to impress him on her memory for the thirty lonely years to come.

'Sorry, Beth,' he growls yet again, to which she replies as patiently as ever, 'You have no need to be sorry. I keep telling you.'

No need to regret the interests they never shared, the friends they never made, the holidays they never took or the places they never visited. Instead they sit in a slowly darkening room, trying to compress the thirty missing years into as many days.

29

The Show

Every year after the Show there is a double-page spread of colour photographs in the next issue of the Herald.

The Herald has a reliable local photographer and he does a good job whatever the weather, and this year we had unbroken sunshine from start to finish. The double-page spread always includes a massive shire-horse jingling with harness, a hot-air balloon, riders coming a cropper in the water jump, green-and-gold traction engines belching smoke, the silver band puffing their cheeks, children in mid-air on the bouncy castle, and a baby in a pram with ice cream smeared all over its chops.

If the Herald's photographer has a fault it is that he spends far too much time pursuing girls with bare midriffs or wearing skimpy summer dresses. Girls can always be persuaded to pose for the camera and one of them showing plenty of leg astride a roundabout horse is a sure thing for the front page. The same could be said of the man with the banner, who never fails to have his photograph featured prominently every year.

In our nearby market town eccentricity is not only tolerated it is highly regarded and appreciated. Anyone willing to brighten the day with a little harmless odd behaviour is encouraged to do so and given credit for taking the trouble to stand out from the crowd. The man with the banner is a farmer by the name of Phipps. His farm is in the neighbouring village of Huckle and he is known by the wildly unsuitable nickname of 'Tiger'.

At the Show every year Tiger Phipps wears an old-fashioned brown pin-striped suit with a yellow rosebud pinned to the lapel. His outfit includes a white shirt with a stiff collar and a neatly knotted black tie as though off to chapel. This is contrasted by the straw boater he wears on his head. It has a vivid red and blue ribbon and he wears it at a raffish angle, which fits in with the sense of occasion. His banner is a piece of plywood nailed to a broom handle. On one side is written WINE IS A MOCKER, on the other appear the dire words, STRONG DRINK AN ABOMINATION.

Tiger Phipps strolls round amiably in a one-man procession, exchanging friendly banter as he goes. It is a slow procession because he is asked to pose for a photograph every few minutes. Whole families like to be taken with him in the middle holding up his temperance banner. Tiger is endlessly good-natured and patient. If he is aware that people are making fun of him he gives no sign.

Eventually his circuit of the showground takes him close to the beer tent where not surprisingly he is greeted with cheerful ribaldry. By this time it is high noon and the young men inside have been drinking steadily for several hours and are well tanked up. The tug-of-war team, thirsty lads all, raise their glasses and invite him in for a bevvy.

'Not a bad drop of stuff, Tiger,' they call out. 'Why don't you try some?'

The reason being that Tiger Phipps is an arable farmer who grows only one crop, the same crop year after year. And far from being the backward old codger you might suppose he has a big chemical store filled with all the latest pesticides, and big spray booms on his tractor to drench his crop from end to end during the growing season. He grows barley but it is a variety used exclusively for malting and is of such high quality that his entire crop is purchased every year by one of the big brewing companies to make beer.

This is what the lads in the refreshment tent are politely drawing to his attention as they hold up their pint mugs with one hand and point to them with the other. There are none so deaf as those who won't hear and Tiger wanders by looking studiously elsewhere.

In the course of a very long day I must speak to half the population of Mardle. Few local people miss the Show, hardly surprising as Beckles Court and its large park are within the parish boundaries. Mostly they tell me how much they are enjoying themselves, which is nice, and makes all the hard work worthwhile. They enjoy themselves, and they eat. It is a food-fest, the best of the year, and an excuse to over-indulge. Everyone begins eating, drinking or licking ice creams the moment they arrive in the showground. The most elaborate picnics go on all day in the car park and around the main show ring. Lined up one after the other in an avenue known as Food Alley are vans selling tea, coffee, sandwiches, fish and chips, burgers and kebabs. An appetising smell of fried onions drifts around the ground for most of the day. This comes from the big hot-dog stall, which is doing well, judging from the queue of people waiting to buy.

As for the Members they look forward to a posh sit-down lunch of salmon and white wine in their marquee. Among them are a smartly dressed couple I intend to write about shortly. They are the Egg Man's brother Clive, and his wife Trixie. Joining them at the table are their two French poodles, one black, one white. The poodles are elaborately clipped, coiffed, scented and bejewelled, a description that could apply equally well to Trixie. But as promised, more of them later.

The ideal weather has brought out the crowds and it is heartening to see so many family groups. Society needs families, and in our part of the country they are still the rule rather than the exception. Not that all family groups are necessarily what they seem. For example the youthful looking Ian Maynard is having a splendid day out with his wife and four children. There are two strapping sons and two bonny daughters, and they all adore their father. His wife, otherwise known as Number Five, watches fondly as he spends time and money at every stall he passes, urging his brood to enjoy themselves, and they munch happily on junk food and ice cream throughout the day. Ian is endlessly generous, as indulgent as an elder brother.

Less happy parents are the neurotic Patersons, Jamie and Agnes.

The edgy compromise with their son Dougal is at an end because Dougal has come down from Oxford and is launched into a successful career. Alas, it is not one that meets with their approval because Dougal parades himself proudly on a tour of the showground to show off his dog collar. He has taken Holy Orders as a Church of England clergyman, and at the Anglo-Catholic end of what is still a fairly broad church. Dougal looks plump and pleased with himself. A bigger cuckoo than ever he towers over his glum Presbyterian parents. They accept the congratulations heaped on them through gritted teeth.

Dougal is one of those fortunate people who seem even bigger than they actually are. His polished Oxford manners and young officer charm breeze him effortlessly through every social situation. He is already earmarked as a future bishop and we all know it, Dougal best of all. He has found his parents easy to annoy. They would have much preferred him to be a rugby playing veterinary surgeon but cannot be seen to be disappointed in a son who has done so well. They smile bravely in public but in private they deplore the glimpse of purple and the whiff of incense that their son trails behind him on his lap of honour round the showground.

After which it is a relief to be able to smile approvingly at the four healthy Batty sisters who lead much happier and less complicated lives. They are having a really good time and as usual are doing everything together. Today it is not frolicking in the swimming pool or kick-boxing classes, today it is pretending not to notice that they are followed everywhere by an admiring fan club of boys and young men. I do not know all of them but I can recognise one of Banjo Goodey's sons, and at least two members of the Hounsome tribe. Which means it is a serious pursuit and there can be no doubt that the boys mean business. The four sisters revel in the power of sexual attraction but are grateful to have safety in numbers as they approach uncharted and dangerous territory.

By the time a scented dusk falls on the more remote corners of the showground it might be a different story. At least so think the boys, their faces expressionless but full of hope. Divide and conquer is their plan of action but they know it won't be easy. Even less so if Sue Batty can rescue her daughters in the nick of time. So it is a fine calculation, a minuet of teenage love and seduction that will go on all day. Meanwhile the girls parade, giggling and whispering, while the boys pursue.

My contribution on Show days is to help keep track of the winners and account for the trophies and prize money. Mostly I do it well, except when Nicola Baigent distracts me by riding past on her horse. It is a big horse but she is a firm rider and has it well under control. Some people are born to look down on the world with their feet in the stirrups of a sixteen hand hunter, and Nicola is one of them.

She has not remarried after the suicide of her husband, Peter Baigent, and as far as I know has not even dated anyone. Her elder son intends to take over management of the farm when he has finished his agricultural degree course at university, which seems a sensible arrangement. The younger son has opted for the military, following his father's early career path. Perhaps when they are safely married off, and their futures secured, Nicola will devote more time to her own life, though I think it will be a while before she is in a romantic frame of mind after Peter's violent death at the barrels of a shotgun.

Even so she makes a most handsome widow and is such a splendid sight in the saddle that I have to admit to some slight confusion with one or two of the minor placing rosettes. All that hauteur, sweat and creaking saddle leather! But my wife is anxious to tell me something so I tear my gaze away and pay attention.

She whispered, 'Ralph has just arrived. I hope he's going to be all right.'

There was a ripple of interest as news of Ralph Chadwick's arrival was passed on round the showground. Reports of his illness had been circulating for weeks but no one was quite sure how serious it was. Rumours cannot be long suppressed and his absence from the farming scene generated an air of mystery. Was he really going to die, and quite soon? His family weren't saying, allowing people to draw their own conclusions.

Ralph's unexpected appearance was a source of much relief and pleasure to many of the people attending the show. He was obviously sufficiently recovered to have an outing in public and they turned to look or altered direction to see him for themselves. His wife Beth must have been instantly aware of the concern and goodwill towards him, and reassured that they had done the right thing in coming.

They were among friends, and there is no better feeling.

30

A Reluctant Death

Ralph had been mentally preparing himself for many weeks and was determined not to miss this last chance of a public appearance with his wife Beth. His family were divided between those who saw it as a heroic gesture and by the others as an ordeal he was unlikely to survive. They were both right.

Ralph and Beth were driven to the ground by the ever-faithful Hud. They were met at the main ring by Trevor and his wife Vicki and their two small daughters. Hud was now in his seventies and white-haired but still completely devoted to Ralph, his boss and companion for fifty years. They were quickly joined by an entourage of officials and other guests so that it became almost a royal procession with people lining up to be introduced. It was a slow procession because so many people wished to shake Ralph's hand and say how glad they were to see him out and about again. And to express the hope that he had made a complete recovery from his illness.

Ralph's outward appearance was not much different from normal but the old formidable presence that made people take a step back was exchanged for an eagerness to be recognised. He looked keenly from side to side in order not to miss anyone he knew. He was particularly anxious to greet those who might know his wife Beth, or to whom he could introduce her. He was intent on involving her in his farewells, for this is what they were rather than greetings, keeping a protective arm close to her waist while he did so. I watched as he shook hands with his friends and neighbours and fellow farmers, marvelling at the animated discussions he was having with them, knowing how close he was to death.

By a prodigious effort of willpower Ralph stayed on his feet for four hours, a massive drain on his strength. He had hardly eaten for weeks and was existing mainly on glucose drinks but his eyes were burning with determination and his face was lit up with a desire to meet as many people as possible. He dearly wanted to impress them on his memory but instead it was they who would remember him as he made this one last circuit of a familiar scene.

He said to Beth suddenly, 'I want to meet some of our own people. Let's go down and take a look at Trevor's bull.'

By his own people he meant his many employees and former employees and their wives and families who clustered around the cattle lines in the hour before the Grand Parade. He left the Members to sip sherry in the luncheon marquee and headed for the villagers with Beth by his side, seeking out everyone he knew and offering his hand.

'How long have you been with us?' Ralph asked the older members of his farm staff one by one, and the answer was always the same – a long time. Sons had followed their fathers at Giants Farm for many years and few left the Chadwick fold once they had become part of its big extended family. Ralph then held out his hand to wish them good luck for the future. A strong clasp and a straight look in the eye that many found hard to meet and turned away.

'He's not really going to die, is he?' they asked one another when he had gone. 'Not a tough old bugger like Ralph.' 'Why is he saying goodbye to us then?' was the reply, but without the joshing and wisecracks that normally defuse a grim situation. They were quiet and subdued for a long time afterwards but consoled themselves with the thought that at least the guvnor had a son to carry on the business, so their own jobs were safe.

After this Ralph led the way back to the Members Enclosure where his son Trevor and daughter-in-law Vicki were having their salmon and white wine lunch. Vicki is the mother of two charming little girls and Beth had passed on to Ralph the good news that she had relented and agreed to become pregnant again in the hope of conceiving a son. This cheered him up but we were all equally aware that he would die without knowing the outcome. This, more than anything else, was making his approaching death even unhappier than it might have been otherwise. He was dying with the fear that there might never be another male Chadwick to carry on the name and the farming empire.

Vicki tested positive first time round, and so had soon conceived the longed-for grandson. Knowing the two people involved I was not surprised, and would have bet on it, because Trevor and Vicki are a gilded couple accustomed to having things work out the way they want them. So it proved and a year later when the next Show came round Vicki was proudly holding up the latest Chadwick for all to see, a fortunate baby boy who had chosen a good bed to be born in. Ralph would have given anything to see it for himself so I sorrowed on his behalf.

Whether by chance or merit, or more likely by the good common sense of the inter-breed judge, the huge Simmental bull entered by Trevor Chadwick on behalf of the family was awarded the sash as Supreme Champion of the Show, and led the Grand Parade of animals into the ring, bedecked with rosettes. Ralph was unable to hide his delight and when the trophy was awarded went forward into the ring to receive it himself. This was the opportunity people had been waiting for, a chance to show their feelings, and they gave him a big cheer and a prolonged round of applause.

It was a memorable last appearance for a man held in great respect, and his death a week later came as a shock.

He knew, just as Beth and I knew, that the effort needed to attend the Show would precipitate his death, but still went ahead. On returning home with his duty done he staggered and had to be helped indoors by Hud. By the evening he had drowsed away into a coma and the next day was taken to hospital. He never regained full consciousness and died a week later. But it was by no means an easeful death and his angry struggle prolonged the ordeal, not only for himself but for his family. Ralph was a man of great possessions and he held on to them until the last possible moment in a reluctant death.

So many people arrived for the funeral service that for the first time in living memory Mardle church was full, with extra chairs and people standing at the back. All whispering to one another, 'We could hardly believe it either. Ralph seemed so well at the Show.'

Sitting across an entire row of pews near the front I could see a phalanx of Ralph's enemies from the Beckles Valley Trust, prominent among them the retired archdeacon who was Amelia Ashby's most loyal henchman, but whose name I can never remember. If they had come to mourn they concealed it well behind cheerful faces and much loudly whispered conversation. Some were even smiling and giving every impression of enjoying the occasion. Leading the gloaters from the Trust was Ms Amelia Ashby herself, and she had not dressed to go unnoticed.

In a church full of soberly attired mourners she looked as if she was headed for a posh day out at the races. She wore a white suit trimmed with navy blue, and a wide-brimmed Lady's Day hat. Her high-heeled shoes showed off her exquisite ankles to perfection, her gloves she removed finger by finger during the first hymn as though starting a striptease to music, and she carried her handbag jauntily over her arm in the best 'Hello Sailor' tradition. She refrained from bursting into song and dancing on the coffin but did not bother to hide the triumphant smirk on her face. Her pleased expression conveyed the message that Ralph Chadwick had got the punishment he deserved. She might have lost the battle over Packhorse Meadow but she had won the argument and the war with it, and there is no more conclusive proof of whether you have won or not than to stand beside the dead body of your enemy.

The burial was private, only members of the family being present when the coffin was lowered. My wife Ruth cried, and I must confess to feeling very emotional myself. I was thinking of the missing thirty years that Ralph minded so much, and which his wife Beth would have to live out on her own.

He would have traded his wealth for as many days but the angel of death could not be bribed. However rich you were you had to go when the bony finger beckoned, and for all his strength and willpower Ralph had been unable to prolong his life by a single hour.

After the funeral I stood with Tom Mundy for a few moments while we looked at the mounds of flowers. My neighbour has one big advantage over the rest of us. By virtue of his calling as the village sexton and grave-digger he can always have the last word if he wants it, and invariably he does. As he picked up his spade to begin filling in the grave he mused aloud with his verdict on the dead man's life, work and achievements.

He shook his head in stern disapproval. 'Ralph didn't pace himself. It was nature's way of slowing him down.'

31

Princess Claudia

Only one wrong family came to live in Mardle but they were brave about it and did not flinch from the mud and the healthy country smells. Guy and Pandora were economists of the academic kind, indispensable from every fashionable left-wing think tank.

They wore their learning lightly so as not to embarrass us in the village, just as they were discreet about their considerable wealth, and they both milched huge sums of money from impoverished countries by advising them how to manage their affairs. Why were they living in Mardle? Because they had produced a daughter and being conscientious parents thought it would be nice for her to have an idyllic few years in the countryside while they wrote some more books.

Claudia was five years old when they arrived in Mardle, and only ten when they left, but during that time she was easily the most prominent person in the village, and the centre of attention wherever she put in an appearance. She was a tremendous hit with everyone, doted on by old and young alike.

During the five years they lived in Mardle I do not think either Guy or Pandora learned anything about the village, or the people who lived in it. They turned up at most of the annual events, such as the church fete, the ploughing match and the village bonfire, but always seemed to be watching from a distance, their faces expressionless. They were as perpetually baffled by Mardle folk as they were by them. Every so often Guy would put in an appearance at the Shorn Lamb and sup a manly jar of ale in an attempt to be matey with the locals but he could find nothing to say to them, nor they to him, so as an exercise in social mobility it was not a success.

True to their socialist principles Guy and Pandora sent their daughter to the village school. This accounted for much of Claudia's popularity as she became known not only to the other children but to their parents as well, and of course to the teachers. Not that they were able to teach her much since at home she conversed in German with her mother, and in French and Russian with her father, who also taught her calculus and to play chess to international master standard.

In appearance Claudia was alarmingly fragile. Because her parents were vegans she grew up in a household where they studied a lot but ate sparingly. Deathly pale and with emaciated arms and legs she had a waiflike appearance that triggered instant sympathy in the warm-hearted country folk who knew a neglected child when they saw one. The village mothers who waited outside the school on the seats by the war memorial would dearly have liked to take her home and give her a good feed, and to tell the truth a good scrub as well, for the angelic Claudia was none too clean by their standards. Her parents were anxious that she should have a grasp of macro-economic theory but seldom remembered to run her a bath.

The inhabitants of Mardle took to the sickly Claudia in a big way. She was the village pet admired for her cleverness and treasured by everyone, including the local children, who boasted to children of other schools about her tremendous brainpower. Perhaps people felt protectively towards her? That was the most likely reason but I don't think anyone has yet worked out exactly what governs acceptance or rejection in a society.

It was my wife Ruth who pointed out that Claudia accepted our homage with all the graciousness of a princess. She began calling her Princess Claudia and others did the same, without sarcasm I may add, because she really did behave like a princess, and she was certainly treated like one. So although not quite in the way that her parents intended Claudia still achieved the golden childhood they had planned for her. She may not have wandered carefree in flower-strewn meadows but she had basked in the admiration of a rural community, and not many people do that.

Our final glimpse of the ten year old Claudia was at the village concert in December. She dazzled us with three pieces from *Kinderscenen*, remarking casually by way of introduction that Robert Schumann was the composer whose music she most enjoyed playing on the piano.

Claudia's departure was mourned not just with regret but with genuine sorrow. She was showered with gifts, accepting them with the gracious condescension we had come to expect of her. Normally when someone leaves the village they are quickly forgotten and we seldom hear from them again. Mostly they disappear without trace but for years afterwards Claudia continued to be much discussed, and reports of her activities filtered down to every level of village life.

'What on earth will that poor girl be able to do?' This was the question people asked of one another, and the concern was genuine. How would such an unworldly child be able to support herself and earn a living? Everyone blamed her parents, the unpopular Guy and Pandora, who had completely failed to prepare her for adult life.

They need not have worried because Claudia did very nicely, thank you. After going up to Oxford to read some obscure subject, duly getting her First, she joined a small firm that made reproduction musical instruments. Period instruments as they are called, the idea being to play baroque chamber music exactly as the composers of the day would have heard it themselves. She soon found this a crowded market place and sought a little more elbow room by going back in time.

To the twelfth century in fact, and she soon set up her own company making even older and weirder musical instruments. Princess Claudia was a perfectionist who had tremendous fun boiling up fish-heads to make authentic glue and chopping down rare trees so that the serpents and hautboys were exact replicas. Cathedral libraries were ransacked all over Europe to provide suitable material, after which she turned her attention to plundering medieval convents of their unguarded priceless manuscripts. Claudia knew a nice little earner when she saw one and wasn't fussy.

There being little in the way of musical notation in the twelfth century the researcher has considerable latitude in arranging and interpreting the music to best advantage. The industrious Claudia soon solved the problem by writing her own twelfth century music. It is a rich seam which she mines assiduously. People buy her recordings and flock to her concerts in ever increasing numbers.

Her concerts are beautifully stage-managed in a mocked-up Venetian chapel. Capped and gowned choristers warble away while the authentic instruments scrape, tootle, whine and drone in accompaniment. Kitsch it most certainly is but for some reason this particular form of artistic chicanery appeals strongly to the educated middle classes. Claudia is on home territory and targets her punters with unerring accuracy.

She was well and truly in business, and still is, alert to every opportunity for folding an honest dollar. All too often these days I tune in to one of the music programmes and know immediately from the doleful twang and jangle that yet another of her best-selling recordings is being played. Medieval music is a gold mine, and she quarries it rapaciously.

We are understandably proud of Claudia in Mardle and still count her as one of our own, even though she has never once returned to the village. She is now unlikely to do so from her villa in Crete, her colonnaded white-fronted house on New York's Brighton Beach, or her vineyard in the Loire valley.

The reason I am reminded of her now, and moved to write, is that a few minutes ago I heard my wife calling out to me urgently and supposed that the house must be on fire. I was upstairs at the time and rushed down only to find that she wanted me to watch something on television.

'It's the Princess,' Ruth explained, pointing to the screen. And sure enough there she was, being respectfully interviewed about her latest successful venture into ancient music. She still looked as if a good feed would do her good, and many of the village mothers would have itched to run a comb through her hair or give her face a wipe. They need not have worried because Claudia knew what was good for her and tickled the interviewer's tummy as skilfully as she had the villagers eating from her hand when she was a child.

Softly and exquisitely spoken, breathlessly persuasive, sweet little Claudia has her world by the goolies in a vicelike grip and never intends to let go. Successful parents have successful children so we were naive to suppose they had not prepared her for the hard knocks of a commercial world. She shakes the money tree every day of her life and never grows weary.

Perhaps one day I will send the Princess an invitation to perform at the village concert in December. If she could still play Schumann's *Kinderscenen* half as well as when she was ten I might even think about forgiving her for the capped and gowned choristers and the Venetian chapel.

32

Rich People Have Their Troubles Too

Few shepherds are talkative and the shepherd on the Beckles Estate is no exception. He makes it plain that he prefers his own company and always works alone. He never speaks unless spoken to, and sometimes not even then.

Nor has he ever been known to smile, still less to share a joke. He does not seem to need friends, which is just as well, as he doesn't have any. He answers to his trade name of 'Shep' and there must be many people who have never known his real name, even his fellow workers on the estate.

Shep has held the job for over twenty years. He looks after a lot of sheep and has a wide area of hillside to cover. He takes very little time off and puts in a long working day. He has a big four-wheel drive truck and two dogs that sit patiently in the back until he calls them down to help him. He operates from some old buildings away from the main farm and looks after his own equipment. He accepts only essential help and is taciturn to the point of rudeness. In spite of these shortcomings he is acknowledged to be good at his job. Whatever the weather or the state of the farming economy his flocks always make money for the estate so he is left alone to get on with it in his own way.

Shep is a man of striking appearance. He is tall and lean with pale blue eyes in a weather-beaten face. And if anyone does succeed in coaxing a word out of him he is betrayed at once by his accent, which is not that of a village farm worker. No one can help the way they speak and Shep's vowel sounds can only have been acquired at the most expensive of English public schools. No one needed a social science degree to work out that here was a man who had seen better days. This was certainly true in Shep's case, or Milo to give him his real first name.

Twice a year during the school holidays, once in the summer and once early in the new year, my mother took me to stay for a few days with my aunt, her sister. Her sister's husband managed a farm some thirty miles distant, which is a long way in the country since most people are concerned only with what goes on in their own village and take little notice of goings-on elsewhere.

My father told me that my uncle possessed that most enviable of all farm jobs, one with virtually no interference from the owners. These were members of a rich cosmopolitan family with residences in London and abroad. This was their English country house where they did a bit of shooting and kept a few horses, ideal for a family weekend when they wanted a change from London. Milo and his wife were the owners in residence and used it as their main home, although they were often away for weeks at a time. Milo was someone's spoilt son who had crashed a few racing cars before marrying into this wealthy family of European bankers and industrialists.

My aunt acted as housekeeper while they were away. When they were due back she would arrange a vase of flowers in every room, put out clean towels and make sure everything was to hand, including plenty of food. On their return Milo and his wife and their two small daughters would find it all unlocked and warmed up ready for them to walk in and continue their comfortable lives with scarcely a ripple of inconvenience.

I can remember the first time I was allowed to accompany my aunt into the big house. This was a country mansion, exquisitely furnished and maintained. I would have been about twelve years old at the time and followed my aunt in wonderment from room to room as she busied herself making up bunches of flowers. She hummed to herself as she worked so I guess that she enjoyed her privileged position and protected it carefully.

'Never intrude,' she instructed me. That was the golden rule. She set it all up for them and then disappeared from view. The family liked to be completely private and everyone who worked for them took care not only to keep out of their way but out of their sight as well.

I did not intrude but could never see enough of the house and visited it at every opportunity when my aunt allowed. It was the first such house I had ever seen from the inside. There were large pictures on every wall, beautiful carpets on the floor, polished tables and antique furniture in every room, a library of books with a ladder, a gun room, a billiard room and a music room with a grand piano. I never stopped marvelling that one house could contain so many wonderful things.

At the same time I can also remember the sense of shock I experienced. This was because I had listened from infancy to the advice doled out by my parents who took pride in coming from good yeoman stock where Jack was as good as his master, and usually better. They preached the virtues of sturdy independence, and the need to succeed by one's own honest endeavours. I was shocked because I had expected my aunt and uncle to be the same. Instead of which they were fawningly deferential.

Their eagerness to make life even more pleasant for Milo and his wife was matched only by their refusal to see anything wrong with the wealth and privilege this fortunate couple took for granted. At the first hint of criticism my aunt and uncle sprang to the family's defence, telling me that you had to understand rich people and how they led their lives.

'Rich people have their troubles too,' my aunt told me, but I did not believe her. It seemed to me that they led very agreeable lives with no money worries, and no need to work unless they felt like it, which wasn't very often.

Milo and his wife divided their time between her family's many establishments. They moved smoothly from the castle in Scotland to the villa in Lombardy, then to the bungalow in Barbados, and from there to the apartment in New York for a shopping spree. Plus lots of little impromptu holidays in between, mostly spent on the family yacht moored at Cannes. They still had to fit in their three weeks on the ski slopes, their champagne picnics at Royal Ascot and Goodwood, and their fox hunting in the winter.

Horses they took a bit more seriously. Milo's wife was a fearless rider to hounds and they liked to hunt during the season. She bred her own hunters and they travelled round in their own sumptuously appointed Mercedes horse box. It was a pastime they shared with equal enthusiasm, ignoring the protesters and determined to hunt abroad when it was finally banned in this country.

A scarlet coat does something for a man, particularly a tall athletic young man able to spring from the ground straight into the saddle. If someone called out to Milo he responded with a flashing smile, and the general opinion was that he had plenty to smile about. Before the hunt moved off he always had an admiring crowd clustered round him as he laughed and joked and patted the neck of his horse. Even the hunt saboteurs liked him, and they would exchange the banter appropriate to the occasion. Nor did the animal rights activists need to concern themselves unduly on behalf of the foxes. Milo's interest in the hunting scene was directed at quarry on two legs rather than four, and he certainly found them easier to catch.

The men who carried out the work on the farm were not quite so reverential as my aunt and uncle. When I was a little older and they knew me better they became less guarded in what they said in front of me. Their views were considerably more robust, despising their employers as idle and degenerate. About Milo himself they were slightly more divided. Yes, he was a playboy but he was also a sportsman. They admired him for that even if he was much too fond of the ladies for their liking. Puritanism is imprinted deeply into the rural subconscious. Those who work hard for a living frown at too much casual sex.

'Our young guvnor isn't fussy,' they told me, although not without some pride in his sexual exploits. 'That big horse box of theirs has seen some action. Not half it hasn't!'

This was because Milo could never resist the many young lady huntresses who shared the saddle with him. There were plenty of these to choose from and he took his pick. He pleasured as many of his companions of the chase as would allow it, and they mostly did.

'No good his wife complaining,' the tractor driver told me. 'Because she's just as bad if not worse. My ferrets have got better morals than those two.'

No doubt an extreme view but a well-aimed criticism even so. Reckless horse riding is a dangerous but thrilling pastime. Milo and his wife and their friends were young, they were rich, they were healthy and beautiful, the men just as much as the women. They were a hard drinking, hard riding set of young toffs with plenty of money, plenty of free time, and the inclination to enjoy themselves.

It worked because they operated within the bounds of a convention. They kept the promiscuity within their own circle, and more importantly within their own class. It was an unwritten code of conduct which they all understood and obeyed.

Until one day Milo breached it, with dire consequences. I heard the full story from my aunt and uncle who witnessed the confrontation at first hand. It made a deep impression on them at the time, and on me too when they told me about it at my next visit. It ended with them losing their comfortable jobs so for once they spoke freely and with much bitterness about Milo and his indiscretion.

'A barmaid?' cried his wife disbelievingly when she heard the news. 'A bloody barmaid! Someone tell me it isn't true.'

Unfortunately it was true, a transgression of their code for which Milo was to pay dearly. He had been unable to resist when this voluptuous young creature appeared in the village pub and began wiggling about behind the bar in a skin-tight mini-dress. His wife refused to overlook it, outraged by this breach of the social niceties.

'A slut of a barmaid,' she continued to wail. 'He's gone

too far this time.'

And so it proved. She mobilised her family and much to Milo's surprise and annoyance they insisted on throwing him out. He was rich but they were infinitely richer, and much better organised. The house was in trust to his wife, which made his position hopeless from the start. He could still not believe it. He had always thought that he and his wife had an understanding, that a little semen spilt here and there would never be sufficient reason for a permanent rift.

'What about the farm?' he asked her. 'The house? The children?'

But his wife's sensibilities had been offended and she would not be reconciled. 'You should have thought about all that before you started fucking the barmaid,' she told him candidly. And meant what she said, refusing to be talked round and insisting on punitive terms for the divorce.

With the result that he had soon lost everything, a devastating blow made worse by his refusal to accept defeat. In a competition to see who could hire the most expensive London lawyers he was always going to lose. He still fought on through the courts, borrowed more money and changed his advocate, but with the same outcome. Except that by this time he was completely ruined and deeply in debt.

So to help matters along he quarrelled with one of his wife's male relations and almost killed him in a fight, inflicting so much damage that he spent two years in prison as his punishment. There was a lesson in it for me, which I duly learned. I was sorry that I had not believed my aunt when she told me that rich people had their troubles too, and even sorrier that I had been jealous of Milo on whom the iron fist had fallen so heavily.

His wife sold the house and farm the moment she filed for divorce, and was never seen in this country again. She went to live in South Africa, taking the two small daughters with her, while Milo disappeared into prison many miles away. A new and more popular owner soon took up residence and Milo and his family were instantly forgotten. They had never bothered to befriend their workers, or engage with the villagers, so it was no surprise that local people were pleased to see the back of them and swiftly erased them from their communal history and memory as if they had never existed.

My aunt and uncle felt the same way and could not have cared less what became of Milo when he left prison. It would have been easy for him to give way to drink or despair but instead he took advantage of the service for the resettlement of offenders in order to make a new life for himself. Because he was seen to be making an effort the authorities found him employment as a farm worker, which was how he came to be living in one of the workman's cottages on our Beckles Estate. He was put to work with the sheep and a few years later, by a gradual process of transition, took over when the foreman shepherd retired. He was considered to be good at his job, and left alone to get on with it, since this was obviously what he preferred.

Twenty years have passed and he is still working out his penance.

Milo the playboy sportsman with the flashing smile disappeared while he was in prison and bore no resemblance to the taciturn man who came out. He morphed into the unsmiling Shep, a man without friends, tight-lipped and un-communicative to the point of rudeness. He still discourages all attempts at conversation, thus avoiding any risk of being questioned about his past. He speaks to no one and so is able to lead a solitary life away from curious or pitying eyes. What dark thoughts occupy his mind during all those hours when he is alone on the hills with his sheep no one but himself will ever know. Failure is bitter, but only for the man who experiences it.

However he has one great consolation. Through all his troubles the barmaid stood by him and was waiting at the gates to meet him when he came out of prison. They were married soon afterwards and she is still with him now in his shepherd's cottage. A comely and pleasant woman in middle age to whom he has not once been unfaithful.

33

Four Jolly Farmers and their Racehorse

My parents belonged to the Agricultural Society and liked to have their lunch in the Members Marquee on Show day. They took me with them and it was during one of these leisurely midday lunches that I first saw the four jolly farmers. I was ten years old at the time and it has been a lasting memory. It is difficult to judge age when you are ten but I can remember how big and strong the four farmers seemed to me. I know now that they would have been in their late twenties or early thirties and I guess they had been friends for most of their lives.

They were certainly jolly. Every time they met they advanced on one another with glad shouts, followed by much handshaking, back slapping and hearty laughter. People turned and smiled indulgently at the sight of these healthy young men enjoying one another's company so much. During the next eight years I saw them regularly because they were convivial fellows who would attend anything that was going, and liked their food. Sunday dinner at the Bear Hotel was the treat my parents awarded themselves to mark family birthdays or other special occasions, and if the four jolly farmers were there too you soon knew it because of their hearty laughter.

Eating was their favourite pastime. They were men of voracious appetite who were always first at table, calling loudly for the menu and the wine list. In appearance they were much alike, with big red healthy faces and huge muscular forearms. These were usually on show, for they were serious shirt-sleeved eaters. When they sat all four at table the outside world was excluded. They would sit talking for hours on end, ordering up fresh supplies of food and drink but never tiring of one another's company. When eventually they stopped eating the cigar smoke would billow instead, the whisky bottle would be passed round and the laughter would ring out louder than ever.

Next to food their big interest in life was horse racing, in their case the more affordable winter sport under National Hunt rules. They were never happier than on a windswept racecourse where they were a familiar sight to the regular race-goers in their caps and sheepskin jackets. Such was their pleasure in the sport that they clubbed together to buy a succession of racehorses.

This was a severe test of their friendship because they were bound to lose money. And did, but within reason they could afford to lose, and considered it money well spent on something they all enjoyed equally. If their horse and its jockey parted company at the first fence they would curse loudly, and then laugh. Their fellow race-goers considered there was not much wrong with men who could laugh when that happened, and rated them highly as good sports. Not that they lost all the time. They were shrewd businessmen with a good working knowledge of livestock and enjoyed some modest successes on the track which offset their losses. And when they had a winner they celebrated mightily.

'By God but our racehorse is in fine fettle,' one of them boasted in my hearing. This was at another of the agricultural society's annual dinners. By this time I was eighteen years old, and remember the occasion well, because it was the last outing I had with my parents before going to university. It was a rite-of-passage event that marked the end of my village upbringing and the start of adult life.

The four jolly farmers were on good form that evening. Eating and drinking hugely, and as always laughing. Always they laughed. But the unguarded remark about their racehorse being in fine fettle struck me as odd. It was immediately talked over by the others and I saw my father look at me and shake his head imperceptibly as a warning to say nothing.

The next day he took me aside and explained that the four

jolly farmers shared another interest. Next to eating, drinking and gambling on horses they enjoyed a little healthy fornication and would regularly desert their wives for a debauch in the red light districts of Hamburg or Amsterdam. However, my father told me, this was risky and expensive so they hit on an easier way. They clubbed together to buy a woman at home so that they did not need to go abroad for their extra-marital sex fun.

The four jolly farmers would have been about forty years old when they exchanged the pleasures of horse racing for the delights of the bedroom. Looking back on it I realise now that my father was acknowledging my adult status by explaining this dubious arrangement to me. It took place during the boom years so the four farmers were affluent enough to afford someone with a bit of class.

After a careful search they found themselves a widow whose husband had been a young army officer killed abroad. According to my father she was very regimental, with impeccable manners. They set her up in an apartment twenty miles away where they were unknown, and in a town large enough for such an arrangement to go unnoticed, whether taking their pleasures jointly or severally.

My father swore me to secrecy. 'It will end in tears,' he predicted confidently. 'Tears and disgrace, or worse. Murder, most likely. Men always end up quarrelling over a woman. They won't be satisfied with a quarter share each.' He chuckled, and obviously found it amusing. 'She must be costing them plenty. They haven't been near a race track for months, and never will again probably. Can't afford both!'

I had my own way to make in the world and after university and beginning full time teaching at the College I had little contact with rural affairs. It was some years before I encountered the four jolly farmers again. By this time I was in a relationship with Ruth and one day during the October half term I accompanied her to a farm sale where she was acting as clerk to the auctioneer. I had not been at the sale many minutes before I heard a familiar sound, the sound of four jolly farmers laughing. Four jolly farmers who went everywhere together and always succeeded in having a good time. They had been firm friends when I last saw them and apparently were still friendly and still went everywhere together. The four jolly farmers soon became bored with the auction and drifted outside to the refreshment caravan where some hot food was available. It was a cold day and the four big men, now in their fifties and somewhat larger round the middle than I remembered them, munched on burgers and drank soup from plastic mugs while continuing to laugh heartily.

'Where's the whisky?' they asked next, and soon homed in on the barn where the drinks table was set out. After this their bursts of laughter grew even louder, drawing indulgent smiles from their fellow farmers who had also taken time out from the sale for a bite to eat and a visit to the empty calving box that served as the Gents.

Any form of friendship is rare, enduring friendship rarer still. It was certainly a big surprise to me to see them still together and apparently still enjoying one another's company.

I continued to come across them at regular intervals, in the Members Marquee at the Show every year, for example. They spent most of the day occupying one end of a long table, eating, drinking and laughing. Always they laughed. However often they met, and they met frequently, it was like a joyful reunion with much handshaking and back slapping as though they had not seen one another for many years instead of a few days.

The College where I teach is in the old part of the town, laid out long before the invention of the motor car, so there is only a minimal amount of parking space. Most people find it quicker to walk from one of the town's large public car parks than waste time searching for a space. I have written earlier about College Close, saying that it is the best address our small market town has to offer. Visitors have to pass through a medieval archway to reach the curving spread of lovely old town houses overlooking the College playing fields. For those who seek privacy and elegance, and can afford it, College Close is the place to live.

Perhaps I am slow on the uptake but it puzzled me how often I saw one or other of the four jolly farmers in and around this old part of the town. I assumed they must be visiting a maiden aunt, and there several single ladies living on their own in the Close. Slow on the uptake is right because it finally dawned on me who they were visiting. Not only were they still together but they still had their same woman! And so it proved. At some stage in their relationship they must have felt sufficiently confident to bring her to the more convenient assignation venue of College Close. No doubt she had means of her own but would have appreciated some help from her friends to set up home in this much-prized secluded enclave.

It did not take me long to identify the woman in question and I have to admit that I looked at her with some curiosity. She was every inch the military widow and fitted easily into the town's polite society. She was even on sherry drinking terms with Amelia Ashby and her chum the retired arch-deacon who lived next door, but whose name I can never remember. Class will always tell, my mother used to say, and as always she was right, because the woman behaved with unshakeable respectability in a town where good manners are still valued.

My father was long since dead so I was not able to confront him indignantly and tell him that he was wrong in all his predictions. Whatever the odds against such a precarious arrangement lasting more than a few weeks before ending in acrimony or violence I should have taken them, because here it was still surviving amicably many years later.

The lady in College Close is a great traveller. She is always going or coming back from somewhere, not that this is unusual in a community where single elderly ladies are expected to have independent means. Where does she go? And who with? Any of her four husbands is my guess. To Ireland with one, to Jersey with another, I am sure they have it well worked out and take it in turns to have little holidays and honeymoons discreetly apart. In spite of their advancing years they still eat as heartily as ever, and I am sure are just as active sexually, being men of rude appetites.

Moving forward now to the present day I have to report that the four jolly farmers are finally showing signs of age. One has arthritis and walks with a stick, another has recently lost his wife, but they do not look out of place when I see them making their way slowly into the Close. The lady in question is older too, so no eyebrows are raised, not even in the alms-houses opposite.

It is a shame that we all have to grow old and forgo our pleasures one by one. As a teenager I found it heartening to see the four jolly farmers at table together, tucking in with their shirtsleeves rolled up, clinking their glasses and calling for second helpings. They lived life to the full and I for one would consider it a privilege if I could hear the laughter ring out just once more as it did when they were young and in their prime. I fear it never will.

Leaving aside any slight moral issues the five of them have stayed together for over thirty years. Any woman who has had four lusty lovers and kept them as friends afterwards has not missed out on much. To have ended up with a house in College Close overlooking the cricket pitch and the medieval chapel is to have played her hand well. I would rate it as a success story, and think it does them credit, all of them.

But especially the racehorse.

34

Waiting for the Wind

One dark windy night in January, in the early hours of the morning, we were woken by shouts and repeated rings at the doorbell. We put our heads out of the window and saw Tom Mundy in the drive. He was fully dressed and wearing a heavy coat with the collar turned up. He pointed, but did not need to explain why he had woken us.

The night sky was lit up by a lurid glare, and we could hear the sound of flames. A barn fire would have been bad enough, tons of valuable winter feed destroyed in half an hour. There were no barns in Beckles Lane, but there was an old cottage with a mother and her severely handicapped daughter inside.

Ruth and I dressed as quickly as we could, and followed Tom Mundy's example by putting on our warmest outdoor clothing, knowing that there was a bitterly cold wind blowing. Tom's wife Joan was waiting for us outside their house and we walked together down the narrow lane to the blazing cottage at the end. It was two o'clock in the morning and we were the only witnesses as Molly's cottage was destroyed by fire. We did not need to get very close because the flames lit up the scene. And fortunately for the safety of Tom Mundy's cottage the strong wind was blowing the huge streams of orange sparks in the opposite direction.

Even so we stood as close as we could by way of neighbourly support. I watched with Tom while our wives cried with their arms round one another. 'Poor Molly,' Joan sobbed. 'And poor little Polly. They can't possibly be alive in there, can they?'

'No,' her husband replied. We knew he spoke the truth.

Eventually some more people arrived, although not many.

It is an isolated lane where the houses cannot be seen from the village. In any case most people are asleep at two o'clock in the morning, rightly so in the depths of winter. The weather had been mild and wet since Christmas but a few days ago the temperature dropped to freezing, and a vicious wind sprang up from the north east. It strengthened steadily, a dry, icy, penetrating wind that fanned the flames like a bellows.

A house fire is compulsive viewing. As though transfixed we stood and watched as a section of the roof collapsed suddenly with a dreadful rending noise. It cascaded down into the bedroom and the crash was followed by a fountain of blood-red sparks. Once a fire takes hold it is unstoppable. It generates a fierce internal energy out of all proportion to the humble ingredients it devours.

Wind and fire. Nothing can resist them when they team up to destroy something. The arrival of a fire engine at the scene of a disaster is a riveting event, a vivid piece of live theatre with flashing lights and much running about and shouting. A drama in which we participated just by being there.

'How many inside?' the fire officer asked, and seemed relieved when told there were only two. 'Any children?' he asked next, grim-faced, and no one envied him the task of bringing out the incinerated bodies.

We stayed a long time although there was nothing we could do. 'Poor Molly,' Joan Mundy kept repeating. 'And poor Polly. What a terrible way to die.'

She was extremely upset, understandably so as she and Tom had been their nearest neighbours, the only people who had any regular contact with the two women. Ruth took her arm and we walked slowly back to the Mundy household where she made us hot drinks. We were all chilled to the bone after standing around in the icy wind.

'Not so terrible as all that,' Tom muttered gruffly as we sipped mugs of scalding hot coffee and munched on biscuits. 'People die pretty quick in a fire. They inhale the smoke and soon pass out. The girl wouldn't have known a thing about it. Or her mother.'

A merciful end. As I walked back with Ruth to our own house I could not help remembering the question she had asked me many times. 'What will become of poor Polly when her mother dies?' Now we knew.

When it was light I went back with Tom to wait until the bodies were found. Only the walls were left standing and it took the fire crew quite a while to remove the fallen roof timbers and tiles and what was left of the furniture.

'Cancer?' I enquired while we were waiting.

'Yes, cancer of the colon,' Tom replied. 'A nasty one, according to Joan. And too late for anything to be done.' Tom said that Molly had consulted his wife Joan in her capacity as the village nurse and she had arranged for her to see a specialist at the General Hospital. The diagnosis was not long in coming, and what Joan had feared it would be. No form of cancer holds out any hope of a quick cure and for Molly and her mentally retarded daughter it was a double death sentence. She had been offered a course of treatment but declined, opting for her own swift closure instead.

'She was waiting for the wind,' Tom said. Not that I needed to have it explained to me.

Over three weeks had passed since the hospital report, three weeks of steady rain and unseasonably high temperatures. Life is precious, even more so for the doomed perhaps. Molly would have made sure that every extra day she shared with her daughter was spent as happily as possible. Until one morning when she awoke to find that the weather had suddenly changed. Instead of mild drizzly rain there came a thin drying wind from the north east. A grim discovery.

As my friend the grave-digger has told me on more than one occasion, death is never easy. Molly must have put it off for two or three days before deciding that the house had dried out enough to burn quickly. We tried not to imagine her lying awake in bed listening to the wind. Waiting until it was time to come downstairs and begin the preparations for burning herself, her home, and her sleeping daughter.

One of the fire-fighters is Tom's nephew. He told us that

the charred bodies of the two women had been recovered from the same bed. They had died with their arms around one another and it was not possible to separate them.

As in life, so in death.

35

The Egg Man's Brother

I hope you remember the story about Eddie Pritchard, better known locally as the Egg Man. This story is about his younger brother, Clive Pritchard. Although in appearance the two brothers are similar, both being bald in the same leathery sort of way, they are not at all alike in temperament. Clive is also a farm owner but even in these troubled times for the agricultural industry he remains the most amiable of men. He is well-disposed to the world in general and has never suffered from the mental anguish both real and imagined that beset his brother Eddie.

When writing about the Show a few chapters ago I described Clive and his wife Trixie, and promised to say more about them and their two French poodles. This is it. Clive and Trixie are happily married, they go about together, and they believe in enjoying themselves and having fun. The collapse in farm prices which so demoralised the industry and brought countless farmers to the brink of suicidal despair did nothing but good for Clive Pritchard.

As an easy-going sort of chap he would never have roused himself to change his way of life voluntarily. But change was forced on him, as it was on all other farmers confronted with some hard choices. Farming was out of favour – with the press and media, with the government, and more importantly with the public. Pesticides, subsidies, cruelty, disease and general bad practice were held against all farmers whether guilty or not. They had to change their ways, and most were either unwilling or unable to do so.

Not Clive Pritchard though. Never one to be daunted by a challenge he soon found other ways of making money from his land and his farm buildings. Diversifying as it is called in agrispeak, but as a result he has fared better than most other farmers in these unhappy times. In one field he has a holiday caravan park which is full all the year round. In another he runs a weekly clay pigeon shoot where he hires out guns and sells cartridges at a profit. Pick-Your- Own strawberries and raspberries takes care of another field, and in his biggest field he grows grass seed, both proper crops requiring considerable expertise.

More ambitiously he converted some barns into business and storage units, he built some stables and set up a horse livery business, and in his old pig-house he grows mushrooms successfully. This is a specialist crop with a high failure rate but Clive applied his mind and overcame the difficulties. He dammed a stream where he rears fingerling trout, he advertises good quality turf, a commodity always in demand, and somehow contrives to conjure a regular income from all these precarious enterprises.

He has had his failures along the way but being possessed of a resilient nature he just shrugged them off and tried the next thing that occurred to him. Clive is endlessly ingenious when it comes to different ways of making money. He refers to it as ducking and diving, which sums it up accurately, since he will abandon any of his pet schemes overnight if they stop bringing in the cash, and will do so without a moment of regret.

Clive is therefore a modern farmer. He is resourceful, opportunist, skilled at drawing up business plans to bamboozle experts, and at charming money out of bank managers. Venture capital is available if you know where to get it, and how to apply, and he always does. Because of the shameful way that farmers and the countryside have been treated in recent years he has no scruples when there is a grant to be applied for, or a subsidy to be claimed. He sees it as fair game, and is unrepentant.

His wife Trixie is equally versatile. She had her own flock of sheep when Clive married her but retrained as a chiropodist and now includes reflexology and aromatherapy among her accomplishments. The old milking parlour, long disused and smelling strongly of cows and disinfectant, was converted into her salon. It is now snugly warm and sweetly scented, decorated in soothing colours and padded out with the softest upholstery imaginable.

Anger management and stress counselling are her latest cash earners and between all these various occupations she is kept busy all day long. You would have to say that she was a good match for her husband being equally sunny and sociable in temperament. She has the happy knack of getting on with people and appearing to enjoy her work, an attractive trait, and not very common. Trixie dresses smartly and expensively, always wearing the latest in middle-aged chic, and is a great favourite with her clients, women as well as men.

Between them Clive and Trixie make a reasonable living, even though it is not the same as proper farming, which is what they would much prefer. Personally I think they would miss the constant hustle and bustle their new way of doing business has created, and will now never be able to return to conventional farming, even if economic conditions made it possible. All day long Trixie's clients come and go in the tarmac driveway leading to the farm, as do the pony girls from the livery stables. Salesmen and delivery vans jostle with the people working in the business units. This stream of visitors never stops and contrasts favourably with other farms in the area, those which were unable to make the transition, and have become gloomy and isolated places as the depression deepens.

Clive and Trixie also have a project which they run together, and this is a pricey Bed and Breakfast, using their farmhouse. The accommodation and the food are both excellent so the guests do not complain at paying more than they might elsewhere. When the B&B is in full swing Clive and Trixie move out of their bedroom and spend the summer months in a caravan. In recent years the holiday period has extended fore and aft to such an extent that they live outside for months on end. If there is money to be earned they do not complain.

They have a son living at home and he keeps the farming side of the business ticking over. This preserves the hope that one day they can resume their normal line of work, always assuming a miracle happens and the economic situation perks up sufficiently to make it possible. Until the recovery comes their fields still have to be fenced and drained, grass has to be cut, hedges have to be trimmed, gates mended, tiles replaced, rabbits and foxes and other pests and predators kept under control. In addition to carrying out this routine maintenance Clive's son is following in the family footsteps by setting up in business as a farm contractor, buying his own machinery and hiring himself out by the day.

Clive is often invited to give talks to farming groups about his diverse business enterprises, such as charging townies money to come and watch lambs being born, or just to sit behind the wheel and drive a tractor up and down a field. They pay money to do that? They surely do, and Clive trousers it without a qualm. The tax position is rather tricky when defining what is or is not a farming activity but there are no flies on the Egg Man's brother. He knows all the dodges and willingly passes them on.

Such as tips on portion control, and how to buy muesli and quinoa in economy catering sacks for the B&B. How often can you get away with not changing sheets and pillow cases? What do you do about people who turn up with unsuitable pets, or unruly children? Clive always has the answers, and can explain the legal position. It may not be pukka farming but it will do until the next upturn comes along.

'We need a nice war,' Clive says wistfully. 'A big, proper war, preferably a world war. We're just about due, aren't we?'

Clive is a blazer man. When he takes off his overalls and seeks his pleasure he likes to dress smartly. Not feeling comfortable in a buttoned-up collar he has taken to wearing a cravat instead of a tie with his blazer. Unfortunately he is either colour blind or completely lacking in colour sense. For some reason he prefers pink shirts, which would be all right except that his favourite cravat has orange, green and purple stripes. Mercifully he is spared this migrainous clash of colours himself, it is only those sharing his stretch of the golf club bar who have to wince and turn away.

His wife Trixie no longer has time for cooking. Since the new way of life began they have eaten their main meal out every evening. There is no shortage of bars or eateries and they patronise them all in turn. Much of the money Trixie earns in her salon she spends on clothes and cosmetics. Elaborately coiffed, jewelled and beringed she is a good match for her husband with his blazer and cravat. They are a lively couple who do not dress to go unnoticed.

Accompanying them everywhere are their his-and-her French poodles, one white, one black. Both dogs are extravagantly clipped and adorned with fancy red-leather collars. Every Sunday for many years Clive and Trixie have eaten their Sunday dinner at the Bear Hotel. Their arrival causes much commotion. Led by the poodles Clive and Trixie make a grand entry and for the two hours they stay they are the centre of attention, with much banter and bonhomie all round. They know the staff and many of the customers, mostly regulars like themselves, and are greeted everywhere by name, including the dogs.

Clive's is the white poodle, by name Fido. On Fido's collar is a shiny nameplate giving his name as 'Phaideau.' Clive is a former pupil at the College and not above making this heavy-handed play on words.

Because he and Trixie enjoyed eating out so much he began to contribute a weekly restaurant column to the Herald. On and off it ran for several years and has to be counted a success. 'Trencherman Eats Out' was not the snappiest strapline on the Leisure and Pleasure page but it led to some free wining and dining, just as the local newspaper benefited from the extra advertising that resulted, so everyone was happy.

However dire the meal or undrinkable the wine Trencherman still managed to enthuse about the decor or the attentiveness of the service. He sprinkled praise like stardust and for many years afterwards his enthusiastic comments continued to be quoted in hotel brochures, as in *'Trencherman of the Herald particularly liked our coq au vin menu'*. In truth Trencherman and his wife liked anything eatable at the end of a long working day, and liked it even more when it was free, and it often was.

Eventually Clive tired of writing his weekly column. Although not until he had extended his reports to include fish-and-chip shops, takeaways, and insanitary burger wagons parked in roadside lay-bys. Even filling-station microwaves used to heat up pies were given the Trencherman imprimatur. Clive Pritchard was too kindly a man ever to say anything bad about anyone and his column gave innocent pleasure to the Herald's readership for many years.

In a town with a great many clubs and social organisations there are plenty of honorary secretaries desperately in search of speakers. Clive will always oblige when asked and in consequence is recommended from one group to the next. Invited to address the Women's Institute recently he launched enthusiastically into a talk on badger gassing, his scheme of the moment. Not quite what they had in mind.

He is also a willing after-dinner speaker, although if you have heard him once you could give the speech yourself next time, complete with all the dismal jokes and one-liners. Ruth's favourite is the one about the sermon using the text of the Widow's Mite (Luke 21.2), and the verger's advice. 'Don't waste your breath, vicar. There's only two widows come to church regularly and there's no 'might' about it. They're both happy to oblige.' Not many people get as much fun out of life as the Egg Man's brother. 'Why should anyone object to vicars with knickers?' he wonders aloud, continuing the religious theme with his thoughts on women priests. 'Or without knickers, come to that!' And so on.

It is harmless enough but he always gets a laugh and plenty of more polished speakers fail to do that. 'I do conjuring tricks as well you know,' he tells his audience. Who, like me, have mostly heard it all before. Including the one about the salesman with a new brand of embalming fluid, the one that stops you feeling quite so stiff the next day. Personally I always find it hard to smile at that one. Clive may not be very good but he is not the worst after-dinner speaker in the world and we all give him a clap for doing his best.

In spite of these shortcomings he is surprisingly public spirited. Everyone in the district owes him a debt of gratitude for his efforts in obtaining the town a bypass. Yes, virtually single-handed. Years of patient council negotiation failed to solve the traffic problem so the Egg Man's brother applied his mind and did it for them.

He won the day by making a nuisance of himself rather than by the force of intellectual argument. Clive was some-what short in that department but to make up for it he was imaginative, and by nature, mischievous. This scratch-and-sniff brew of amiable eccentricity, peasant cunning, lateral thinking, opportunism, persistence, civic pride and local knowledge soon obtained our small market town its bypass.

Actually what we got was a ring-road system with four big roundabouts, north, east, south and west. In other words a bypass on the cheap but it was sufficient to ease the traffic congestion to the point where it ceased to be a problem. And it certainly was a problem when it used to wind its way miserably through the town centre.

Clive did it by creating havoc at peak times. At weekends and public holidays throughout the summer months he would emerge from his farm on a tractor. Not his new speedy tractor but an old museum piece kept for sentimental reasons. This belched out black smoke and chugged along at a steady five miles an hour. Behind him he towed a trailer stacked high and wide with bales of straw so that the ever-lengthening convoy queued up at the rear could not see past.

This was great fun and snarled up the traffic nicely. He would pass through the town and then on the return journey have a breakdown. His favourite place was the narrow river bridge in the town centre, creating a traffic situation that needed the best brains of the county police force to sort out. It is surprising what one ingenious and fun-loving man can do to disrupt the traffic and after several months of this the authorities capitulated and agreed to act. Clive was genuinely sorry when the transport department bowed to the inevitable and made funds available for the ring-road system, finally putting an end to his weekend fun and games. I would rate it as a significant civic achievement for which the council officers naturally took the credit.

Nor was this the sum total of his contribution to the common weal. Five years ago there was a shortage of magistrates. Clive modestly answered the appeal for local worthies to put themselves forward and has graced the local bench ever since. Clive is an admirable choice. Saloon-bar middle England could produce no better.

He is without doubt the most lenient magistrate in the history of the town, if not the entire kingdom. He never fails to be moved by the hard luck stories put forward in mitigation. He can be heard murmuring sympathetically at every mention of an unhappy childhood while the police witnesses grind their teeth in fury. The local offenders consider themselves lucky and thrice times blessed when their cases are dealt with by our indulgent and sunny-natured local farmer.

Clive is touchingly proud of being a magistrate and will always find a way of inserting it into the conversation. Just in case you did not know, or had temporarily forgotten, that he was the local lawgiver and upholder of moral standards. For once he takes something seriously. Jokes about the magistracy are considered bad form.

'I'm sitting,' he will say by way of apology and explanation if you want him to do something. He has an impressive ritual of producing his pocket diary, putting on his gold half-glasses, checking the date and then shaking his head. 'Sorry, Alan. Can't make it. I'm sitting.'

My advice to anyone unfortunate enough to be summoned

to appear in front of the beaks in our local Court House is firstly to hope that it is a day when justice is being dispensed by the Egg Man's brother. And secondly to have their hard luck story ready, and to make sure it is a good one.

36

The Boy Jack Made Drunk

A generous benefactor is a prized resident in any community and we are fortunate in having Jack Hignett to live among us. In his youth he had been a famous rugby player and he not only possessed wealth of his own but had married a young and pretty wife who had inherited a large amount of family money. No one could be jealous because they were a friendly and hospitable couple who spread their money around. Between them they supported all our local good causes. My wife Ruth was pleased because they were sponsors for the Show and I was pleased because Jack Hignett supported the College rugby team and often turned up to watch them play.

Every time we met he never failed to remind me of the occasion, many years ago now, when I had called on him to deliver a parish magazine. This was an incident I would have preferred to forget but Jack was amused by it and always laughed and put a big arm round my shoulders when he told the story. I was eighteen at the time and waiting to go to university. Someone had forgotten to deliver the small church magazine to their house and asked me as a favour to deliver it for them, knowing that it would not take me many minutes on my bike.

I did so willingly, glad for something to distract me during these last few anxious weeks. I had been allocated a room in a hall of residence in central London and found the waiting time passing slowly in a mixture of excitement and apprehension. My destination for the magazine delivery was a lovely old house with a wide curving gravel drive. The Chantry is on the parish boundary between Mardle and Long Beckles and I would have liked to look at the view for a moment, the house being on the slope of Beckles Hill. I didn't get the chance because as soon as I came to a stop I heard a voice calling me round to the back of the house.

It was a man's voice and I found him slumped in a big cane armchair on a wide terrace overlooking the large garden. I realised that he had heard my tyres on the gravel so I propped my bike against the wall and handed over the parish magazine.

'Must be for the wife,' he said, throwing it aside. He indicated a chair. 'Take the weight for a few minutes. Tell me all about yourself.' He held out an enormous hand. 'I'm Jack Hignett by the way. What's your name?'

If there is one thing rather than another that pleases a student of eighteen it is to be treated as a man rather than a large schoolboy. I took immediately to Jack Hignett for this reason. I told him that my name was Alan Ablewhite, that my parents were farmers, and that I was waiting to go to university.

He said, 'You look as if you could use a beer. Stay there and I'll fetch a couple of tinnies from the fridge.'

It was a roasting hot day and I was certainly in need of a drink after my cycle ride, most of it uphill. I would have preferred fruit juice to beer but Jack Hignett was not the sort of man you could argue with or mess around. After he told me his name I remembered that he was once a famous international rugby player.

'Best Number Eight we ever had,' my father told me later when he asked where I had spent the afternoon. 'Didn't miss much in the line-out either. Super chap.'

Jack Hignett would have been fifty years old when I delivered the magazine that hot summer afternoon, so his rugby playing days were long over. I watched appalled as he began the process of heaving himself from his chair and beginning the short journey indoors. He was a huge man but I had never seen anyone quite so unhealthy in all my life.

After much grunting he struggled to his feet then hobbled slowly into the house, returning as promised with two cans of beer. On reaching his chair he flopped backwards with a sigh of relief, panting heavily. Sweat poured down his face. It was a hot day but not nearly hot enough to justify all that sweat after so little effort. As he settled into his chair I watched in horrified fascination as his paunch began to settle also, sliding slowly downhill until it came to a stop against his belt. There it piled up in a great soft mound, then spread itself oozily on either side.

'You'll have a great time in London,' he assured me as we sipped our beer. He had already asked me where I was going to university and enthused about London, although mainly I regret to say about its low life and the availability of women. He told me some stories of the great times he and the rest of the team had enjoyed after matches against the other London clubs. 'You don't play rugby?' he queried disbelievingly. 'Man, you don't know what you're missing.'

Well, I suppose I would be missing the injuries for one thing and from the way he hobbled I guessed his entire skeleton had been battered so much that every joint had been weakened beyond repair. He had played several seasons too many, and judging from his squashed nose, his crumpled ears and slightly slurred speech, far too often without his scrum-cap also. He was the wreck of a man and I did not need to be told that he got through quite a few tinnies in the course of a day.

It got worse. He lit a cigar and began inhaling the smoke deeply, blowing it out in tremendous gusts. Here was a man killing himself before my very eyes! He was breaking every health rule in the book and I did not see how he could possibly survive for much longer. He continued to pant and sweat while lying back in his cane armchair smoking and drinking beer.

Looking back on it I guess that he was bored and glad of my company. Having been provided with an audience he told me still more anecdotes about his rugby playing days, not only the testicle-squeezing antics in the scrum but the fun and games in the pubs and clubs afterwards. I was equally pleased to be distracted and listened indulgently as he told me lurid stories about the naughty ladies they hired, and how they and the team entertained one another back at the hotel.

Every twenty minutes or so he would struggle to his feet again and waddle painfully into the house, returning with two more ice-cold cans of lager. I did not like to refuse and it turned out to be a long afternoon. Every time I said I had to leave he insisted on just one more little tiddly, by which time my head was swimming. I can remember laughing loudly at his stories.

I was saved by the arrival of his wife. The gravel scrunched as her brand-new silver Mercedes came to a stop. She jumped out, waved and smiled brightly, then skipped up the two or three steps on to the terrace and kissed her husband on the forehead.

'This is Alan,' he introduced me. 'Lucky bugger is off to London. Wish it was my turn again. Students have all the fun.'

His wife's name was Gemma and she was not only athletic and pretty but much younger than her husband, by at least fifteen years at a guess. She began darting about tidying up, removing the ash tray full of cigar butts and gathering up the drink cans. She smiled at me kindly, telling me not to move. She said sternly to her husband, 'I hope you haven't been telling Alan any of your rude stories. He's going to university to study, not to spend all his spare time in the rugby club bar. Isn't that so, Alan?'

'Gemma is the Lady Captain this year,' he informed me proudly. 'Of the Golf Club, that is.' He held out his hand to her. 'Did you win today, darling?'

'But of course!' She turned to me and said, 'I would never have dared come home if I had lost. Jack likes my winning ways, don't you, sweetheart?'

She gave him another kiss and I have to say that she seemed very fond of her husband in spite of the difference in their ages. After growing up in a village as quiet as Mardle I was greatly taken with the wealthy and worldly-wise Hignetts, certainly by the delectable Gemma Hignett whose perfume I could smell from the other side of the wide terrace. She was wearing white trousers and a navy blue summer jacket with gold buttons. She was as dashing and nimble as her husband was obese and sluggishly unhealthy. The cumulative effect of the alcohol was making me amorous. I was smitten, and followed her lissom movements with spaniel eyes.

'This is going to be the last one before dinner,' she informed her husband when he asked her to fetch him yet another frosty. 'And no, Alan is not going to join you. I think you've given him quite enough to drink already. Or a cigar,' she added when he offered it to me. 'Young men have quite enough bad habits without you starting them on new ones.'

She treated me to a little wink and a smile before disappearing through the open doors and returning with the can of beer. I watched her with the same fascination I had watched her husband, although for exactly the opposite reason. His panting and sweating filled me with distaste while his wife's short brisk dainty steps as she bustled about made me more amorous than ever.

Jack insisted on seeing me off, grunting with the effort of heaving himself out of his wickerwork armchair, then puffing and blowing as he accompanied me to the drive where my bicycle was still propped against the wall of the house. Gemma came too, thanking me for delivering the magazine.

The next thing I knew she was helping me up from the gravel. Having swung my leg over the saddle I had promptly fallen off the other side, and lay there giggling helplessly. 'Oh Jack, you've made him drunk,' she scolded. 'He's only a boy from the village, he lives on one of the farms. You should be ashamed of yourself.'

So a somewhat ignominious end to my visit but I managed to arrive home and soon afterwards made it safely to London, which was just as exciting as Jack Hignett had predicted it would be. I soon forgot about him but from time to time memories of the charming Gemma rose to the surface. She had put her arms round me to help me up and check that nothing was broken. The lungful gush of heady scent and feminine breath I experienced has stayed with me ever since.

Lady golfers are not all muscular big hitters. Firmly lodged in my memory was my first sight of the lively Gemma as she jumped out of her car and skipped up the terrace steps to kiss her husband. She was blithely happy and deft as she tidied away the drink cans and Jack's cigar butts. So it came as a pleasant surprise some years later when Ruth asked me to visit the Hignetts in connection with the Show. They had been long-term sponsors she reminded me, as well as generous contributors to every good cause in the village.

Then she told me the bad news, lowering her voice appropriately. 'Poor Mrs Hignett is in a bad way. Not long to live, I'm afraid.'

'Surely you mean poor Mr Hignett?'

'Jack? No, he's still going strong. Gemma is the one who is ill.'

'She is?'

'Leukaemia,' Ruth informed me, spreading her hands in a gesture of hopelessness. 'In and out of hospitals and clinics for the last two years. But I think they have done all they can for her now.'

My second visit to The Chantry was a less happy occasion than the first. It was dark winter instead of high summer, and indoors rather than on a sun-drenched terrace. I was invited through into their kitchen dining alcove where Gemma Hignett was sitting at the table.

'She likes it in here,' Jack whispered to me. 'Warmer for her.' His wife sat motionless on her chair, her hands clasped under the table. At first sight she did not look much different. She was beautifully made up and expensively dressed, with her hair nicely done, and from across the table I could still smell her perfume. But instead of darting from place to place with little birdlike steps she was keeping completely still. A profound and saddening change.

Hardly moving a muscle she whispered, 'You're the boy Jack made drunk.'

'Yes.'

'You fell off your bike and I helped you up. That was funny, wasn't it?'

'Yes.'

'And now you're finished with university and teaching at the College?'

'Yes.'

'Do please sit down and have a cup of coffee with us. Or a glass of something if you prefer.'

'He didn't come on his bike today,' Jack said, laughing as he clamped a big arm round my shoulder. 'Better have coffee, old chap. Mustn't get you squiffy a second time.' He treated me to a conspiratorial nudge, briefly removing a bottle of whisky from the cupboard beside his chair to show me what he was drinking himself. He gave a boyish grin. 'No need to look so worried. I'm not driving anywhere today. Or riding a bike!'

His physical condition was no worse than when I had last seen him, although this was not saying much. But at least he was still around, not something I would have bet money on. He still panted after the slightest exertion and his vast sagging paunch would have fallen to his knees without the support of the thick leather belt he wore to hold it back.

I suppose it was the unfairness that troubled me, as it must have concerned others who knew them better than I did – the paradox that he should have made it into his sixties while his delightful little golf-playing slimming-club wife was waiting to die. She had that fixed empty stare I have only seen a few times but which I guess priests and doctors see all the time and know it for what it is. She was staring death in the face and did in fact die not long afterwards. In great pain I regret to say, and the foreknowledge of this showed in her frozen smile and frightened eyes.

'It's been a bloody frustrating few years,' Jack told me when I visited him again a few months after her death. 'I know the doctors tried, but it was hopeless from the start, they might as well not have bothered. She would have died just the same whatever they did.'

'That's how it is sometimes.'

'We kept hearing about new treatments and wonder drugs. None of them worked.'

'I suppose there are some things it will always be impossible to cure.'

'I was bloody fond of her. You know that, don't you?'

'She was fond of you, too.'

'Keep coming to see me, Alan. I don't intend to get married again but it's going to be bloody lonely on my own. I miss her all the time.'

Love affairs come in all shapes and sizes and do not necessarily end with death. I kept my promise and called on Jack once or twice a year, and on occasion met him at a function, and in spite of his bulk and lack of mobility he never turned down the chance of a big feed and a few little tiddlies. The cigars he smoked seemed even bigger than on our first meeting, and he still inhaled with long greedy gulps. A healthy lifestyle it wasn't but many years have passed, and as Ruth frequently reminds me, Jack Hignett is still going strong.

'Fancy that!' she said recently when she opened the mail one day and held up a card. 'We've been invited to Jack's eightieth birthday party. Organised by the Rugby Club. A dinner.' She frowned and reconsidered. 'It will be a boozy affair, you can be sure of that.'

'A very popular man, our Jack. The cricketers will be there as well. And the golfers. Should be a good evening.'

'Rowdy as well as boozy,' Ruth predicted with a sigh. 'But we shall have to go, he has been very generous to the Show. Jack can always be relied for a donation.'

So, more than thirty years after our first meeting, I found myself at Jack Hignett's eightieth birthday celebrations. Sportsmen for miles around had answered the call, and with their wives and guests made it a sell-out dinner.

I have to report that Jack was in good form on the night. True, he walked in slowly with the aid of two sticks but put away a good dinner and a couple of bottles of wine. Called on to speak he struggled to his feet, just as he had done on that first meeting when I was eighteen years old. I braced myself for some sentimental reminiscences, the usual valedictory fare to accompany the coffee and mints, but not for the first time where Jack Hignett was concerned I was proved wrong.

His speech was neither rambling nor unduly nostalgic but full of good jokes, compliments to all the right people, and contained some shrewd comments on the state of the modern game of rugby and the direction it was taking. He spoke a lot of good common sense and was obviously well informed, not just about his sport but also about the wider world in general. It was a polished performance that thoroughly merited the loud applause it received.

While he was speaking I could not help remembering that hot afternoon on the terrace when I had viewed his grossly unhealthy body with distaste. Watching him pant and sweat had almost made me feel ill myself. Cigar smoke and booze, not the healthiest of diets, yet here he was again, and as Ruth often reminded me, still going strong.

He must have been in better shape when he persuaded Gemma to marry him but their affection for one another was plain to see, even to an eighteen year old country boy with a swimming head after drinking too much beer. And although I had often been slightly irritated by his insistence on reminding me of the incident every time we met I realised at that moment with a poignant stab of insight that he was remembering his wife rather than me, and how she had skipped and danced around the terrace on that hot afternoon, elated after her win at the golf club.

Had anyone told me that Jack would outlive his much younger wife by so many years I would not have believed it likely, or even possible. Yet such is the mystery of life, or rather death, and I would like to think that I had learned my lesson. Which is not to make hasty judgements about people, and certainly never to predict which of us will die and which of us will live a little longer. Because for all of us it is the great unknown.

37

Knee Deep in Feathers

Every year Tom Mundy's daughter Valerie takes a week of her annual leave to help prepare the Christmas poultry. She has made a life for herself away from the village and is rarely seen except for this annual appearance. She followed her mother into the nursing profession and has a senior position in a London teaching hospital.

My neighbours Tom and Joan Mundy would dearly have loved to be grandparents but their daughter Valerie was too keen on pursuing her nursing career to risk the distraction of having children. Since this is the same reason why Joan had only one child herself she cannot complain, although now that she and Tom are older it was a decision she regrets. They are proud of Valerie and try hard not to sorrow over the absence of grandchildren, but still feel it as a loss.

When Valerie and her father get together they tell jokes and behave more like children than adults. From the moment they start work on the poultry it is one long laugh from beginning to end. Almost anything will set them off and the peals of merry laughter last the whole week. Joan also sets the week aside to help Tom with the birds. She is quieter by nature but loves this annual family reunion and joins in the laughter.

I suppose it is less fun if you happen to be a turkey but only town people are sentimental about farm animals and the three Mundys are soon hard at work. It is a production line. Tom does the killing and legs up the birds from nails in the rafters. Val expertly removes the feathers without a single blemish or tear of the skin, while Joan cleans and trusses them ready for the oven.

It is always instructive to watch experts at work and I usually call round a couple of times to talk to Valerie and ask about her life in London. And to find out her views on the current state of the national health service, always worth hearing. It is nice to see a family that gets on well together. Mother and daughter both wear brown housecoats and head-scarves, and they chatter away far into the night. To keep themselves awake they drink endless mugs of strong coffee and munch on chocolate biscuits. Nurses are no strangers to unsocial hours and can work round the clock if they have to, although not always knee deep in feathers.

Once having started they need to keep going until all the geese, turkeys, ducks, guinea fowls and cockerels have been trussed and floured ready for collection or delivery. Tom does not have a big freezer so they need to work fast and pray for cold weather. A mild spell is bad news for the independent poultry-man who has of necessity to start proceedings well ahead of the big day.

It is a team effort and they have always taken it seriously as a family business. After all that work they are pleased to gather in the money for there is a considerable outlay on food as the birds reach table weight. Tom's regular customers know that he prefers cash, and mostly that is what he is given. The end result is superb, repeat orders are taken as a matter of course, and Valerie books her Christmas holiday well in advance.

I have made no secret of my admiration for the Mundys, husband and wife, who if anything are busier than ever. What impresses me is not that Tom and Joan are hard at work from the moment they get up until they go to bed but that they are not aware of being at work, in fact seem not to know the difference between what is work and what isn't. They have yet to discover what is meant by leisure time and the fact that they earn money from their labours is incidental. They both bustle cheerfully all day long and the moment they finish one job they start the next. In this way they get through a tremendous amount of work without seeming to notice.

Every village should have someone like the Mundys. Many of the older people in the village prefer Joan to the doctor, particularly where feminine ailments are concerned. A local woman with a lump in her breast might well seek Joan's opinion first before making the fateful visit to the surgery. Women whose babies she has delivered now book her for the confinements of their daughters. At the other end of the facts-of-life cycle she is first choice to lay out the dead, and does so knowing that her husband will go along to the churchyard later and start digging the grave.

Although Tom and I often visit one another's houses, and usually have a drink of some kind, we rarely invite one another for a sit-down meal with our wives. So it was something of a surprise when he came to see us one December evening and asked if we would share their Christmas dinner with them this year. It had been a difficult year for several reasons, beginning with the fire in January which had resulted in the deaths of our neighbours Molly and Polly. Tom said that Valerie would be helping them with the poultry as usual but would have to drive back to London on Boxing Day.

We guessed there was a reason why we had been invited but could not work out what, and agreed to be patient until it was revealed. The three Mundys were hearty eaters so we skipped breakfast to leave room for the generous helpings we knew we would be given. We joined them for their Christmas dinner at two o'clock in the afternoon but it was a leisurely affair and we were still finishing off with nuts and wine long after it grew dark.

Our curiosity was satisfied when Tom and Joan said they had something they wanted to show us. They led the way into their sitting room and on a small side table were two plastic containers with lids. I had seen similar containers before and knew what they were.

'Yes, ashes,' Tom said. 'I went back and collected them from the crematorium last January.' He pointed to their labels in turn. 'This one has Molly's ashes. This one has Polly's.'

'Where did you have in mind to scatter them?' Ruth asked

him.

'Joan and I waited until now so that Valerie could be included. She was very fond of Polly.'

Valerie nodded. 'Yes, I was. Such a happy little thing.'

Tom said, 'We thought that you and Ruth would like to come too, Alan.'

'Yes, of course. We would love to be included. Where did you have in mind?'

'We couldn't decide. Do you have any ideas?'

Ruth had the answer. 'I know exactly where I should like to scatter their ashes. They loved that path coming down off the hill, the one we can see from our bedroom window.'

Joan nodded in agreement. 'We know where you mean, we've seen them there too, many times. Yes. The ideal spot.'

Valerie said, 'I have to go back to London early tomorrow morning. Do you think we could do it as soon as it gets light?'

Which we did. Early next morning we trudged in silence up the long field-edge path down which we had seen Molly and Polly walk so many times from the windows of our house. Tom carried one of the urns and I carried the other. We were fortunate with the Boxing Day weather which was cold but dry, with pale December sunshine. It was a solemn occasion and we were in a suitably sombre mood.

We came to a stop when we were high enough up to look back down over the village. Tom removed the lids and we took it in turns to scatter the ashes of mother and daughter along the path, mingling them so that they could be as together as possible.

When the urns were empty we embraced one another in an instinctive gesture. Ruth and Joan wept a little, for all of us it was an emotional occasion. Together we marked the closure of Molly's tragic life and celebrated the happiness she had shared with her daughter. I think we were saddened to realise that the five of us were the sum total of those who had ever cared about Molly and Polly, who had grieved over their deaths, and who would remember them for the rest of our days.

Long after the event I still seem to see them, always when my mind is preoccupied with other things. Without warning their distinctive silhouettes will loom out of the headlamp beam as I drive home on a winter evening. Cloaked and hooded, leaning forward as if battling against wind and rain, they are the ghostly apparitions of two women who might have lived here a year or a century or two ago. I pass them by almost before my eyes have registered their presence so that I cannot be sure whether I have actually seen them, or just imagined them, because I saw them so often in the past.

I see them in the summer too, again when I am least expecting them. I pull open the bedroom curtains and there they are, just as they always were, ambling without haste as they begin their long slow descent of the field-edge path where we scattered their ashes. The younger of the two women keeps stopping to pick flowers, poppies her favourite, and white marguerite daisies, holding them up to show us when she passes the house.

And in my head I still hear Ruth's heartfelt words. 'What will become of poor Polly when her mother dies?'

38

Nothing More to Prove

Observe the man walking downhill towards Giants Farm.

He saunters slowly down one of the long track-ways that radiate out from the farm to facilitate the movement of machines or livestock. This one runs along the side of a recently cut cornfield, a cornfield of immense size, and the track itself has come from far off on the horizon.

The man is nearer now. It is a warm evening of brilliant sunshine, the combines have stopped work for the day and the dust has settled. The man is in shirtsleeves with a jacket thrown casually over his shoulder. Behind him trails a liver-and-white spaniel that seems to be enjoying the walk a lot less than he is.

It is a broad view he sees, many square miles of prime farmland, much of it belonging to him, for the man is Trevor Chadwick. Nothing else moves on this hot evening in late summer as he alters course towards Giants Farmhouse. Below him there is an enormous complex of buildings. In addition to the original huge barns that enclosed as much space as a cathedral there have been added many purpose-built implement sheds, workshops and dairy units. Taken together with his own large farmhouse, and the houses of his workers, Giants Farm is a self-sustaining community almost as big as a village.

Trevor strolls without haste because he has little left to learn and nothing more to prove. He takes the ownership of this huge farm with its land, property, machinery, livestock and inherited wealth very much for granted. After all he was born here, as was his father before him, and trained almost from birth how to run it and look after it.

True, he inherited well ahead of time because of the premature death of his father, Ralph Chadwick, but no blame can attach to him for this and no one begrudges him his good fortune. He now has a son of his own so the continuity of family succession is assured. Farming methods are changing fast and Trevor as usual is well ahead of the game. He follows the Chadwick tradition of embracing change and profiting from it, rather than putting up futile resistance.

He has already reduced his workforce considerably and the farm will shed still more jobs in the years ahead. The houses once lived in by farm workers he lets out at high rents, a handy addition to the annual cash flow. Conservation and land management have begun to replace traditional cropping and the emphasis will steadily shift to supplying the leisure market.

The jobs may be different from those in the past but in many ways they are better, being less back-breaking, and less dirty. A new range of skills is called for and Trevor is an optimist who sees a bright future ahead, not only for himself but for a new generation of country workers. His original garden centre and nursery is now one of the largest in the land, it is a money tree that will bear golden fruit for the rest of his life. He has since bought up similar businesses elsewhere and expanded and diversified them with a range of leisure and outdoor activity products that will keep the tills ringing until his young son takes over. He will have been well trained so that in his turn he can think up new and even better ways of keeping the Chadwick coffers full to the brim.

When at last Trevor reaches the house and goes inside he finds this equally silent and deserted. The reason being that his wife has taken their three children to stay with her parents for a few days. His own mother, Beth Chadwick, has moved into the town where she was able to afford an exquisite small Georgian house in College Close. She occupies her time pleasantly enough, and is well provided for, although he knows it cannot be the same for her as being the chatelaine of Giants Farm.

Trevor does not mind being on his own occasionally and searches for something to read while he eats his meal. There are a great many rooms, all elegantly furnished, but the lasting impression is of spaciousness. With so many large and lofty rooms there is no need for them to live on top of one another. He and his wife Vicki and their three children have spread themselves comfortably all over it, and live in style.

Nor does such a big house and garden lack people to look after it. There are plenty of local men and women eager to be involved with the house and its ruling family. It would be unkind to call them servants, even if they behave like servants, because they do not come entirely for the money. They love coming to the big house to use the kitchen, and to prepare Mr Trevor's meals when his wife goes away. When they both go out for the evening they can be sure that their children will be well looked after, just as there will always be someone to water the pot plants, walk the dog, or load the dirty plates into the dishwasher when they have a dinner party. It is very agreeable to have so many people willing to make life easy for them and Trevor and his wife appreciate it very much.

In return they are careful to avoid any display of wealth and are seen to be living modestly below their considerable income. Their cars are big but old, far older than those driven by their employees. The two girls share a moth-eaten pony and are unfailingly polite if anyone speaks to them. Vicki Chadwick does her share of good works in the village and is not afraid to get her hands dirty. Even their two cats try hard to be as ordinary as possible.

'There's no swank about the Chadwicks,' is the general opinion, and they are rated as good people as well as good employers.

The truth is somewhat different. In a quiet way Trevor and his family mop through a fair old whack of money every year but they spend it elsewhere and their extravagance goes largely unnoticed. For example the two girls go to a very expensive boarding school but they too read the game and play everything down. If asked where they have been for their holidays they will say they have been to stay with their granny. Omitting to mention that it was their other granny, the one who lives in Chamonix and pays for their skiing lessons.

As for Trevor and Vicki they were fortunate at an early stage in their marriage to find something they enjoyed equally. They both love going to stay in swish hotels. This is something which does not need much forward planning so there is always a pleasurable feeling of anticipation. It is a self-indulgent but blameless enough pastime which they can well afford. They slip away unobtrusively and are back again before anyone notices. Usually it is for one or two nights only, occasionally for a long weekend, but this is how they choose to spend their money on themselves.

Mostly they go to London, or to Paris now it is so easily reached through the tunnel. They never tire of it and at one time or another have stayed at all the famous hotels in both cities. They love the ritual of booking in and having their luggage carried, they love room service, they love eating in the elegant restaurants, and most of all they love the deference of hall porters and head waiters which they accept without demur. It has kept the romance alive in their marriage, and they are well content.

'Never leaves the farm,' is a commonly heard remark, and it is widely believed that Trevor follows the family tradition of never taking a holiday. He doesn't, but makes up for it with lots of little mini midweek holidays that go unnoticed.

There is a dining alcove next to the kitchen where one of the house helpers has left his meal ready on a tray covered by a starched white cloth. This consists of a beautifully prepared salad, a plate of brown bread-and-butter, and a bowl of succulent shrimps. He is fond of these and starts eating immediately. There is also a bottle of white wine which has been chilled and is now just right to drink. Golden evening sunshine streams through the window as he runs his finger appreciatively up the condensation on the outside of the bottle before filling his glass.

The struggle of the earlier Chadwicks to establish themselves at Giants Farm has been long forgotten. Even the prodigious efforts made by his father to expand the business have begun to fade. This is partly because Trevor's diverse financial interests no longer rely on farming to maintain his income. Property development, many shrewd investments, and profitable retailing from his shops and garden centres have made him richer than all the other Chadwicks put together. As a qualified accountant himself, and with a merchant banker for his father-in-law, he has all the financial expertise he needs to keep the money rolling in.

Through the window he can see the spire of Mardle church where his father and all the earlier Chadwicks are buried. It will be many years yet before he joins them there in the long sleep and the time will pass very agreeably. The only problem on his mind at the moment is that his wife's parents are in the process of buying a new yacht and are trying to persuade him to take a share, something he is determined to refuse. He does not like boats or sailing, apart from which his Chadwick instincts tell him to keep the money in his own pocket.

So he eats his shrimps and drinks his wine and ponders the problem of how to decline the offer without causing offence or appearing to be mean. He goes on to reflect that it might after all be fun to own a yacht and take a real holiday for once in a while. To sail down the west coast of France perhaps, maybe even as far and Portugal and back.

Apart from this he does not have a care in the world.

39

Mardle Churchyard

Another Show has come and gone, so many of them now that they are starting to merge together in my memory. Some will always remain special and different. The one attended by Ralph Chadwick a week before his death will never be forgotten.

I still teach at the College and when I drive out of the village towards our small country market town there is a high point in the road where I always sneak a glance to my left. This is because it allows a brief glimpse of the former Packhorse Meadow, now a large cornfield. In the autumn it is ploughed, the freshly upturned earth a rich brown. Then sown, once more setting in motion the miraculous cycle of the seed and the harvest. From my car window I monitor its progress week by week from light green shoots to leafy dark green, then coming into ear and finally ripening. The combines make short work of harvesting the precious grain, leaving behind a huge gleaming rectangle of clean stubble to await the plough. It is such a tranquil sight in autumn sunshine that it is hard to recall the angry confrontation between Ralph Chadwick and Amelia Ashby. I doubt if few people other than myself have any memory of the events leading up to the disappearance of Packhorse Meadow. The lesson being that all conflict ends up as history, and soon fades into memory.

Nicola Baigent is another who has seen many Shows come and go. Although I would never mention it to her I am sure that every time the Show comes round she is reminded of her husband Peter, the trimly stylish little Captain who blew his brains out one fine summer morning. She has never remarried but still rides her horse every day. It is another sixteen-hand hunter able to jump gates and fences when she is in the mood for a gallop across the fields.

There is a high wall of brick and flint between the Glebe House and Mardle churchyard. Many years ago the original occupants made a doorway in the wall, which we keep locked. Only very occasionally do I unlock it, usually on a summer evening when I am tempted to take a walk round the church-yard. Many of my relatives are buried here, including both my parents, and I like to see that their graves are tidy, and to bring flowers on the anniversaries of their deaths.

As I walk slowly round the churchyard my eyes register the names of many people known to me. Howard Noyce for instance, the fat boy in the class who liked dressing up to go to meetings. It was easy to poke fun at Howard, the pig farmer with pretensions to gentility, but he made the best of what he had and forced people to take notice of him, an achievement in itself.

Nigel Maynard of Bellwether Farm lies nearby. If you remember he was the chief livestock steward at the Show and fathered four children with the student known as Number Five. Whatever the moral rights and wrongs of his solution to the family problem he had succeeded in his intention, which was to pass on his land and property to his son Ian. To him nothing else mattered, whatever he had to do to achieve it, and he died with the satisfaction of knowing it had been a job well done.

The Chadwick family purchased a group of plots in advance so that they can all be buried together. Ralph's father Lionel Chadwick is the only ostentatious oversized grave among them, as you would expect from someone who believed in putting on a show. The others are all of modest proportions, again as you would expect from prudent farmers who mostly lived below their income. I am saddened to see that Ralph's headstone is already scabbed with lichen, a reminder of how quickly time passes, even for the dead.

Hans the old soldier and his own soldier son from the Falklands War are always on my list for a visit when I have one of my churchyard tours. Gemma Hignett is another. There is a space below her name waiting for Jack's name to be added. He is still going strong well into his eighties, so it has been a long wait.

Even more poignant is the lonely and neglected resting place of Fred Harmer. His wife Doris the bag lady no longer lays out flowers all over his grave. She died and was cremated with a social services grant, having no money of her own, nor any relatives to do it for her. Her wish to lie beside Fred in death was therefore not respected, for which I am profoundly sorry.

The churchyard is plagued with rabbits at the moment. I have complained to Tom Mundy who has promised to do something about it. Not only do the rabbits eat the flowers as soon as they are placed on graves but their tunnelling has undermined many of the older graves and caused the headstones to lean in all directions.

I reminded him again a few days ago when we met by chance. It was early on a Sunday morning and we were both descending the field edge path which runs down off Beckles Hill. Tom was surprised to see me so far up the hill, and said so, which obliged me to supply an explanation. I told him was that I putting on weight and that Ruth insisted I take a walk occasionally, both true statements. Tom was not impressed and just sniffed. However he managed to make it a meaningful sniff, implying that life was very pleasant for some.

'Mossing,' he explained when I asked what had brought him out to the hill on a Sunday morning. He carried a short rake in one hand, a hessian sack in the other. It was stuffed with soft green sphagnum moss which he had raked from the steep northern-facing slopes of the hill. This has moisture retentive properties and there is a florist in the town who will always buy the moss from him to use in packaging, or to protect tender plants.

It was a salutary lesson in free market economics. We had both been for an early morning walk but while I had spent much of the time standing around with my hands in my pockets musing on the past Tom had busied himself by earning some petrol money. As always his industry and application could only be admired. He was never idle, always doing something useful and usually making money at the same time. His disapproving sniff had been an admonishment I deserved, and it struck home. I resolved to be more diligent in future, and to spend my spare time in some worthy occupation.

Growing up as boys together forged a lasting bond between us. Yet although we are pals and on friendly terms it would not be true to say that we are friends, as such, because we have nothing in common except for our shared heritage of a village childhood, and by living together as near neighbours. Even so we are both aware that a special relationship exists between us and after mulling it over for several years the answer eventually percolated through. The casual way we behave towards one another is because we are more like brothers than friends. Brothers do not have to like one another, and often don't, yet the bond is always there.

So it is with Tom and me. If we are busy or preoccupied we pass without speaking, secure in the knowledge that doing so will not cause offence. And just as brothers are often jealous of one another I know it has crossed our minds more than once that it would be nice to change places sometimes. When it is cold and wet Tom thinks of me in the cosy staff room at the College, and in younger days I was certainly envious when he sauntered down to the river with his fishing tackle while I sat at my desk studying.

Not for Tom the anguish of sitting examinations and sweating on the results, or the nervous tensions that go with a professional career. To be permanently freed from the bondage of ambition is to ensure a good digestion for life, and the guarantee of eight hours of peaceful slumber every night. Never to have suffered the humiliation of seeking preferment, or the agony of rejection, and never to have endured the tedium of idleness even for a single hour, is to have led a fortunate existence.

We carried on down into the village and came to a stop by the war memorial. Before we parted company Tom put aside his rake and sack of moss to fold his arms and ask me a question. 'What do you make of the world these days, Alan? Me, I can't make head nor tail of it. Tell me what's happening.'

'I can't make head nor tail of it either. And given up trying.'

'You don't suppose it's because we're getting on a bit, do you?'

'Us, Tom? Never.'

At which moment an unfamiliar sound was heard, bringing our conversation to an end. Once a month Mardle Church comes into use again with a nine o'clock Holy Communion service, and the tenor bell was being rung to summon the village faithful. We watched as along they came, passing through the lych gate and up the flagstoned path to the open south door. Not just elderly ladies with prayer books in hand but also several husband and wife couples, and most pleasing of all, some of our young people as well.

It was a warm misty morning, pleasantly still, which prolonged the sound of the bell as it echoed slowly down through the river valley. Neither Tom nor I are regular churchgoers but we are traditionalists and regret that our village church is not more widely used. We had waited by the War Memorial so that we could watch the communicants arrive, both of us sufficiently curious to find out which of our neighbours still attended these monthly church services. Soon after nine o'clock the bell stopped ringing, the door was closed, and with the worshippers safely pewed up inside we parted company.

My lifelong friend Tom Mundy took a look round at the village and gestured with his rake. 'What do you think, Alan? Not a bad place to live, is it?'

'No,' I said. 'Not bad at all.'

End

Printed in Great Britain
by Amazon.co.uk, Ltd.,
Marston Gate.